**HIGHEST HONORS FOR
PAMELA THOMAS-GRAHAM AND**

BLUE BLOOD

"Thomas-Graham's precisely rendered campus background, vivid characters, easy dialogue, and fluidly entertaining narrative mark a robustly talented new recruit to the genre."

—*Kirkus Reviews*

"A writer of outstanding talent and promise . . . a strong series."

—*Library Journal*

"Definitely a writer to watch."

—*The Mystery Review*

"Thomas-Graham weaves a deft plot, offering many possible suspects."

—*The Pilot* (Southern Pines, NC)

"The observations of [Thomas-Graham's] sleuth, Nikki Chase, are still sharp, particularly when it comes to snotty preppies, fashion, and racial politics."

—*Daily Camera* (Boulder, CO)

"*BLUE BLOOD* is suspenseful enough to win the neophyte novelist a wide audience. Beyond the swiftly moving plot, the book poses some thought-provoking questions about race."

—*New Haven Register* (CT)

"Thomas-Graham skillfully portrays the academic worlds of Yale and Harvard and the distressed black community of simmering resentments and incendiary elements waiting to explode."

—*Booklist*

"Thomas-Graham has given Nikki a keen sense of humor as well as the 'insider' savvy to ferret out the secrets behind ivy-covered walls. She deserves top marks for this fast-paced read."

—*St. Petersburg Times* (FL)

"This professionally accomplished author certainly conveys an 'insider's knowledge' about the characters in *BLUE BLOOD* and the worlds they occupy, with a great deal of creativity and fun."

—*New York Law Journal*

"An enthralling whodunit."

—*Ellery Queen Magazine*

A DARKER SHADE OF CRIMSON

"A fast and funny debut whodunit—with A+ insights into the churlish world of academic politics and keen observations on middle-class race relations, [this] graduates with honors."

—*People*

"Deftly blends fast-paced storytelling with a thoughtful exploration of the human faces behind the racial diversity rallying cry heard on the nation's university campuses. . . . It offers an abundance of suspects, plot twists, and clues . . . and a convivial blend of light-hearted escape and social critique."

—*Chicago Tribune*

BY
PAMELA THOMAS-GRAHAM

Blue Blood
A Darker Shade of Crimson

Pamela Thomas-Graham

Blue Blood

AN IVY LEAGUE MYSTERY

POCKET STAR BOOKS

New York   London   Toronto   Sydney   Singapore

A Pocket Star Book published by
POCKET BOOKS, a division of Simon & Schuster, Inc.
1230 Avenue of the Americas, New York, NY 10020

Copyright © 1999 by Pamela Thomas-Graham

Originally published in hardcover in 1999 by Simon & Schuster Inc.

ISBN 0-671-01671-7

First Pocket Books Printing April 2000

10 9 8 7 6 5 4 3 2 1

POCKET STAR BOOKS and colophon are registered trademarks of Simon & Schuster Inc.

Front cover photo by Steve Murez/The Image Bank

Printed in the U. S. A.

For Lawrence Otis Graham
and Gordon Graham,
the brightest stars in the firmament

ACKNOWLEDGMENTS

The past year has been quite a journey, and I've been blessed to have some truly extraordinary individuals alongside me for the trip. So, in no particular order, I'd like to say thank you:

To the many Yale students and alumni—and current and former residents of New Haven—who helped me decipher Eli's secrets, including Anna Barber, Chris Todd, Josh Galper, Mark Templeton, Kenny Hill, Nancy Marx Better, Alan Miles, David Hecht, Victoria Holloway, Doug Moser, Jennifer Beckendorf, Lieutenant Brian Sullivan and Judy Mongillo of the New Haven Police Department, Melissa James, and Heidi and her staff at the Three Chimneys Inn;

To Leigh Bonney and Lauren Tyler, dear friends

who went above and beyond the call of duty by sharing their Rolodexes and their memories of Yale with me;

To the many members of the Harvard and Radcliffe communities who generously assisted me as a new author, especially Sally Gable, Tamar March, Lindy Hess, Ellen Reeves, Bruce Hubbard, Peter Bynoe, Amy Taylor, A'Lelia Bundles, David Goodman, Jim Conner, John Cosgrove, Nick Lemann, Emilie de Brigard, Regina Montoya, Nash Flores, Richard Tiedes, Tony Tesorerio, Harold Binder, Jim Relle, and Motoko Huthwaite;

To Jimmy and Jetta Jones, Desiree Saunders, Bennie and Flash Wiley, Marcella Maxwell, Audrey Thorne, Gerri Warren-Merrick, Dedra Davis, Deborah McHamm, Deborah Bibb, Michelle Studemeyer, Sandra Jackson-Berger, Fayne Erikson, and Melissa Walsh, who so kindly gave their enthusiastic support to my first book;

To my colleagues and friends at McKinsey & Company for their unfailing generosity, including Pete Walker, Rob Rosiello, Don Waite, Tom Woodard, Andrew Parsons, Stacey Rauch, Peter Flaherty, Rajat Gupta, Juan Hoyos, Dana Norris, Lauri Blitzer, Stefano Proverbio, Roger Abravanel, Tom Barkin, Jan Elstub, Saadia Khan, Vivian Reifberg, Elaine Bortman, Amy Brakeman, Margaret Loeb, Fred and Patty Eppinger, Mike Sherman, Mark Leiter, Mark Loch, John Rose, Roger Kline, Marshall

Lux, David Court, Claudio As pesi, Haniel Lynn, Steve Pamon, James Costantini, Andre Dua, Robin Ebenstein, John Andersen, Arthur Armstrong, Jerome Vascellero, and my friends in the BCSS;

To Angelo Barozzi, Ron Frasch, Wayne Markowitz, Robbin Mitchell, and all my friends at GFT;

To Bob Johnson, Debra Lee, Byron Marchant, George Curry, and the terrific team at BET;

To Ann and Andrew Tisch, David Acorn, Norman Selby, James Cash, Rosabeth Moss Kanter, Elisabeth Radow, Elizabeth Rose, Marty Staff, Deborah Taylor, Adrienne Lewis, Dora Hurt, Dolores Hurt, Laura Josephs, Jerry Stacy, Simone McBride, Rosina Costantino, Don and Ruth Boyce, Julie and Earl Greene, Robert and Virginia Crilley, Lorraine Manos, Bill and Virginia Johnstone, Julie Ciarmitaro, Lelia Finzel, Margaret Morton, Kristine Langdon, Ruby Chandy, Dauna Williams, Andre and Alysson Owens, Marguerite Gritenas, Jay Ward, Gail Busby, Bruce Wilson, Nancy Linnerooth, Larry Reitzenkamp, Larry and Betty Lauer, Ann and Al Gottlieb, Helen and Milton Williams, Connie Claytor, and Elliot Hoffman;

To Jennifer McGuire, Ellie Hirschorn, Susie Huang, Christy Parsons, Michelle DiLorenzo, and Julia Knight, my Wyoming pals;

To Drs. Anne Carlon, Chris Creatura, and Kathryn Cox, and to Clara O'Neal and the wonderful nurses in the Ante-Partum unit at New York

Hospital, for their extraordinary warmth and care;

To Betty and Richard Graham, Richard, Jr., and Sheri; to "Thomases" far and wide, including Vince, Barbara, Mary, Julia, Magnolia, Bessie, Frances, and James; and to Mattie, Azalia and Michael Hosey—you've all taught me what family really means;

To David Rosenthal for his vision; to Michael Korda and Chuck Adams for their insight, dedication, and charm; to Jack Horner and the team at ICM;

To my incredible agent, Esther Newberg, who always delivers;

To my parents, Albert and Marian, for a lifetime of love and care;

To Gordon, my precious boy,

And most of all, to my darling husband, Lawrence Otis Graham, whose courage, brilliance, energy, and integrity are a continual source of inspiration and joy.

Good night, poor Harvard,
Harvard, good night
We've got your number,
You're high as a kite.
Oh, good night, poor Harvard,
You're tucked in tight
When the big blue team gets after you,
Harvard, good night!

YALE FIGHT SONG

What did I do
To be so black
And blue?

THOMAS "FATS" WALLER

Blue Blood

Blue Blood

CHAPTER ONE

We're Not in Cambridge Anymore

Georgian. *Gothic*. Houses. *Colleges*. The Yard. *Old Campus*. Widener. *Sterling*. Finals Clubs. *Secret Societies*. George Plimpton. *William F. Buckley*. Conan O'Brien. *Dick Cavett*. John F. Kennedy. *George H. Bush*. Shabby chic. *Just plain shabby*.

The differences between Harvard and Yale are limitless and distinct, and none more important than this: while a Harvard graduate invariably bleeds crimson, at Yale the blood always runs blue.

I jumped into the left lane. But the Buick got there first. So I signaled right and floored the gas. Anticipating me, the Buick glided back into the right lane and mockingly flashed its taillights. I pumped hard on my brakes. The Buick slowed down even more. No jury would have convicted me at that point, so I decided it was time to run him off the road.

The third Monday of November found me racing down I-95 South on my way from Cambridge, Massachusetts, to New Haven, Connecticut. It was pouring rain, and I was tailgating a dark brown Buick station wagon being driven by a maddeningly oblivious elderly man. I was about to escalate from riding his fender to full-blown light-blinking, horn-blowing, and cursing.

Because I had to get to Yale. Fast. Even though it was too late.

Amanda was already dead.

Finally, the Buick drifted casually into the middle lane and I jetted past, my foot pressing the accelerator so hard that the car doors rattled. My landlady had loaned me her red '87 Chevy Cavalier for the day, after I'd promised to treat it gently. But there was no gentleness left in the world that morning.

Amanda Fox, the wife of one of my oldest friends, had been found dead the night before on a deserted street in New Haven, on the outskirts of the Yale campus. She'd been stabbed five times, and her left hand had been severed at the wrist. I was trying not to think about it. If I thought too much, I'd have to pull over again; then I'd never make it to New Haven.

And Gary needed me. Really needed me.

My name is Veronica Chase, Nikki to my friends.

An Assistant Professor of Economics at Harvard, I am the only black in the fifty-person department. At thirty years old, I feel alternately exhilarated and overwhelmed by the responsibility that my position entails. That morning, overwhelmed didn't even begin to describe how I felt.

I first met Garrett Fox eleven years ago when I moved into Dunster House, my undergraduate dorm at Harvard. Ten years my senior, Gary at the time was a resident tutor and an Associate Professor in the History Department. We became friends because we both studied every evening in the House library, a cozy, wood-paneled room with an expanse of French windows and a working fireplace, and we fell into the habit of grabbing coffee at Tommy's Lunch after the librarian shooed us out at closing time. Gary was bookish, gangly, and unreasonably attractive: behind his wire-rimmed glasses were a pair of mesmerizing gray eyes, and he usually wore thick, nubbly sweaters of the type that made me want to crawl right into them. I had a huge crush on him for about a week, but it quickly receded into a lasting friendship. Since he was half a generation older than me, he became like the big brother I never had—counseling me on classes, summer jobs, and numerous affairs of the heart. I treasured his advice, and there was nothing that I wouldn't have done for him.

At least, until the day he announced that he was marrying Amanda Ingersol.

Amanda was the golden girl of my college class: five feet ten, with tawny blond hair, piercing blue eyes, and legs a mile long, she was always suspiciously gorgeous, even at 9:00 A.M. She was fourth-generation Harvard by way of Manhattan, and as a freshman exuded an aura of WASP affluence and bored sophistication that I immediately both loathed and envied. It became clear to me during my first week in Cambridge that being from the Midwest was second only to hailing from the South in inspiring disdain and pity from the likes of Amanda and her Upper East Side, private-school crowd—and being treated like a bumpkin tended to make me testy. My irritation bordered on the homicidal after an episode at a black-tie dinner in the Master's House our sophomore year. "Nikki," she called out to me as I sat between a Dean and a visiting scholar from Oxford, struggling to eat my first lobster, "I wish I had a video camera. It's so refreshing to see someone attack their food with such childlike innocence."

Since Amanda lived in Dunster House, it was impossible to ignore her, although it would have been difficult in any case, given her penchant for striding around campus with a three-quarter-length raccoon coat tossed over her shoulders. ("It was my grandmother's at Smith," she'd explain.) She managed to infuriate almost every woman I knew, usually as a result of her irritating ability to fascinate every male with whom she came into contact. My differences with her, however, went well beyond minor skirmishes over boys: she was madly conservative politically, which in my book is the one truly unforgivable sin. As the editor-in-chief of *The Salient*, the Republican rag on campus, Amanda wrote more than one editorial about affirmative action that nearly brought us to blows. Conveniently ignoring the fact that as an alumni child she herself had received preferential treatment from the admissions office, she openly derided the university's desire for diversity in the incoming class and once actually challenged me to reveal my SAT scores during a particularly heated argument. By graduation day, I hated her with the kind of passion that only a twenty-one-year-old can muster, but took consolation in knowing that soon I'd be rid of her. And then Gary announced that he was marrying her.

Calling this news earth-shattering would grossly understate its impact. I felt utterly betrayed. As far as I knew, Amanda and Gary had never exchanged more than casual greetings in the dining room. He had never said a word about her to me. And now they were getting *married?* Everyone had assumed that Amanda either would return to New York and become a Republican-party fund-raiser, or move to DC and disappear into some far-right yahoo congressman's staff. Either way, we figured that in three or four years, she'd have married a man twice her age and be living on Park Avenue or ensconced in a town house in Georgetown. But instead, there she was, standing beside Gary in the Dunster courtyard, sweetly proclaiming that they were moving to New Haven, that Gary had an exciting opportunity at Yale, that she would be entering Yale Law School, that her aim was to become a law professor. A professor!

Why would a budding politico such as she take up with an impecunious academic? And how could he do this to me? Gary was *my* friend, *my* father-confessor. Not *her* secret lover.

They were married in a very small ceremony at Cambridge City Hall three days later.

Silence prevailed between Gary and me for almost two years afterward.

But then I stumbled across him in a New Haven pizzeria while on a road trip to the annual Harvard-Yale Game, and somehow all of my anger and resentment suddenly seemed very distant and petty, and I was instantly reminded of how much I missed his friendship. Soon we fell into the routine of regular phone calls and an annual rendezvous at The Game. Whenever we spoke, it was like picking up the last conversation in midstream, and I luxuriated in the warmth of an old, stimulating friendship that had been renewed.

Of Amanda, we spoke very little. I knew that she was becoming very well known and highly controversial. She'd clerked for the most conservative Supreme

Court Justice after graduating from Yale Law, and had networked her way around Washington so well that she was publishing a steady stream of op-ed pieces in the far-right press and in addition to her legal writing had regular gigs as a substitute for the major conservative commentators on the Sunday-morning talk shows. I read an article that referred to her success as the "talking dog" syndrome—a beautiful, smart, truly conservative woman being as rare as a canine who can speak. My feeling is that just because a dog can talk doesn't mean that it should be listened to, but apparently her shtick of rabid conservatism plus her shiny blond hair had mass appeal. The Beltway crowd certainly couldn't get enough of it. The grapevine had it that she was in DC as often as she was in New Haven, and that she was being considered for early tenure, given her growing national stature. Meanwhile, Gary's career had taken off just as rapidly: he was made a Dean at Yale in record time, and the rumor was that he was actually on track to be the next President of the university. I still had never figured out how he and Amanda came to be married, but they were a true "power couple" in academic circles, and our few mutual friends reported that they seemed blissfully happy—a state far more exalted than any I had ever achieved in a relationship, which, of course, made me dislike Amanda even more.

And now she was dead, at age thirty. It didn't seem possible.

The sight of the exit off I-95 for downtown New Haven yanked me out of my reverie. Despite the rain I had made excellent time, shaving half an hour off the normally two-hour trip. I cut across two lanes and careened off Exit 47, steering with one hand while I fumbled in my purse for the slip of paper on which I had scribbled directions to Gary's campus apartment. *Take the 3rd exit off the Connector*, it read. *Then right on* . . . some street that I couldn't make out, even though it was my handwriting.

Damn.

What had Gary said? I'd been no more than half awake during our conversation, and it showed in my scrawl. The street name looked like a four-letter word ending in "k." Given my current irritation, I could think of at least one word fitting that description, but I doubted that was the name of the street.

Looking up as an exit ramp whizzed by, I wondered uneasily if I had just missed my turnoff. Despite my biannual trips to The Game, New Haven was totally foreign to me, and given the town's less than savory reputation, I wasn't keen on getting lost. Never mind that I had grown up in Detroit and seen more than my fair share of rough urban neighborhoods. Even *I* was intimidated by the specter of New Haven. Especially after Amanda's murder. Everyone I knew, including native New Yorkers, said it wasn't safe. I forcibly resisted the urge to snap the door locks shut as I eyed the burned-out buildings lining either side of the overpass. That was what a timid suburban housewife would do, and I fancied myself a fearless black urbanite. Trailing clouds of bravado, I turned off at the next exit ramp.

I was immediately plunged into a neighborhood of dreary wood-frame houses, most of them covered in peeling pastel paint. The lashing rain had slowed to a steady downpour, and the narrow streets were gloomy and desolate. A small black child opened the front door of a dilapidated house, staring at me as I slowed down to look for a street sign. The ferocity of his expression startled and saddened me, so much so that I rolled through the next intersection without really registering the name of the cross street. Half of the next block was cordoned off with sodden yellow "crime scene" tape, and I could see two white men in dark slickers hunched over the sidewalk inside the barrier, with what appeared to be tape measures in their hands. A cluster of black men huddled inside a bus shelter on the next corner, their breath visible in the icy air. Craning my neck to see the street sign, I floored the accelerator. OLIVE STREET, the sign read. No luck.

That was when I saw the flashing lights in my rearview mirror.

Just what I needed. A policeman on my tail.

Slowly, I pulled over to the side of the street, fighting a rising tide of impatience and apprehension as a silver Ford Crown Victoria came to an abrupt halt behind me. Despite a recent successful collaboration with the Harvard cops, I hadn't shaken my instinctive mistrust of the police. I had plenty of male relatives, and I'd gritted my teeth through a heart-wrenching array of stories of official intimidation and abuse. A black activist had recently coined a phrase for the only crime any of them had committed: "DWB." *Driving While Black*. After rolling down the window, I carefully placed my hands on top of the steering wheel. Things were bad enough without some trigger-happy cop turning me into a statistic.

It was just as I'd feared: the patrolman was stout, white, and unsmiling. Rain streamed off his navy blue New Haven Police poncho as he stood beside the car. I caught the name Timothy Heaney as he flashed his badge.

"License," he barked.

"Just a minute," I snapped back, fumbling in my purse. "What's the problem?"

"What do you think? I just clocked you at forty-five in a twenty-five-mile-an-hour zone. Registration."

Registration? *Great.* Where did Maggie keep it?

I smiled my best shit-eating grin. I was going to have to get this guy on my side fast, before he arrested me for stealing the car. "You know, Officer Heaney, you're going to have to give me a minute to find it. I borrowed a friend's car this morning, and I think she probably keeps it in the glove compartment—"

"Uh-huh." He cut me off. "Step out of the car."

"All right," I said pleasantly, between gritted teeth. *Would he be searching my car if I were a cute little blond girl?* I thought not.

Moving deliberately, I slid out of the Chevy, my blood pressure spiking up another few points as the cold rain hit me full in the face. I pulled up the hood of my yellow slicker, then watched while he rummaged through the glove compartment and emerged with a tattered piece of white paper.

"What's the friend's name?" he grunted.

"Magnolia Dailey, 25 Shepard Street in Cambridge, Mass.," I said impatiently.

"Fine," he said, nodding impassively. "Get back in the car."

Neanderthal, I fumed. A great big man, bossing around a defenseless, lost woman.

"You're getting one summons, Miss—Chase," he said, squinting at my driver's license. "Although this inspection sticker is out of date, too."

"Damn, that's awfully nice of you."

"You want another ticket, Miss Chase? Because I'd be happy to write it." He leaned closer to the window for emphasis. "This is a residential neighborhood, and there are a lot of little kids on these streets. They should be in school, but some of them aren't. With all these leaves on top of a slick road, you could've killed someone racing through here like that."

Our eyes met. I hate being lectured, and the fact

that he was right did nothing to mitigate my intense annoyance. I considered trying to defend myself. But I had broken all laws human and divine on I-95 trying to get to Gary, and I didn't have time to convince this cop that if I was speeding, it was for a good reason.

I took a deep breath. "Sorry, Officer," I said briskly. "What I meant to say was thank you for not issuing a ticket on the inspection, too. I'll get it taken care of as soon as I get home." *Which couldn't be soon enough.*

"Get used to our speed limit, Miss Chase," the cop said grimly as he handed me the ticket. "You're not in Cambridge anymore."

Cursing violently under my breath, I drove a few more blocks and then got directions to the campus from a toothless elderly black man who was standing in the midst of traffic hawking copies of the *New Haven Register*. He pointed me toward York Street—which turned out to be the mystery scrawl on my sheet of directions—and I followed it to Chapel Street, which was where Gary said I should park. The rain began to slack off as I threw the car into a space on the street and set out warily on foot.

New Haven was seriously depressing me, and the dilapidated storefronts, empty restaurants, and deserted sidewalks that I was passing weren't helping. Fully half of the buildings had been abandoned, and their windows bore printed and hand-lettered signs proclaiming SPACE FOR RENT. A hotel advertised "Single Room—$29." Blue and red graffiti scrawls marred several of the storefronts. The awning over a small deli valiantly proclaimed "Fresh Salad Bar," but when I peered through the rain-spattered glass, I saw no occupants save a lone Asian counterman. The place had an air of defeated resignation, as if the worst had already happened, and all that remained was to survive. These Yalies were crazy. Why would anyone in their right mind voluntarily spend four years in this place?

My dispirited mood lasted until a sign proclaiming High Street loomed over my head and I turned left.

And saw before me a vista that seemed at first like a mirage.

Through an immense stone archway I could see a narrow, tree-lined street, which swept past towering slate gray stone Gothic buildings on either side. Stately turrets and chimneys wreathed in fog were faintly visible in the distance, and a majestic stone clock tower with lacy filigrees presided imperiously over the lesser buildings. Where there had been deserted sidewalks, now there were students walking resolutely, carrying books and backpacks, and the very air was misty, and hushed, and contemplative. It was as if Carcassonne, the medieval French walled city, had been transported intact to Connecticut.

I walked slowly down High Street, past brooding

stone buildings with moats and arched gateways, and paused at the center of the block. I still had no idea where I was, but I wasn't minding quite so much now. On my right was a large grassy quadrangle surrounded by lofty brown and gray stone buildings that I knew was Old Campus, where the freshman lived. That much I remembered from road trips to The Game. But what intrigued me more was across the street. Under the imposing stone clock tower was a slate archway guarded by an ornate wrought-iron gate, through which I could see a large courtyard enveloped in gray mist. Surrounded by stately Gothic buildings, it was beautifully landscaped with weeping willows, maples, and shrubbery. Above the archway was carved an inscription: FOR GOD, FOR COUNTRY, AND FOR YALE.

The lure of the courtyard was irresistible. I crossed the street and gently pulled one of the gate's large round iron handles, but it was locked. Disappointed, I glanced down at my watch. It was almost noon. I had to find Gary.

"Excuse me," I asked a tall, lanky redheaded man walking past me. He was wearing a Yale sweatshirt underneath his windbreaker, and looked as if he knew where he was going. "Do you know where Branford College is?"

"You're looking at it. Right through that gate." He gestured. "But it's cursed." He frowned.

Despite myself, I recoiled from the gate as if it had

become electrified. None of us needed any more bad luck.

"The legend is that if you pass through that gate before Commencement, you won't graduate," he said, grinning at me. "Come on. I'll show you the main entrance."

We walked back a few feet, and then turned onto a flagstone walkway flanked by Gothic stone buildings on either side. Over a gateway on the left, I read the words JONATHAN EDWARDS. I recognized the name as one of the residential Colleges.

"This is Branford," he said, gesturing to the building on the right. "Here." A ponytailed girl was just opening a heavy wooden door that appeared to be the dorm's main entrance, so I ran a few steps and grabbed it, shouting my thanks over my shoulder.

I was immediately plunged into a narrow, dimly lit arched corridor that quickly opened onto a small courtyard. A towering elm stood at its center, encircled by a stone bench. Beyond the courtyard was another narrow corridor, this one with a painted wooden map of Branford College on the wall. I located the room marked DEAN'S APARTMENT. That would be Gary's. Shaking the rain from my hood, I passed through the corridor and found myself in the large, verdant courtyard that I had originally seen through the forbidden gate.

It was every bit as beautiful as it had seemed from outside, a medieval cloister in the heart of a decaying city. From this vantage point, I could see the intricate details of the beige and gray stone Gothic buildings that surrounded the courtyard. The tall leaded-glass windows glittered, even in the cold, gray mist, and the profusion of trees and low bushes softened what would otherwise have felt harshly monastic. Two wooden benches nestled invitingly under a tree, and a wooden swing hung whimsically from a towering oak on the far side of the courtyard.

A wailing police siren from the street outside broke the almost holy stillness, and I turned abruptly toward an arched wooden entry door marked "784–788." That was where I'd find the Dean's apartment. I peeled off my raincoat as I climbed three flights of well-worn, narrow, circular stone stairs, pausing to look through the thick leaded windows at the courtyard below. I was high enough now to see the maroon, green, and charcoal gray roof tiles of the building's adjacent wings, and the sharp contrast between the homespun redbrick of Harvard's dorms and the somber stone stateliness of Yale's was becoming increasingly apparent. At its heart, Harvard's campus exuded an all-American simplicity, functionality, and optimism, whereas this place, in its soul, seemed quintessentially European: sophisticated, ornate, and world-weary.

On the third-floor landing, I arrived at a heavy arched wooden door marked DEAN. Gary Fox opened the door on the first knock, and we regarded each

other wordlessly for what felt like an eternity. It
had been almost exactly a year since I had last seen
him, and he looked much the worse for wear. His
face was a great deal thinner, making his large gray
eyes even more striking, and his shiny black hair
was much more liberally sprinkled with silver. He
looked tousled and unkempt, as if he hadn't slept for
days.

"Oh, Gary." I breathed slowly. "I'm so sorry."

My jacket slipped to the floor, and then we were
holding each other, and I felt sobs racking his body.
Sadness shuddered through me in waves, and I held
him tighter, absorbing the blows. The persistent feeling of unreality that had shadowed me all morning
slipped away. This was real. She was dead. Just like
that.

"Come in, Nikki," he said finally, removing his
glasses and wiping his eyes with the back of his hand.
"You're soaking wet. You must be freezing. Come on
in."

The suite was surprisingly large: the spacious living room had a dark hardwood floor covered by a
faded Oriental rug; there was a low beamed ceiling,
and a row of tall-leaded glass windows overlooked
the courtyard. I could see three additional rooms
beyond heavy oak door frames. I instinctively moved
toward the large stone fireplace before I realized
that the grate was cold and full of ashes. I *was* freezing, and it was going to take more than a fire to

make me feel warm again. Gary watched me as he stood awkwardly in the middle of the room.

"I hope you're not going to be in trouble for missing your lectures today."

"Don't be silly," I chided, glancing around the room. A single lamp burned in what was otherwise an oppressive gloom. "That's what teaching assistants are for."

"Do you want something to drink, or—" His voice trailed off.

"No, I'm fine." I purposefully turned back toward him. I had come here to comfort him, and it was high time I started. "Come on, let's sit down."

He sank into the brown leather sofa adjacent to the fireplace, and I sat beside him. Turning to face him, I gently laid my hand on his arm. "Tell me everything." He'd been practically hysterical when he'd called earlier that morning, and my grogginess had only made it harder to understand exactly what had happened.

He took a long breath, and then began speaking. "It all started because she was teaching last night."

"On a Sunday night?"

"Yes, she taught an undergraduate seminar on the Constitution. Fifteen students." In contrast to his tone of urgency earlier that morning, his voice now sounded dispassionate and almost aloof, as if he were telling someone else's story, not his own. "The seminar was in a classroom up on Science Hill. In the

Klein Biology Building. It ended at about nine-fifteen."

"And did she leave when all the students left?"

"No." He shook his head. "The police told me that someone in the class said that she stayed behind to talk to one of her students. A kid named Marcellus Tyler. They questioned him this morning, and he says he didn't walk out with her. He claims that they talked for about ten minutes about a paper he was writing for the class, and then he left the building. He said she was packing up to leave, but she had to use the ladies' room or something. At any rate, he says she told him to go ahead, that she'd be fine. And no one seems to have seen her after that until . . ."

He paused for a moment and swallowed hard. "They found her body around one o'clock this morning. In the middle of a poor black neighborhood about a half a mile from Klein." He looked at me. "She was stabbed. At least five times. She was covered in blood when they found her, and her hand—her left hand was severed at the wrist."

He had told me that much over the phone when he called that morning, and I still felt nauseated at the thought of so vicious an attack. Who on earth would do such a thing?

"They don't know yet," he said, sounding anguished. "They don't know if she was raped."

"Do they have any suspects?" I asked.

He nodded slowly, and I felt my heart breaking

for him. "This student, Marcellus Tyler. He was the last one to see her alive."

"Do you know anything about him?"

Gary shook his head. "I don't have much information. I think the police said he was a sophomore. I know he must be a big guy, because they said he's a linebacker on the football team. Oh, and he's black."

Holy shit.

Amanda was found dead in the middle of a poor black neighborhood, and the last person to see her alive was a black Yale student? Gary really *did* need me. He was sitting on a racial powder keg.

"I hope you're not automatically assuming he did it."

"I don't know, Nikki." He sighed distractedly, raking his fingers through his hair. "I really don't."

Please don't let a black man have killed this girl. "I'm just thinking about what his motive could possibly have been," I prodded. "He was her student, right? So why would he want to kill her? Had she just given him a bad grade or something?"

"I don't know," he repeated numbly. "I just hope to God they find the son of a bitch who did it. Because if it's not this kid, then it means the killer is still out there."

A gust of wind rattled the windows. "What was the weather like last night?" I asked.

Gary looked at me quizzically. "It was raining. Hard. Why?"

"I was just thinking that it seems more likely that since the weather was bad, it was someone specifically out to get *her*. No random criminal would be out on the street if last night was anything like it is today. Bad guys hate to be cold and wet, same as the rest of us."

He stared at me. "That's exactly what the policeman said."

"Don't mind me. I seem to be channeling Nancy Drew these days." I shrugged lightly, my eyes searching his face.

There was something he wasn't telling me.

"Gary, are there any other suspects?"

"Yes," he sighed heavily. "There's one more."

He rose and looked out onto the enchanted courtyard before he turned back to me. "Some of the cops seem to think that *I* was the one who killed her."

CHAPTER TWO

The Neutron Blonde

"Large pie with pepperoni, garlic, and mushrooms. That all for now, Dean Fox?"

The waitress slid a metal tray loaded with an oversized pizza and three glass jars of the usual accouterments between Gary and me, then waited expectantly.

"That's all," Gary said, quickly glancing up to meet her eyes. "Thanks."

We were sitting at a table in the front window of Naples Pizzeria, a Yale student hangout that I vaguely remembered from prior road trips to New Haven. Across the street, the outline of a tall stone building was barely visible in the torrential rain, and I caught glimpses of torsos, jawlines, scarves, and locks of hair as a parade of umbrellas passed by. The restaurant was an amiable, fragrant refuge from the frosty damp air outside: rows of wooden tables surrounded an open kitchen with a roaring fire, and photographs of Yale sports teams and color sketches of the crests of each of the Yale Colleges and graduate schools covered the walls. The spicy air was rich with the smell of baking bread and roasting tomatoes. Now I just had to coax Gary into eating something.

I pulled two gooey slices from the round silver tray and slid one onto his plate.

"This going to be as good as Pepe's?" I teased gently.

He smiled weakly and stared down at his plate. "Sorry, Nikki. I thought this was a good idea. But I can't."

It had surprised me that Gary was even willing to leave his room, given the shock of Amanda's death, and what must have been a night without sleep. But he had seemed anxious to be gone from the suite at Branford, and I thought that somehow food might help.

"I know," I said gently. "But you'll feel better if you eat something."

"They really think I did it, you know," he said abruptly.

"I know. You said that earlier. But why? Why would they ever think that?"

He frowned. "Because I have no alibi for last

night. And because I didn't seem alarmed by her absence—I hadn't called the cops. I was working in my office at Branford from dinnertime until about midnight. By the time I got back to our room, it was almost twelve-thirty, and normally Amanda would have been back by then. But she liked to stop in on friends on Sunday nights, and sometimes she'd go to her office after class. So I wasn't that concerned. Just when I had decided to call the police, they called me to tell me—" His voice trailed off.

"Lack of an alibi hardly makes you a prime suspect, Gary. And she was only 'missing' for a couple of hours. I think it would have been more suspicious if you *had* called the police that quickly."

"Well, there's more." He sighed heavily. "Amanda and I had a pretty bad fight Friday night. Publicly. In fact, in front of everyone. At a dinner party at the President's house. And someone obviously couldn't wait to tell the police about it."

"What were you arguing about?"

"She made a speech at the Political Union last week that went way over the top." He idly rearranged the glass condiment jars on the table as he spoke. "It seems stupid now. But the topic of her speech was 'The Idiocy of Feminism,' and she insulted a number of Yale faculty members. She started by calling the feminist movement arcane and irrelevant, and it went on from there."

"Well, what do *you* think?" I said, trying not to

bristle. There was no point in being irate that Amanda had been given an incredibly prestigious platform to spew right-wing vitriol at impressionable college students.

"You know I don't care about politics, Nikki. I'm a historian, remember? But I felt that in the last year or so she had become far too strident, that she was beginning to look a bit foolish. Those television producers kept egging her on, but people here were starting to call her 'the Neutron Blonde,' and it wasn't meant as a compliment. I suggested that she modulate her tone in the future, if she expected to be taken seriously. But she took my comments completely the wrong way, and accused me of trying to stifle her to protect my own status. She even said that I was jealous of all the attention she was getting."

"She stepped on some important toes, eh?" I knew the academic power game well enough to know that pissing off the wrong person at a critical moment was career suicide. And if Yale was anything like Harvard, the powerful faculty members were more likely to be liberal than conservative.

He nodded. "Yes. She'd made a career out of skewering sacred cows."

"So who was the 'someone' so eager to fill the police in on your little tiff?" I asked.

He sighed in exasperation. "I don't know exactly. But there are several people who would be happy to see me embarrassed—or worse—by this."

"Like who?"

"A lot of people think I'm in line to be the next President, Nikki. Some of them would rather have themselves or their protégés in that position. So it would be very convenient if it looked like I was furious with my wife for having such extreme views that she was becoming a liability for me. Makes me look desperate, which is just what they want."

Being a power couple clearly had its drawbacks when one partner stepped out of line.

"I hear what you're saying, Gary. But no one can seriously believe that you'd be capable of killing your wife. I mean, a public spat is hardly proof of murderous intent. If it were, I'd be behind bars."

He smiled faintly. "Still into volatile relationships, eh? I'll never forget the fights you used to have with that guy that you had the huge crush on your senior year. What was his name? Dante—"

"Dante Rosario," I said quickly, the unexpected sound of his name sending an involuntary flush to my face.

Gary peered at me quizzically. "I seem to have struck a nerve."

"I haven't talked to you for a while, have I?" *Snap out of it.* "He's back. We're housemates, actually."

His face momentarily brightened. "You've got to be kidding! I haven't heard anything about him in years. So you're living together now?"

"It's a long story. But he happened to move into

my house in Cambridge two months ago, and we're—we've been—we're—"

Gary raised his eyebrows. "Apparently so. Go on."

I shook my head adamantly. I was there to help him, not cry on his shoulder.

"All I can say is, for a die-hard liberal, you have awfully retro tastes in men," he gently needled me. "As I recall, he was *almost* as conservative as Amanda."

"Don't remind me."

A sharp rapping sound on the restaurant window interrupted us. I looked up to find a short man with spiky black hair peering through the glass and waving at us. He was wearing denim overalls, a blue scarf, and a plaid flannel jacket, all of which appeared to be soaking wet from the rain hammering insistently against the pavement. Gary beckoned to him, then leaned back in his chair.

Whoever this man was, his presence had immediately recast Gary's entire demeanor: he suddenly seemed both calmer and more vulnerable, as if the cavalry had finally arrived. For the first time that morning, he actually looked alive.

Within seconds, the man was sliding into the chair next to Gary, his hand on Gary's shoulder.

"Hi, I'm Lancelot." He smiled at me, then immediately turned back to Gary. "I just got back from New York. We *finally* found those hats we've been looking for—in a magic shop in Chelsea, can you believe it? They're absolutely *fabulous*." He turned to me again. "I'm stage-managing a production of the Scottish play that opens at the Yale Rep in two days, and we've been looking all *over* for these incredible habits worn by Sicilian nuns in the fifteenth century. For the witches."

"The Scottish play?" Even though I knew we should inform him about Amanda, I couldn't help asking.

"*Macbeth*, you know," he whispered. "It's bad luck to say the name out loud. Curses the production. Everybody knows that. I knew a man who *died* on a production because the director didn't believe it."

"Lance." Gary cut him off abruptly. "There's something you need to know."

I watched the color drain from his face as Gary began telling him about Amanda. He was out of his chair before the story was complete, enfolding Gary in an awkward, damp embrace. "Man, I'm so sorry. I'm *so* sorry." He knelt at Gary's feet and searched his face. "Do they know who did it?"

"No." Gary shook his head as Lance slowly returned to his chair. "The last person to see her alive was a student in her seminar. The police think it may have been him."

"They should check his records," Lance declared. "You know, see if she was about to give him a bad grade or something. These kids are crazy today, you know," he said, turning to me. "Did you hear about those boys in Chicago that dropped another kid out of a window and killed him just because he wouldn't give them a stick of gum? What can I do to help?" he asked, turning back to Gary.

"Nothing right now."

"Why didn't you call me?" Lance said, sounding hurt. "If I hadn't happened along here, I still wouldn't know."

"I left you a message last night," Gary said. "Several messages, actually."

"Well, there you go." Lance reclined in his chair. "I haven't been home yet. The train from the city was late this morning—what a surprise—and I was on my way to a production meeting when I saw you all." He quickly glanced at his watch. "Let me call and tell them I won't be there."

"Don't miss your meeting for me," Gary said. But it was clear to both of us that he really wanted Lance to stay.

"Don't be ridiculous! Of course I'm skipping it. Just give me a minute. Save me a piece of that pizza," he whispered in my ear as he headed toward the pay phone.

Twenty minutes later we were crossing Old Campus on the way back to Gary's suite. The rain had slowed to a drizzle, but the sky was so dark that it seemed like dusk, and the damp November chill had left the quad nearly deserted. The wind rattled through the naked branches of the elms lining the pathway as a carillon tolled a mordant hymn, leaving me feeling unexpectedly forlorn. I was cold in my very bones. A couple of students stopped Gary to express their sympathy over Amanda's death. It was clear that word was starting to spread through the campus.

At the intersection of two walkways covered in sodden autumn leaves, we passed a statue of an elderly man wearing a flowing robe and seated in a chair. What caught my attention was that while most of the statue was the pale green color of oxidized copper, the toe of the man's shoe was bright gold.

I touched Gary's arm, interrupting his conversation with Lance, and looked quizzically at the statue.

"That's James Woolsey. A former Yale President," Gary said, answering my unspoken question.

"But why is there one gold spot?"

Gary shrugged lightly. "You're supposed to rub his shoe for good luck. The freshmen tend to do it right before exams."

Cursed archways, "the Scottish play," and now ritual shoe-rubbing? These Yalies were a superstitious lot. Must be a side effect of living in the shadows of so many ponderous Gothic buildings.

As we approached the door of Gary's entryway at Branford, I could see a broad-shouldered young black man sitting on the rain-soaked stone steps outside the door. He had dark, flawless skin, and his hair was shaved close to his skull, making his luminous brown eyes even more prominent. He scrambled to his feet as we approached, and I realized that he was well over six feet tall. And big—he could have easily weighed two hundred and fifty pounds.

"Dean Fox?" he asked anxiously, looking down at Gary.

"Yes," Gary replied wearily.

"I just wanted to say how sorry I am. I—I'm Marcellus Tyler."

Gary recoiled in surprise as I viewed the boy with new interest.

"What the hell are you doing here?" Gary said coldly. A young woman passing us in the courtyard glanced curiously in our direction.

"I just wanted to say how sorry I am, sir," the student said. He had a brown Kangol cap in his hand, and was twisting it nervously as he spoke. "I should have waited for her. Professor Fox, I mean. I knew it was late, and I should have walked her home."

"So why didn't you?" Gary said harshly. Several other students had now slowed down to listen in, and I tried to signal to Gary that he was attracting an audience. But his eyes were locked on Marcellus Tyler's face.

"She kept telling me to leave, that she had some things to finish up. I asked her a couple of times if she wanted me to wait, but she said no. I really did." The student's eyes were pleading, and I couldn't help feeling touched. If the police really did consider him a prime suspect, then Marcellus Tyler had plenty of problems himself. He probably should have been out looking for a good lawyer. Instead, he was standing on Gary's doorstep in the cold drizzle, seeking absolution.

That was when I noticed the cut, an angry red gash on his index finger, about an inch in length. The cap in his hand partially obscured it, and I could tell that Gary and Lance hadn't noticed it.

"Get out," Gary said. "Now." His jaw was trembling, and he looked as if he were about to explode.

"Please," Marcellus entreated. "I—"

"Get. Out. Before I fucking kill you." Gary had spoken so softly that the full impact of his words took a moment to sink in. Marcellus looked at me and I shook my head slowly.

"You should go," I said softly. "This isn't the time."

He reluctantly turned away, and within moments had vanished through the darkened corridor leading toward the street. The cluster of students in the courtyard began to disperse.

"That kid knows something." Lance's pronouncement broke the silence between us. "I can feel it. He knows what happened last night. But he's not telling."

"Yeah, he knows because he killed my wife," Gary said angrily. "I'm sure of it now." We started up the winding stairs to Gary's suite, our words echoing off the thick stone walls of the entryway. "What I want to know is, why hasn't that—why hasn't he been arrested? What the hell are these cops doing? The longer they wait, the more time he has to destroy evidence and cover his tracks."

"But what would his motive be, Gary?" I prodded gently.

"I should have thought of it before," he said, seething, as he ushered us into the living room. "Things have been happening so quickly, I hadn't even remembered it until now. About two weeks ago, Amanda started getting these strange phone calls."

"Obscene phone calls, you mean?" Lance interjected.

"Not really. If I answered the phone, the person would immediately hang up. But if she answered, a male voice would start asking her questions."

"What kind of questions?" I sat on the edge of one of the armchairs, as Lance appropriated the space on the sofa beside Gary.

"Where she was going that night," Gary answered. "What she was wearing. Who she was thinking about. Silly, juvenile stuff."

"Did you recognize the voice?" I asked sharply.

"She said that somebody in her seminar had a crush on her, and she thought he was probably the one calling, although she wasn't sure."

"I knew it!" Lance said triumphantly. "I told you, these kids are nuts."

"And you think the student was Marcellus?"

"Why else would he be here?" Gary exclaimed. "He was obviously—"

"Obsessed with her," Lance interrupted. "She probably told him last night to cut it out, that she wasn't interested in him, and then he waited for her and killed her."

Gary glanced at him and nodded soberly.

"You think the kid carries around a huge knife, just in case things don't go his way?" I said skeptically.

"I don't know, Nikki!" Gary was on his feet, pacing before the fireplace. "Maybe he found a knife lying around in the street or in an alley somewhere, and that's what gave him the idea."

"This is New Haven, remember?" Lance chimed in. "The boy could get his hands on any kind of weapon he wanted."

The two of them continued to discuss how Marcellus was the most likely suspect, and Lance urged Gary to call the police to tell them about his visit and the mysterious phone calls. The two men were clearly very close. Lance continued to complete Gary's sentences, and the frequency with which they exchanged glances was beginning to make me feel like an interloper.

So I listened to them silently, because I knew better than to say what I felt.

But I was hoping like hell that they were wrong about Marcellus Tyler.

CHAPTER THREE

The New Black

Five o'clock Monday evening found me shivering in the rain outside the Elm Street gate of Calhoun College, waiting vainly for someone to come along and admit me. It was dusk now, and the stately limestone building loomed forbiddingly as I huddled in its shadow, trying to avoid being splashed by the passing traffic. Wearing a miniskirt and short boots had seemed like a great idea this morning, but now I was soaking wet and miserable—the ultimate fashion victim.

I had spent the rest of the afternoon with Gary, helping him fend off the steady stream of callers wanting to offer their condolences. The word of Amanda's murder was now out all over campus, and

Gary had achieved the instant celebrity status that accompanies violent crime. In addition to his friends, the local press had begun to swarm: five reporters had materialized at his front door at Branford, and three more had contented themselves with shouting questions up from the courtyard until they were ejected by the Yale cops. Lance and I kept the mob in the hallway at bay after Gary almost slugged a stringer for *The New York Times*. Finally, at about four o'clock, we were able to persuade him to accept the sedative offered by the Yale Health Services physician who had stopped by to check on him. Gary was now sound asleep, and Lance had promised to stay with him for the night. The doctor had said he was unlikely to awaken before morning.

I needed to get back to Cambridge at some point that evening, but I had decided to stop in on Lily Cho, a graduate student in the Yale Economics Department whom I had met at a conference over the summer. Lily was a resident fellow at Calhoun College, and I figured it would be easy enough to follow someone through its main entrance and see if she was willing to have dinner with me before I hit the road. But the Calhoun courtyard was deserted, and no one seemed to be either coming in or going out. The sound of classical music issued from a window above my head, but repeated shouts brought no response. Freezing cold now, I clutched my raincoat, berating myself for dressing so inadequately. I should have brought gloves and a scarf, but I'd been in such a panic that morning that it hadn't even occurred to me. Across the street, a young woman in a dark blue slicker and jeans dragged a plump and extremely reluctant beagle along by his leash. At the corner stoplight, the dog collapsed mournfully in a heap on the sidewalk, unwilling to take another step. I met the woman's eyes and we shared a moment of mutual frustration, then she knelt and began pleading with her pet to keep moving before they both caught pneumonia. Two more minutes, and I'd have to give up and go find Maggie's car, which I devoutly hoped would still be where I'd left it.

Just then, a statuesque Asian woman wearing a glossy lime green slicker, black leggings, and knee-high black rubber boots emerged through the iron gates of Old Campus and daintily crossed Elm Street, her brown and gold Louis Vuitton bag swinging insouciantly from her shoulder.

"Lil?" I called out.

She turned and stared for a moment. "Nikki!" she cried, her face brightening as recognition dawned. "What are you doing here?"

Lily Cho was by far the most chic academic I had ever met, and she wasn't disappointing me that night. She had an unerring sense of style that was simultaneously nonchalant and utterly composed, and in our brief acquaintance she'd already trained me to laugh off fashion-magazine pronouncements like "brown is the new black" and go with what worked for me. I made a mental note to try the tall black rubber boot thing, but somehow I doubted that they would make me look nearly as elegant and assured as she did.

We climbed a set of well-worn stone stairs to her suite, and paused in the narrow hallway while she fumbled for her keys. Her arched wooden door was littered with sternly worded student reminders: PLEASE USE THE RECYCLING BIN. REMEMBER: NO MEAL SERVICE WILL BE PROVIDED ON THANKSGIVING DAY. NEED TO MISS A MID-TERM EXAM? LET'S TALK NOW. The doorway across the hall from hers proclaimed a series of far more entertaining messages: it was plastered with bumper stickers reading IN GODDESS WE TRUST, SANITY IS THE PLAYGROUND OF THE UNIMAGINATIVE, MY GODDESS GAVE BIRTH TO YOUR GOD, BUILT TO SEE ACTION, and MEAN PEOPLE SUCK. A photo of a blond, curly-haired Cupid sprawled on the ground with an arrow in his back was captioned BE AFRAID. BE VERY AFRAID. A white message board hung from the door handle, commanding callers to leave messages for Cherry, Amy, Justine, or Cynthia.

"Your neighbors seem like nice girls," I commented dryly, as Lily looked up from her purse.

"You can't *imagine*. Come on in," she said, opening the door.

I felt my spirits lift the moment I stepped across her threshold. Her place was similar to Gary's, only smaller: dark wood floors, a fireplace, low ceilings, and leaded-glass windows. But where Gary's had been spartan and grim, Lily's was warm and inviting. A huge overstuffed sofa upholstered in ivory damask lounged in front of the fireplace, flanked by a dark pink armchair. Pink, ivory, and green pillows were everywhere, potted plants lined the windows, and the comforting scent of vanilla wafted through the air. She leaned over a small stereo and a stream of jazz music immediately filled the air. Leave it to Lil to transform a dingy dorm room into a garden of earthly delights.

"So what are you doing here anyway?" she asked as she dumped her bag on the sofa.

"Well," I said as I shrugged off my jacket, "you know my friend Gary Fox?"

"That's right, you told me you all were old friends. Incredible thing about his wife, isn't it? I heard this afternoon at the TAs' meeting. Somebody said her arm got chopped off, too." She tossed a log from an orderly stack near the hearth into the fireplace, shooing me toward the armchair as she reached for a matchbook.

"Well, that's what I'm doing here," I said, settling into the chair. "He's a wreck, as you can imagine. I've been with him all day."

"So I guess that rumor about her gun wasn't true."

"What rumor?"

"She used to tell people that she carried a handgun in her purse. She told somebody in the Economics Department that she even slept with it under her pillow."

"Knowing Amanda, I'm sure that was just another way to attract attention," I said. "That girl would do anything to get a rise out of the gullible liberals in the crowd." Because if she *had* carried a gun, she still might be alive.

Lily rolled her eyes. "Not just the liberals. That woman defined the phrase 'media whore.' She'd say anything if it got her a sound bite. So do they know who did it?" She perched on the arm of the sofa as flames began to crackle in the fireplace.

"They think it may have been one of her students. He may have had a crush on her that turned violent." I unlaced my soaked boots and slipped them off.

"Wow. This is juicy! You want a drink?"

"Can you scare up one of your famous Fuzzy Navels?"

"*Mais bien sûr!*" She grinned as she rummaged through the bottom shelf of her bookcase and produced half-empty bottles of peach schnapps and vodka. "So they think some student with a crush killed Amanda Fox? And I thought *I* had it bad. Last fall, I had this lovesick kid in my Labor Economics course offering to fly me to Puerto Rico for the weekend. He kept telling me that if we only spent some time together, I'd see how special he was." She shook her head wryly as she poured a generous amount of liquor into two glasses. "Nineteen years old, and still had pimples. But I gotta tell you—when I saw the resort brochure, I almost went!"

"I must only attract the poor ones. No one's ever offered me more than a cup of coffee in exchange for my favors. But seriously—there's a long way between a schoolboy crush and murder."

Lily disappeared into what I assumed was her bedroom and emerged with a half-gallon carton of orange juice and a tray of ice. "They should check and see who's gotten bad grades from her. My students are so ambitious, it's more likely that they'd go postal over a 'D' or an 'F' than they would over an unrequited romance."

"Especially the men," I said, nodding.

Lily deftly mixed the orange juice, schnapps, and vodka, added ice cubes, and then passed me a glass. "To us. And to our darling students, who care more about admission to Harvard Business School than life itself."

I smiled appreciatively after I sipped the tangy-sweet cocktail. "Girl, you still make better drinks than most bartenders I know. And from a dorm room, no less!"

"It's a gift."

"Listen, I'm heading back to Cambridge tonight, but can we grab dinner before I go?"

"You know I'd love to, but I have a command performance tonight. The Fisches are having a cocktail party for the faculty at the Yale Art Gallery, and I have to be there."

"Who are these fish, and why do you have to obey their commands?"

"They're this big, rich Yale family from Savannah. Forbes 400, *Town & Country*, but really loud and pretty low class. Two of the brothers—Max and Jared—are members of the Yale Corporation—the university's Board of Trustees."

"They let two members of the same family onto the Board?"

"Are you kidding? For the money the Fisches throw around here, Yale would let the family's yellow hound dog be on the Board. Rumor has it that they're planning to donate another seventy-five or hundred million, so we all have our orders to play nice-nice." She glanced at her watch. "Hey, why don't you come with me? Then we can dish on the way over, I can score some attendance points, and you can still make it home at a decent hour."

"That sounds great, but I didn't happen to throw a little black dress in the car this morning."

"Oh, don't sweat *that*. I've got a killer Armani frock in my closet with your name on it."

"What about shoes?" I called, following her toward her bedroom in my stocking feet.

"You're not afraid of Blahniks, are you? Because that's all I've got."

A girl with a closet full of Manolo Blahnik shoes? Who was willing to share? This visit had definitely been worth the wait.

A half hour later, we were striding along in four-inch heels on a flagstone walkway that bisected a broad, grassy quadrangle behind Calhoun College. The rain had finally stopped, but a thick fog was settling in over the campus. I could dimly make out a series of hulking stone buildings in the mist, gaslights illuminating their turrets. "What is this called?" I asked.

"Cross-Campus Plaza. That's Harkness Hall—it's all classrooms. That's Berkeley College North. And South. And that's Sterling, the main undergraduate library."

Each and every one of the buildings she pointed to looked like churches to me. Sterling, in particular, reminded me of the Episcopal cathedral in which I used to worship as a child. This was a deeply strange place.

"The Cross-Campus Library is underground, right below us. That's where all the undergrads hang out when they're pretending to study. And that building across the street"—she pointed to a low white stone building that looked exactly like a monastery—"is Commons, the main dining hall."

I wondered if the constant presence of all this religious imagery made the students more pious. Or did it just make sin all the more alluring?

We emerged from the plaza onto High Street. The fog was now nearly impenetrable, and it was impossible to see more than a few feet ahead. I thought again about Amanda Fox.

"Do you feel safe here, Lil?" I asked abruptly.

"Sure," she answered with a shrug. "You learn pretty quickly where you can and can't go at night, and then you just deal with it. You lived in Manhattan for two years—you know what I mean."

I knew what she meant. But New York City has miles and miles of perfectly safe terrain, and taxis handy to whisk you away when the neighborhoods got rough. In a town this small and this troubled, how much safe real estate could there be? And wouldn't you go mad being so boxed in?

"But doesn't it bother you that every few years, there seems to be some random, horrible street crime committed here?" I prodded. "Like wasn't there a kid murdered here a few years back? He had an unusual name—like a martyr's name."

"His name was Christian Prince. I was a freshman when that happened. Really sad. Look, I'm not saying it's Nirvana here," she said flatly. "But New Haven is not nearly as crime-ridden as people make it out to be. Half of the neighborhoods that people describe as 'bad' are just *black* neighborhoods. Which in white people's minds makes them automatically 'bad.' But you don't need me to tell you how *that* works."

On the sidewalk just ahead of us, a wiry black man

in a stocking cap, worn blue jeans, and a tattered army jacket trundled doggedly along with a grocery cart overflowing with pillows, plastic bags, and empty soda cans. Apparently, the stone walls between the campus and the rest of New Haven were porous. The man had swathed himself in a plastic trash bag to fend off the damp night air, and he was humming tunelessly, the sound oddly in sync with the grating of the cart wheels against the pavement.

As he started to cross the street in the middle of the block, I heard a voice call out, "Hey, man!"

A young Asian man in a Yale slicker was coming toward us, pointing at the homeless man and shouting. I braced myself for town-gown relations, New Haven style.

"You dropped something, man!" the student called out. He stepped off the curb and retrieved a couch cushion that had fallen off of the homeless man's grocery cart and lay hidden behind the wheel of a parked car. Briskly handing it over, he loped off toward Elm Street.

Okay, so maybe there *was* something to recommend this place, after all.

In two minutes, the Yale Art Gallery emerged from the fog, looming before us on the corner of Chapel Street, and I realized that I had walked right by it earlier that day. It was stationed amidst the depressed retail establishments I had passed, its brown cinderblock facade blending in all too well.

A welcoming gust of warm air greeted us as we swept across the threshold, and after checking our coats in the vestibule, we were steered toward the first-floor gallery. I was pleasantly surprised to see that in this bastion of Olde English architecture, the current exhibition was of African art: a placard announced that the works on display were sculptures created by the Baule people of the Ivory Coast.

"We encourage you to enjoy the exhibition first, then join the group in the adjoining gallery," a serious young man urged.

"I'll meet up with you later, okay?" Lily whispered. "My dissertation adviser just arrived, and I *don't* want to see him right now."

I nodded sympathetically and spent the next ten minutes wandering through the galleries solo, gradually mesmerized by the intricate masks and sculpture. Eventually, I roamed into a hidden wing that featured glass cases filled with small wooden figurines. SPIRIT-SPOUSES, read the display card, ARE MEANT TO REPRESENT SUPERNATURAL HUSBANDS OR WIVES WHO PROTECT THE LIVING. Given the current state of my love life, a spirit spouse was probably the only type I'd ever have, but it was a nice thought.

The narrow corridor was wreathed in shadows, and it wasn't until an irritated voice somewhere farther down the passageway interrupted my bout of self-pity that I realized I had strayed into a private conversation.

"Brother, you better pull yourself together."

The phrasing and thick Southern accent sounded black, but when I located the source of the gruff voice that had issued the command, the speaker turned out to be a forty-something white man with thick wavy brown hair, dark brown eyes, and a stocky build. He was standing in a pool of light, wearing shirtsleeves and dark slacks. His shirttail protruded from one side of his pants, and he was scowling ferociously at a slender white man with shoulder-length brown hair who looked to be my age. I immediately realized that he hadn't been using the phrase "brother" colloquially: his companion was clearly his younger sibling.

"I don't think I can do this, Max," the younger man pleaded in an equally Southern twang. "I can't do this. I need to be alone." He raked his hand through his hair as he turned away, looking positively Byronesque in his grief.

"For God's sake, of course you can do it!" the older man snapped. "You sound like a damned sissy." As insulting as the word was, it must have been even more maddening when it came out sounding like "sis-uh."

The young one turned back to his brother, eyes blazing. "She hasn't even been dead for twenty-four hours, and you're acting like—"

"Like a fucking *man*. The way *you* should be acting. Life goes on, boy, and you're not pissing away my big night—*our* big night. We've got a major announcement to make, and you're damn well going to stand up there and make it with me."

Could these be the famous Fisches? I wondered, suddenly very intrigued. And was the younger one talking about Amanda Fox?

"Screw you and your announcement, Max. Like any of that matters now."

"Hey. *You* were the one who wanted to keep the son of a bitch from becoming President, little brother. With the cops on his butt, you'll get your wish." "Max" grabbed his brother's arm and pulled roughly. "It's show time. Wipe your nose and let's go."

A look of pure hatred flickered across the younger one's face, but it came and went so quickly that I wondered if I had imagined it. Then he straightened his shoulders and followed his brother. I looked away as they passed, although they seemed so preoccupied that I was certain neither of them would have noticed me, even if I had stared shamelessly.

Wanted to keep the SOB from becoming President. They *had* to be talking about Gary and Amanda.

Which meant that they needed watching.

I followed the men as they passed from the darkened gallery into a glittering three-story hall with towering stone walls and a slate floor. A dozen sparkling crystal chandeliers illuminated a series of tall, startlingly white Greek sculptures and a crowd of chattering, tweedy professors holding wineglasses. A jazz trio in black tie played softly in the background.

The older brother strode purposefully to a small podium near the windows and tapped the microphone impatiently. If this *was* Max Fisch, he was single-handedly dragging down the fashion quotient of the Forbes 400—he looked like he'd just rolled out of bed. The music came to an abrupt halt as a tall, white-haired man joined the younger brother at his place behind the older man's left shoulder.

"Okay, let's get this moving," Max growled abruptly, and the room slowly quieted. "I'm sure you all know I'm Maxwell Fisch, Class of '77," he continued. "And this is my brother Jared, Class of '85. Most of you probably know that we've invested a lot in this school—seventy-five million dollars, in fact, over the last five years."

"But who's counting?" the woman next to me hissed audibly. She rolled her eyes as Max wiped his mouth with the back of his fist.

"We structure our contributions to Yale in the same way we structure our investments in all our businesses," Fisch continued.

"Isn't it enough that he's dragged us out on a night like this? Now we have to listen to this low-class hillbilly compare Yale to a *business?*" the woman said, less quietly this time.

Her male companion placed a comforting hand on her arm. "Money talks, my dear," he said imperturbably.

"So we look at Yale the same way that we look at

Fisch Corrugated Paper Mills," Max declaimed. "As an entity that requires greater investment in order to generate increased returns. And with that in mind, our family will be increasing our contribution to the university. In a *major* way."

The white-haired man smiled benevolently from behind Fisch's shoulder. Must be the Yale President. If the contribution was going to be as major as all that, the big guns would have to be assembled.

"Our gift will total two hundred million dollars, to be given within this fiscal year," Max announced, and the President's smile broadened to Cheshire Cat proportions. After a stunned silence, the room erupted into loud applause. Apparently, a hillbilly could be forgiven a lot if his wallet was big enough.

"But there's one small condition," Max shouted into the microphone as he raised his hands.

I could tell from the look on the President's face that Maxwell Fisch had just departed from the agreed-upon script.

Max smiled coyly. "Like my daddy always says: 'For every gimme, there's a gotcha.'" He paused. "The money must be used to create a required curriculum for freshman students at the College. For the study of the ethics and American values. We'll be contributing money for the construction of a new house of worship on campus, which all undergraduate students will be required to attend once a week." Max glanced at the President. "We will, of course, endow a chair to head this curriculum. And our family will naturally play an active role in the selection of the individual who will hold this chair."

An audible gasp went up from the crowd. The President wasn't smiling anymore. Not even the least little bit.

"Is he *kidding?*" whispered the woman beside me. "What, does he think we're for sale? Doesn't he know we would never allow an outsider to control a faculty appointment? Let alone the freshman curriculum!"

"You've forgotten the most important part, Max." Jared Fisch, who had been standing silently behind his brother, had suddenly revived. He ignored his brother's glare and the buzz of the crowd as he stepped forward to the microphone. "The endowed chair will be named in memory of one of our dearest colleagues, a brilliant scholar whose life and work have been cut horribly short. Amanda Ingersol Fox."

This time it was Maxwell Fisch who gasped audibly. "Amanda was our dear friend, and a true inspiration," Jared continued. "May her passionate commitment to education, principle, and truth live on in this small way." He stepped back from the podium with an enigmatic smile, and his brother was left to conclude the festivities.

The crowd wasn't waiting for him, however. Already the woman standing beside me was loudly talking to her friend. "I don't know what's worse: the fact that they're offering us a bribe, or the fact that its sole purpose seems to be to memorialize that *witch*," she hissed.

"Don't kid yourself," her companion replied *sotto voce*. "From the look on Big Fisch's face, Little Fisch just pulled a fast one on him."

"Well, the Prexy better get on top of this, and fast. It's ridiculous!" she snapped.

I scanned the crowd, looking for Lily. I needed to know a lot more about these Fisches, especially what the younger one's relationship was with Gary. And with Amanda. Ten minutes had passed, and I had traversed the room twice without catching sight of her, when I stepped into the hallway on the far side of the room and paused for a moment at the drinking fountain.

"Excuse me. Can you part my hair?"

I slowly raised my head and found myself confronted with an expanse of delicate pink scalp covered with strands of thinning black and silver hair. Taking an involuntary step backward, I saw that it belonged to a tall, kindly, patrician white man who appeared to be in his late fifties. He was wearing a gray suit, blue bow tie, and a snow white shirt, and was smiling sheepishly at me.

"I don't have my glasses, and I can't see a thing, and my date tells me that I need to do something about my part. It goes on the right side."

"Sure," I said, still taken aback. The man proffered

a thin black plastic comb, which I gently dragged across his scalp. Combing the thin strands over, I met his twinkling blue eyes and couldn't help smiling. "Do you want it combed over, or back?"

"I comb it back," he confided, taking the comb from me. "Like this. What do you think?"

He was grinning back at me, and I leaned toward him conspiratorially. "You look very debonair. Your date should be pleased."

"I'm Reid Talbot. Professor of Law. And you are?"

"Veronica Chase. Assistant Professor of Economics."

"If you'll let me, I'd be happy to escort you back to the party, Professor Chase." He gallantly extended his arm, and I took it as we started across the hall.

"I'm surprised that we haven't met. I thought I knew most of the Economics faculty."

"I have a confession to make," I whispered as we entered the room. "I'm crashing. I'm actually on the Harvard faculty."

"Oh yes, that school up in Massachusetts. I've heard of it." He shook his head regretfully. "It's a pity about that scandal with President Barrett. What brings you to Yale?"

"I'm a friend of Dean Fox. I'm sure you've heard about his wife's death."

The animation drained slowly out of his face, replaced by a deep sadness. "Oh, Amanda," he said softly. "She was a wonderful, wonderful girl."

I looked at him closely, and saw that his sadness

was genuine. "Of course, you were on the Law School faculty together," I concluded, "so you must have known her."

"More than that, young lady. I've known her since she was a first-year law student. I advised her on her first *Law Review* article." He cleared his throat, and I saw the glimmer of tears in his eyes. "I'm so pleased that Jared is going to memorialize her in this way. It's the least he can do."

"Reid?" a voice called out. We turned to find a stately gray-haired woman in a dark green dress regarding us quizzically. "It's time to go. A group of us are headed to Mory's to sort out this Fisch tale."

"We have to hurry, or we'll miss the Whiffenpoofs," said the man beside her as he glanced impatiently at his watch.

"I'm coming, Felice," Talbot said gravely. "Please excuse me, Professor Chase. I thank you for the grooming assistance."

I watched them disappear into the crowd, turning the professor's words over in my mind.

The least he can do?

What exactly had Jared Fisch done to Amanda Fox that required atonement?

CHAPTER FOUR

Tea and Sympathy

It was almost midnight by the time I arrived back in Cambridge, and I paused on the concrete walkway leading up to our house after parking Maggie's car on the street. The welcoming beams of our porch light illuminated the gold and crimson sheaves of Indian corn hanging at the front door, and the stack of fresh-cut firewood beside the doorway. My breath was faintly visible in the clean late-autumn air, which smelled of wood smoke, and damp leaves, and safety. The street was hushed, save for the occasional whisper of a car flying by on nearby Mass Ave. and the wind rustling through the dark, leafless trees, so I could clearly hear the sound of voices coming from inside. The nightly tea party appeared to be in full swing.

I live on the top floor of an old three-story wood-frame house just north of Harvard Square, which is also occupied by my landlady, Magnolia Dailey; her affable black labrador, Horace; my once and possibly future boyfriend, Dante Rosario; his roommate, Ted Adair; and my cosmopolitan cat, John Maynard Keynes. An opinionated fifty-nine-year-old schoolteacher with a Harvard Ph.D. and an Angela Davis afro, Maggie holds court at the end of each day at the kitchen table, luring the rest of us in by providing a steady flow of herbal tea, fresh-baked pies and cakes, and outspoken views on every possible aspect of our lives. The combination is usually irresistible.

"Darlin', is that you?" she called out as I stepped through the front door.

"Yes," I shouted back as I shrugged off my slicker.

"We were about to give up on you," she chided as I swung through the kitchen door and dutifully kissed her cheek.

"No we weren't," a female voice piped in. "No way I was leaving until I got the 4-1-1 on Amanda Fox."

The voice belonged to my best friend, Jessica Lieberman. A fourth-year resident in obstetrics and gynecology at Mass General Hospital, she still managed to find time to hang out at our house at least two nights a week. I'd called her that morning to fill her in on Gary Fox's phone call, since she was well acquainted with both him and Amanda: she'd been in the same college class and the same dormitory as Amanda and me.

"You look great," I said as I settled in next to Jess at the kitchen table. Tall and slender, with a mane of curly dark-brown hair and huge brown eyes, she was wearing a short green skirt and brown crocodile high heels. A matching green jacket hung on the back of her chair. "What's with the interview suit?" I asked.

"Don't you remember? I told you the head of ob/gyn at Brigham and Women's Hospital was having a dinner party at his house tonight. He practically *promised* me that maternal-fetal fellowship next year." She peered more closely at me. "Those earrings are fly! Where'd you get them?"

"Shoot! I forgot I had them on. These aren't mine." Lily had loaned me a pair of gorgeous sterling silver clip-ons as part of my outfit, and I'd been so preoccupied mentally dissecting the Fisch brothers' conversation I'd overheard that I'd failed to return them.

"So how is your friend in New Haven, baby?" Maggie asked as she sliced a generous hunk off of the chocolate cake that sat in the middle of the kitchen table. Always the African queen, that night my landlady was swathed in a floor-length purple-and-orange robe and draped with a long rope of black beads.

"That's right, what's up with Gary and the homecoming queen?" Jess drawled.

"Don't speak badly of the dead, Miss Thing," I chided. Jess had never forgiven Amanda for stealing her boyfriend sophomore year.

"I had no time for that girl when she was alive. I'm not planning to fake it now," she said with a shrug. "But I do feel sorry for Gary."

I was about to fill them in on the day's adventures when I heard the front door open. Two male voices echoed in the hall, and I felt a reflexive surge of electricity flow through my veins. Our housemates were home, and despite my best efforts to the contrary, Dante Rosario's appearance inevitably precipitated a chemical reaction.

"Ted?" Jess called coyly, winking at me. At the moment, Dante's roommate, Ted Adair, was Jess's quasi-boyfriend, which meant that he stood ready to make an immediate commitment while she preserved her right to flirt with all and sundry. It was nice work if you could get it.

"When are you planning to stop jerking him around?" I hissed at her. Having been in the same position as Ted on numerous occasions, I felt obliged to lend him a hand.

"Stop trying to ruin my fun," she said with an evil laugh.

"You're full of shit, Rosario," Ted said adamantly as the two men emerged through the kitchen door. "Giuliani's business development districts haven't benefited anybody except the suburban shareholders of the Fortune 500 companies that are getting the tax breaks. Hey, sweetie," he said, absentmindedly kissing Jess's cheek. Ted was a lawyer at a free clinic in Roxbury, and shared my ferociously liberal political beliefs.

"Do the math," Dante retorted, shrugging off his black leather jacket. "The per capita increase in tax revenue alone was sixty-seven hundred dollars."

"Yeah, but where's the extra money getting spent?" Ted demanded. "Not in the neighborhood. You're a government professor, for God's sake. You know the money flows to the districts with the swing voters."

"Hel*lo*," Jess cried, sounding almost petulant.

"You're not defending enterprise zones again, are you?" I interjected. "We all know they're a Republican scheme to funnel money into the pockets of their largest donors while appearing to do something for minority communities."

"Last I heard, Floyd Flake was supporting them as a critical urban development tool. And last time I checked, he was a Democrat," Dante countered, reaching for a pair of mugs from one of the kitchen cabinets.

"Yeah, and that'll last about as long as Magic Johnson's talk show," I retorted.

"I told you all to stop going to those Kennedy School Forums," Maggie interjected. "Every time you do, you turn my kitchen into *The McLaughlin Group*, and I get enough of that foolishness on the playground at Rindge and Latin School every day. Now stop fussin' and have a piece of this cake. It's fresh made."

"I still think it's despicable that throwing a few coins into a depressed neighborhood is all it takes to salve your conscience," I muttered.

"I know what you think, lady. I just don't happen to agree," Dante murmured, passing me a mug. I looked up to find his eyes on my face. As he read my expression, his brow wrinkled. "What's going on, Nik? You look . . . pensive."

Long ago, a friend asked me to describe Dante Rosario. During my sophomore year in college I'd exchanged a glance with the man from which I was still recovering, yet I'd always found it difficult to accurately delineate him. The specifics were easy: shiny brown hair; huge, intelligent brown eyes; a soft mouth and a hard jaw. But explaining why the whole was more than the sum of the parts was something that I couldn't explain or justify, even to myself.

"Nikki's been at Yale all day with Gary Fox," Jess announced as Ted settled in next to her at the table. "You remember him, right, Dante?" She turned to me. "By the way, is he still wearing those great sweaters?"

"I was wondering where you were today. I stopped by your office, and they said you were out." Dante regarded me quizzically as he leaned against the kitchen counter.

"Gary called me early this morning. His wife, Amanda, was murdered late Sunday night."

"What?" Dante and Ted exclaimed simultaneously.

"I know you two don't have a television, but don't you even read the paper? She was stabbed on a deserted street near the campus, and bled to death before anyone found her."

"My God." Dante's face was noticeably paler.

"Was she a friend of yours?" Maggie asked, regarding him closely. "I thought you all didn't like her."

"Of course I liked her. I just talked to her a week ago," Dante said slowly.

"*What?*" I exclaimed sharply. "You just spoke to Amanda?"

Jess glanced at me, her expression completely transparent. *Calm down, girlfriend.* "I didn't know you kept in touch with her, Dante," she said lightly.

"He talked to her pretty regularly," Ted interjected as Dante slowly sat down next to him.

"I spoke with her last Monday," he finally answered me. "I remember, because we were discussing my freshman seminar on political morality."

This revelation was incredible. Dante and I had broken up the day we graduated from college, and hadn't spoken for eight years until, through total coincidence, he and his roommate moved into my house two months earlier. Since then, we'd been pursuing a uniquely fractious courtship, involving frequent public arguments and private tousling. And now it turned out that he had been talking regularly to a woman that he knew I detested. He'd been in touch with her during all those years that he'd completely forgotten about me, and he'd never bothered to mention it.

"So what happened in New Haven, anyway?" Jess threw herself into the conversational breach before I could react to Dante's bombshell, so I distractedly described the events of the day, concluding with my observation that Jared Fisch seemed especially close to Amanda, which I found surprising, given that he was clearly an enemy of Gary's.

By the time I finished, Dante was looking at me with an exasperated expression. "You can't possibly think that she would betray Gary."

His instinctive defense of Amanda Fox sent me over the edge. Gary was at risk of being falsely accused of murder, and all Dante could think about was *her*—a dyed-blond, race-baiting, gender-betraying Republican. "Hey, I'm just reporting what I saw," I snapped. "The man was clearly devastated by her death. Way out of proportion to his alleged relationship with Amanda. Although that seems to be going around."

"What's *that* supposed to mean?"

"All I'm saying is that Amanda Fox had some kind of very close relationship with Jared Fisch, and he's clearly an enemy of her husband. It seems strange—

if you understand the concept of loyalty. Of course, I'm sure you know all about her extracurricular activities, since the two of you were such *good* friends."

Dante groaned. "Don't even *think* about playing Agatha Christie again, Nik."

"I never said anything about investigating it further. But if I did, it would be none of your business."

"Oh, really?"

"Gee, look at the time," Jess said brightly. "It's almost one o'clock."

"I'll walk you home," Ted said quickly. "Good night, all."

"Since when were you and Amanda such close pals, anyway?" I baited Dante, barely acknowledging their departure.

"Your memory is ridiculously selective, Nik. She and I were always good friends. We went to the Senior Soiree together, for God's sake. I know you remember that."

"Yeah, I do. I remember that we had a huge argument, and that you went with her instead of me. And now that you mention it, I seem to remember that the two of you had just a *swell* time." I'd never forget the sight of them with his arms around her, nor could I forget her mocking expression. And that was only two weeks before she announced her engagement to Gary. Jess was right. Just because she was dead was no reason to pretend to have liked her.

"So *that's* what's bothering you!" he said triumphantly. He was regarding me across the table with an amused expression, which infuriated me even more. "You're jealous."

"Don't flatter yourself, Rosario," I said sharply. "I'm just surprised that you never found your way clear to tell me that you spoke with her 'frequently,' as Ted put it. And apparently, she never managed to tell her husband, either. I mentioned you to Gary earlier today, and he said he hadn't heard your name *in ten years*. But, hey, what do I care?"

"Oh, but you *do* care, Juliet."

"Get over yourself."

"That's enough, children," Maggie declared. Until she spoke, I had almost forgotten that she was still there. "Honestly, the two of you fuss like cats and dogs."

"You're right, Maggie. It's *more* than enough. And I've got an eight A.M. lecture tomorrow." Dante started for the door. "I'll see you in the morning." He paused and whispered in my ear on his way out, "You're adorable when you're angry, Juliet."

"You know, I've killed men with my bare hands for remarks far less sexist than that!" I shouted after him.

"What is going *on* with you all?" Maggie asked as Dante's footsteps sounded on the stairwell. "I know all that fussin' wasn't just over this girl down at Yale."

I sat in silence, still fuming.

"I can't go to bed until you come clean, Sister Professor, so start talking."

"He's taunting me," I snapped. "Because I won't—"

"You won't what?" she prodded.

"Because *he* won't—"

"Won't *what?*"

"Make a commitment. Sleep with him." Maggie looked at me in genuine confusion. "I'm answering your questions. In reverse order," I said, reaching for the teapot.

"Oh," she said, comprehension dawning. "Lord have mercy, no *wonder* you all can't be in the same room together. So since he's been back you all haven't—"

"No," I said adamantly.

"Well, that would explain why you're at each other's throats, wouldn't it?"

In a big way.

"I don't understand," she continued, slicing herself another piece of cake. "You keep makin' eyes at each other, and neither one of you is seeing anyone else, but you won't—"

"I. Don't. Trust him. What's not to understand?"

"Just because you broke up once? Of course, I don't know what you're doing with a white boy anyway, but it *was* eight years ago."

"Well, it seems like yesterday, and he hasn't changed a bit. He hasn't said one word about how he feels about me. And look at this thing with Amanda Fox—you see how he didn't even tell me that he was in touch with the girl."

"You're being a little hard on him, my sister. If they were just friends, and if he knew you didn't like her, why should he tell you? And I don't see why you're so hung up on what he *says*. Actions speak louder than words, and didn't the boy paint your living room last weekend? And doesn't he cook for you almost every night now?"

"Whose side are you on here, anyway?"

"Hey, you know what *I* think about this interracial stuff. Being friends with them is one thing, but cross that line and you'll both be sorry." I could tell Maggie was just getting warmed up. "There are plenty of good black men looking for someone like you," she continued, "and I don't know what your problem is. Okay, so some of our men are threatened by women who are too smart or too independent. But, my Lord, it's better than crossing that line. Seems like every educated brother or sister I hear about is busy marrying outside the race. And where do you think *that's* going to get us? No history, no legacy, no future."

"You're not being realistic," I said defensively. "There aren't enough educated black men to go around. Hear me out—" I continued, as she started to speak. "In this year's freshman class, there are twenty-five black men and *seventy-five* black women.

Even if all those boys are straight, what are the other fifty girls supposed to do? Join a convent?"

"You want statistics, Sister Professor? I'll give you some statistics. One in four black men in this country end up in jail at some point in their lives. Thirteen percent of black men can't vote because they have criminal records. Now, how is your dating some Italian boy gonna turn any of that around?"

"I get the point, Maggie. It's not like I don't think about all of this constantly." I rose abruptly and leaned against the kitchen counter. "Look, this is probably all irrelevant, anyway. Dante is nowhere near ready to bring me home to Mama, and I'm not interested in being featured in some rueful confession to his lovely white wife someday."

"Then, girl, you'd be wise to keep withholdin' the milk—as the old folks would say."

"Well, if it's so wise, then why aren't you doing the same thing with Rafe?" I teased. I had met Sergeant Detective Raphael Griffin, a black Harvard police officer, a few weeks earlier, and after their first dinner party, he and Maggie had become practically inseparable.

"Because, darlin', when you're my age, the *least* of your worries is whether they're gonna bring you home to Mama."

CHAPTER FIVE

You Heard It
Here First

I awakened Tuesday morning before even the first hint of morning light, having spent a fitful night dreaming about Gary and Amanda. Ghostly figures shrouded in fog had pursued me at knifepoint, their whispers taunting me, and I awoke feeling restless and vaguely annoyed. There was something going on down in New Haven—and I was missing out on it.

Slipping quietly down the stairs, I silently closed the front door behind me and started quickly down Mass Ave., headed for Harvard Square. There was plenty of time to fetch breakfast, since I didn't have any commitments until my 10:00 A.M. International Economics section, and I wanted to see how the morning papers were covering Amanda's death.

Dawn was breaking as I passed the Coop, and the Square was just beginning to stir. The counterman at Store 24 was dispensing coffee and doughnuts to a couple of policemen, and a few stray patrons were already seated in the window of the Greenhouse Cafe, their faces buried behind the *Crimson* and the *Globe*. I paused at Nini's Corner and surveyed my choices. The newsstands in Cambridge are bountiful and cosmopolitan, with thousands of daily papers and periodicals available from all over the world. I still remember my awe as a freshman living in the Yard, being awakened every morning to the sounds of an elderly man employed by the Out of Town Newsstand calling out, "*New York Times, New York Post, New York Daily News*" to the commuters streaming down into the T-station. I quickly learned that only the most parochial would read the Boston papers and feel satisfactorily informed.

The coverage of Amanda's death had been spotty on Monday; her body hadn't been discovered until one o'clock that morning, and even the afternoon papers hadn't run lengthy stories. So I figured today had to be the day, and I was right. The story made front page above the fold in the *Crimson*, the *Times*, and the *Globe*. I quickly skimmed their perfectly decorous coverage, and instantly realized that none of these papers was going to tell me what I wanted to know. For detailed information on a grisly murder, what I needed were the tabloids and local papers. So

I gathered up the *Boston Herald*, the *New York Post*, the *Yale Daily News*, and the *New Haven Register*. After a quick stop at Warburton's for a bag of muffins, I headed back home.

Maggie was installed in the kitchen when I arrived, and the fragrant smell of brewing coffee drew me straight to her.

"Sister Professor! You're up early. I heard you go out."

"Had to get the papers," I said, kissing her cheek on my way to the cupboard for a mug. "And I bought muffins."

"You got me a carrot one, right? Let's see what's up," Maggie said, eagerly reaching for the stack of newspapers I had deposited on the kitchen counter.

"Just save me the *Post*, Okay?"

Two minutes later, we were immersed in breakfast and the details of Amanda's murder. Halfway through my first paragraph, I realized that there was plenty that Gary hadn't told me, perhaps because it was too much for him to bear.

YALE BEAUTY STABBED TO DEATH, read the *Post*'s headline. The tabloid reported that Amanda Ingersol Fox, a popular blond Associate Law Professor at Yale and daughter of prominent New York businessman Derek Ingersol, was stabbed five times near the Resurrection Tabernacle Deliverance Church in New Haven at about 9:30 P.M. Sunday, November 17. She had left the Klein Biology Building after teaching a seminar and had been found by the assistant minister at the church on his way home that evening.

The attack was vicious, and appeared to be sexual in nature. "There were two stab wounds in the victim's chest, and three in her upper thighs," Sergeant Sean Kelly was quoted as saying. An unidentified source reported that the pattern of the wounds and the "violent upward thrusts" of the knife indicated that the murderer had sat astride her as he attacked. "The brainy beauty never had a chance," the reporter wrote. "Detectives said it was unclear whether her left hand was severed before or after her death."

Fighting nausea, I pushed my uneaten muffin away and stared at the newspaper. That didn't sound like the behavior of a random criminal. From these details, it sounded like the killer was someone who was intimately and specifically enraged with Amanda Fox. Someone in a frenzy.

The story went on to say that the victim had been found covered in blood, an Hermès purse lying beside her.

"It does not appear that the motive was robbery, because her handbag was there," Kelly said. "But we don't know the contents of her bag when she left the classroom. Whoever did it was clearly crazed with anger. But whether they hated women, or hated her, or hated someone else and mistook her for that person, we don't know."

A choir had been rehearsing at the Resurrection

Tabernacle Deliverance Church earlier in the evening, but no one present reported hearing anything unusual around what was believed to be the time of the murder. So far, no one who might have witnessed the attack had come forward. Officers so far had no suspects, and were going door-to-door seeking witnesses, Kelly said. Police sources said it was unclear whether the attack was completely random or if someone had stalked the victim.

"This is a high-crime area," said New Haven County District Attorney Patrick Casey. "But we haven't seen an attack this brutal in years." Yale officials urged students to take special precautions while walking in the area. The murder scene was within a mile of the school.

The story reported that the deceased professor's husband, Yale Dean Garrett T. Fox, had declined to respond to media inquiries. However, New Haven police had not ruled him out as a suspect. "Right now, we haven't narrowed this down at all. No one has been ruled out."

No wonder Gary was so worried, I thought. A vicious sexual attack on his wife two days after they'd publicly argued? The police would *have* to consider him a suspect.

There was a sickening intimacy to this crime that made me believe Amanda must have known her attacker. Marcellus Tyler's pleading eyes and Jared Fisch's anguished expression flashed before my mind again. Ever since I'd known her, Amanda had generated a passionate emotional response from men.

She'd had that gift.

I turned back to the paper and noted that everyone didn't see it that way. A more political angle was already being spun to the press. "It is highly ironic that Professor Fox, who was an antifeminist, was felled by indiscriminate male violence toward women," said Yale Women's Studies Professor Felice Roberts. "Her death illustrates the concerns of all of us who are fighting for the rights of women. It's a pity that she didn't understand this when she was alive."

Now *that* was a cheap shot. I laid the paper aside and pensively sipped my coffee. Forget my personal feelings about Amanda Fox. *Was* she a random casualty of urban male violence? Or had she been the victim of something much more personal? Something even more sinister?

"Oh my Lord," Maggie muttered under her breath.

"What?" I said sharply.

"Listen to this," she said, reading aloud from the *Herald: "A white female student participating in Professor Fox's seminar reported to police that she observed a man hiding in the bushes on her way home. She described the man as being between five-ten and six-two. 'It was definitely a suspicious-looking black man,' the witness said. 'With really dark skin and short hair.' New Haven police will be releasing a sketch of the suspect later today."*

I inhaled sharply.

"I am too tired of these white people!" Maggie declared, hurling the paper away in disgust.

I knew where she was heading. "The unidentified black man strikes again."

"That's right, my sister. 'Cause you know, every single murder in this country has been committed by the same person: a dark-skinned, evil-lookin' black man. Never mind that half the time it ends up being like in that Susan Smith case," she continued. "Pale as corn silk white girl was busy telling the police that some dark-skinned black man had kidnapped her two kids. But don't you know, a week later she confessed that she had killed them herself? And remember that man here in Boston who did the same thing?"

I nodded. "Stuart. The yuppie. First he said that he and his pregnant wife were car-jacked by a black man in Roxbury, and then later he committed suicide and left a note confessing that he had killed his wife for the insurance money."

"Well, the boy didn't manage to kill himself before they arrested about twenty innocent black folks. Son of a bitch. But it doesn't matter how many Susan Smiths there are, these white folks still think that all the violence in the world can be traced back to us."

"It's not *all* of them, Maggie."

"It's *enough* of 'em."

I nodded soberly, and she resumed reading the paper. "Listen to this," she said. "*Reverend Leroy*

Saunders, head minister of the Resurrection Tabernacle Deliverance Church, was quoted as saying that the black community would not tolerate what it perceived as unfair police harassment in the wake of the murder. 'I'm putting the police on notice right now. We will not accept a rush to judgment. There will be a price to pay if there is. And I demand to be informed at every stage of this investigation on behalf of the African-American community in New Haven.'" Maggie sighed. "I'm glad somebody down there is looking out for our folks."

I frowned. "Leroy Saunders. Isn't he that guy who was just in the paper?" Maggie looked at me quizzically. "You remember," I pressed her. "That *Globe* profile last Sunday on urban ministers. Wasn't he the one who asked all his parishioners to submit their W-2 forms so he could verify their income and be sure they were giving enough money to his church?"

"You're right!" She nodded in agreement. "What did he say? 'The Bible says tithing is giving ten percent of your income. If my folks are doin' right by the Lord, then they shouldn't mind provin' it!'" She laughed under her breath. "What these preachers won't do."

"It's not funny," I said, reaching for my uneaten muffin. "He sounds like a hustler to me. I remember the story saying he lives in a mansion and drives a Mercedes SL. You think *he's* tithing?"

"I don't care," Maggie declared. "If he's lookin' out for our folks, then I'm with him."

She had a point. In this case, I was certain that the usual suspects would be rounded up. A rich white girl was dead, and the local police and the university would be under tremendous pressure to resolve the case quickly and get it out of the headlines.

Suddenly, I was very afraid for Marcellus Tyler.

"Trade liberalization: death knell for the U.S. economy, or a necessary condition for growth? Mr. Hamilton, what's your view?"

"It's quite clear that free trade improves the competitiveness of the U.S. economy," Hamilton said self-assuredly, leaning forward in his chair.

"How so?"

"Because it improves the competitiveness of the imported versions of products by reducing the degree of price distortion, thereby increasing productive efficiency and national income."

"In English, please, Mr. Hamilton." There was an audible snicker from a student in the back row as Hamilton looked at me in shock. It's easy to sound brilliant in an economics course by regurgitating jargon—the hard part is articulating the arcane concepts in clear prose. Hamilton now looked terrified, a clear sign that he'd read the text without understanding a word of it.

"Anyone?" I asked. We were five minutes into my 10 A.M. International Economics section, and it looked like it was going to be a long sixty minutes.

"I'll give it a shot," a voice called from the back.

"Go ahead, Ms. Weber." I leaned against my desk.

"Trade barriers mean that goods produced by other countries incur a duty when they enter the U.S., which artificially increases their retail price. Trade liberalization reduces that duty, and consumers benefit from lower prices."

"Only if the foreign manufacturers *and* the retailers pass the savings along," interjected another young woman. "And what are the chances of that happening?"

"Actually, they're pretty high," I responded. "Here's the scenario: if the retailer doesn't pass the savings along to the consumer, in the short term she earns a higher profit on imported goods than on domestic ones. So she orders even more imported product and less domestic product. Her reduced demand for the domestic product forces the domestic manufacturers to reduce their prices, which in turn increases consumer demand for products made in the United States."

My mind was running on parallel tracks: part of me dutifully continued to recite the accepted theory on international trade. The other part was rehashing what I had just read about Amanda Fox's death. "Retailers settle for smaller profits per unit because they're suddenly selling more units; eventually, the profit-maximizing move on the retailer's part will be to reduce the price of imported product by roughly the amount of the old duty. And consumers will end up paying less for both domestic and imported products." *If this was a random attack, why hadn't Amanda's purse been stolen? And why was the attack so violently sexual? The paper had said she was stabbed in the "upper thighs." I knew what that really meant.*

"That all sounds great, Professor Chase." A bearded student in the front row snapped me out of my reverie. "But what about American jobs? We allow these cheap imports in, and it's working people who suffer."

"That's not true." Mr. Hamilton had regained his composure. "If trade barriers fall, then we'll be *exporting* more, too. So workers laid off in one industry will have new jobs available in others." *Had Amanda pissed off someone important with her unremitting right-wing attacks? Or had she broken somebody's heart? Was this some kind of twisted revenge?*

"Very good, Mr. Hamilton," I said encouragingly. "But what if the jobs are in another state? Or if the new industries require specialized skills?" *Was Gary in danger of being falsely arrested for the murder? And what was going to happen to Marcellus Tyler?*

"Well, you can phase in the reductions in trade barriers so that people can be re-trained," Mr. Hamilton was saying. I nodded with feigned enthusiasm, and he continued. "Or you can provide cash payments to compensate the affected workers."

"Like the Republicans are ever going to go for *that*," scoffed the bearded man.

"Hey, it was a Democratic President who signed NAFTA," Hamilton retorted.

Moderating the ensuing political debate absorbed all of my attention for the remainder of the hour. Afterward, I holed up in my office in Littauer Center and worked through lunch on a paper I was writing for the American Economic Association conference to be held in January. Finally I gave up. It was hopeless. I couldn't get my mind off of Amanda and Gary.

Surrendering to the inevitable, I came home and threw a couple of days' worth of clothes into an overnight bag. Having extracted a promise from Maggie to take care of my cat and not to tell Dante Rosario where I was, I called a taxi and departed for South Station in Boston. There was an Amtrak train heading south at 3:04 P.M., and I was planning to be on it.

Because something was going on down in New Haven. And I wasn't going to be able to rest until I figured out what it was.

CHAPTER SIX

Another City,
Not My Own

"My mother is *totally* freaked out by this."

"I know, my parents are trippin', too. My dad said he wants me to use the escort service just to walk home from Sterling. I was like, Dad, it's like *a hundred feet*, okay?"

It was nearly six-thirty on Tuesday evening by the time I arrived at Lily Cho's door at Calhoun College, overnight bag in tow. She'd graciously agreed to let me crash on her sofa for a couple of nights, and now we were in the middle of dinner in the Calhoun dining room, a majestic three-story stone hall with mahogany paneling, brown leather chairs, two fireplaces, and four immense chandeliers. The four sophomores who lived across the hall from Lily had just joined us at our table in the middle of the room, and it was clear that Amanda Fox's murder was the topic *du jour*.

"Great jacket, Lily," a young woman called out as she hurried by. Lily smiled and waved as I made a mental note of her cropped leopard-print jacket, black turtleneck, and matching skirt. *Consider an animal print. Wear with black.*

"I heard that when they found the body, it was smeared with feces," Amy, a petite blonde, said gleefully.

"*Hello*, we're trying to eat here," her roommate, Cynthia, snapped, putting a plump hand to her cheek as she eyed her plate of baked ziti with exaggerated dismay.

"This is a natural outgrowth of our misogynistic culture. It's clear that some man on a power trip killed her," chimed in the aptly named Cherry, a redhead with corkscrew curls.

"Oh, stop with the feminist theorizing," Amy chided. "We already know you think all men should be castrated." Her voice dropped to a conspiratorial whisper. "I heard the guy was black. Like this really scary black guy with a big Afro—can you imagine?" She paused and took a sip of her Diet Coke. "Do you think it was racial? No offense, of course," she said quickly, glancing around the table.

"Amy, do us a favor and shut up, okay?" Cynthia

interjected. "Justine, what's up with Tyrone? He never sits at the black table."

Justine, a striking young black woman with long black braids, shook her head impatiently, looking briefly over her shoulder at table populated by about fifteen black students. "The Black Student Alliance is having a crisis meeting tonight, and he's going. Some white girl told the police that she saw a black man hiding in the bushes, stalking Professor Fox, and now BSAY is afraid the cops are going to go on a vendetta." The raucous laughter of the three boys wearing Athletic Department sweatshirts at the other end of our table nearly drowned out her sigh of frustration.

"But this is New Haven. It's so diverse. The police here would never do that, would they?" Cynthia's guilelessness seemed sincere.

Justine's eyes met mine. "They'd better not."

"So do you think they'll arrest someone quickly?" Amy turned to Lily. "I don't know why, but somebody said they're even questioning Dean Fox. I mean, he's not black."

"Amy, didn't you just tell me that you had a Biochem midterm on Thursday?"

"Come on, Lily, like anyone's going to study when there's a murderer loose."

The chatter about the murder continued as we poured ourselves coffee from two large silver urns. The girls clearly wanted to appear unperturbed, but

I could hear it—beneath the dishing was an undercurrent of real fear.

"Lily! Thank God I found you!" The voice belonged to a tall, thin young woman who couldn't have been older than nineteen. She was standing next to Lily, looking down anxiously at herself. "Does this scarf work with this sweater? I have to meet Jason in half and hour, and I have to look fierce!"

"The scarf is great, but you need to lose the earrings. They're too big for your face."

Much as I wanted to hang around for the fashion tutorial, it was high time I called Gary to let him know that I was back in New Haven. I found a phone in the lounge adjacent to the dining room. To my surprise, a young woman answered on the third ring.

"Sorry," I said quickly. "I must have the wrong number."

"Who are you looking for?" the voice said smoothly.

"Gary Fox."

"May I ask who's calling?"

Her tone was simultaneously haughty and prying, an instantly irritating combination.

"This is Nikki Chase," I said impatiently. "I'm a friend of his." *Who was this woman? And why did she sound so proprietary?*

"Hold on a moment."

I heard wisps of a muffled conversation which involved the female voice affectionately calling Gary's name, a whispered response, and her announcement that it was me. Then Gary came on the line. "Nikki?"

"Hey, I just wanted to let you know that I'll be in New Haven for the next couple of days. A friend of mine is a resident fellow at Calhoun, and she's letting me stay with her."

"You're kidding! That's *wonderful*, Nikki!" Gary responded. "But can you afford to be away from Cambridge that long?"

Well, of course I couldn't. Even under normal circumstances, November was a busy time, with a second round of midterm exams and a spate of departmental meetings scheduled for the two weeks preceding the Thanksgiving break. Exacerbating the pressure was the fact that the Acting Chairman of my department, Kenneth Irvin, seriously disliked me for having recently helped land his best friend, the former department Chairman, in jail for embezzlement. When I'd called earlier that afternoon to inform him that I would be in New Haven for a couple of days due to the death of a close friend, he'd made his displeasure abundantly clear and ordered me to return as quickly as possible.

"Of course I can be away for a few days," I said brightly to Gary. "You know junior faculty members are entirely fungible. So when can I see you?"

"Why don't you come over now? Jane and I were

just talking. She's been helping me keep the press at bay."

The woman murmured something in the background that solicited a short bark of laughter from Gary. He sounded surprisingly calm. Almost happy. I grabbed my jacket from the back of my chair and was out the dining hall door in no time.

I couldn't wait to meet this Jane.

When I arrived at Gary's suite ten minutes later, there was a fire crackling in the hearth, and a young blond woman was sprawled across the length of his sofa, drinking Orangina straight from the bottle. A red plaid miniskirt and tight black turtleneck lovingly displayed the curves of her twenty-year-old body, and a black velvet headband crowned her head like a tiara. Perhaps it was her presence, but the entire atmosphere of the room seemed transformed from yesterday's gloom—it was undeniably brighter, warmer, and more intimate. I noticed a large bouquet of yellow, white, and russet chrysanthemums on the coffee table.

What a difference a day makes.

"You must be Nikki," the woman called from the sofa, sitting up. "I'm Giselle Storrs."

I glanced over my left shoulder to shoot Gary a look; he was grinning sheepishly at me. Not exactly the grieving widower.

"Jane came over to cheer me up and bring me up to

speed on her senior honors thesis," he said, almost apologetically. "She's answering the phone because these reporters won't stop calling."

"I'm sorry, I thought you said your name was Giselle," I said, turning to the young woman.

"I did," she said petulantly. "I host a TV show on the Yale station—WYBS—and my on-air name is Giselle. Like I could really use a name like Jane on television. All my friends call me Giselle now, but this one just won't get it. The station manager *loves* it, Gary."

"I keep telling her it sounds completely made-up, but she won't listen," he murmured to me. I felt an unexpected stab of jealousy as he crossed the room and smiled at her as he folded himself into the armchair next to the sofa. Gary and I used to while away hours this way—me sprawled on a sofa or an armchair and him stretched out on the floor, talking about classes and boys and dreams for the future. Now Barbie, or Giselle, or whatever her name was, apparently occupied my old spot.

"So do you live in Branford, too?" I asked as I sat next to her on the sofa. Perhaps she lived across the hall, and that was why she seemed so utterly at home here.

"No, I *wish*. I'm in TD—Timothy Dwight. It's ridiculously inconvenient."

"Got screwed in the random lottery, eh?" I said sympathetically.

"No. My grandfather and my father lived there,

and legacies get to live where their parents did." She rolled her eyes. "My mother would have had a cow if I hadn't done it." Of course, I thought. Random housing assignments only befall those of us who are first-generation Ivy League. "Legacies" are alumni children, and the rank confers several privileges, superior living arrangements among them.

"I'm getting another soda," Giselle said, bouncing up from the sofa. "I'm totally dehydrated from lacrosse practice. Anybody want one?"

Gary and I shook our heads, and I leaned toward him as she disappeared into one of the rooms off the living room. "What is she doing here?" I whispered.

"I told you, she's one of my students. What do you mean?"

"You know what I mean, Gary," I hissed. "Your wife has been dead for less than forty-eight hours, and you're entertaining guests?"

Within seconds, all traces of happiness drained from his face. "I know. I'm being selfish," he said, his shoulders drooping. "She came over, and brought flowers, and made this fire, and just for a minute, it seemed like everything was right again, that any minute Amanda would come through the door and—I should send her away but I can't stand to be alone—and Lance has his dress rehearsal tonight—" He buried his face in his hands.

"Gary, I'm so sorry." I was beside him in seconds, my arms instinctively encircling him. "That was a stupid remark, and I am so sorry. Of course you need company. Please, I'm so sorry."

"Don't worry about it," he said, returning my embrace. "I'm just glad you came back."

"Oh!" Giselle exclaimed. I looked up to find her staring at me with a surprisingly cold expression. "Do you all need some time alone?"

"No—" I began, when a loud pounding on the door interrupted me.

Gary glanced at Giselle as he went to the door. A deep, raspy male voice rumbled briefly, then I heard Gary say, "Please come in, Sergeant."

A short, broad-shouldered white man with silver hair, wearing a blue sportcoat and dark gray slacks strode into the room and surveyed the three of us, a mixture of watchfulness and fatigue in his pale blue eyes. As I watched the light glint off a silver badge attached to his belt loop, I realized that he looked strangely familiar.

"Heaney?" I blurted, incredulous. It was the cop who had given me the speeding ticket the day before.

"Have we met?" he responded warily. Recognition spread slowly over his face as he looked me over. "Oh sure. The girl from Cambridge who was in such a big hurry. You get that inspection taken care of?" I could swear that a smile strayed across his lips.

"What can I do for you, Sergeant?" Gary interrupted. His face had gone extremely pale.

"It's about your wife," Heaney said slowly, turning to Gary. "I need to ask you some more questions."

"Sergeant, I've spent hours answering your questions already," Gary began.

"Yeah," Giselle interrupted. "And after what I told you about that man in the bushes, I don't see why you would need any other information. You should be out looking for *him*."

"*You* were the one who saw the black man in the bushes?" I interjected.

"Yes, it's a weird coincidence, isn't it? I was taking Professor Fox's constitutional law seminar." Giselle glanced at Gary. "Gary kept telling me what a great course it was, and I'm thinking about going to Law School, so I signed up for it last spring."

It was weird. But was it a coincidence? "What exactly did you see?" I pressed.

"Pardon me," Heaney cut me off. "But if you don't mind, I'll ask the questions. Starting with you, miss May I have your name?" He was looking straight at me.

"Don't you have it from the ticket you gave me yesterday?" I snapped. "Nikki Chase," I responded, as he frowned at me.

"Nikki's an old friend of mine, Sergeant. She's just here helping me out."

Heaney nodded, appearing satisfied for the moment. "We need to talk, Dean Fox. We can do it here, or down at the station."

Gary looked at Giselle, then at me. "Would you excuse us? I'd just as soon do this here." The expression in his eyes pained me. He looked frightened. And vulnerable. I had thought he was exaggerating when he said the police considered him to be a suspect, but the presence of this burly cop at this hour of the night belied my cavalier attitude.

Gary Fox was clearly in trouble. And his little blond friend Giselle had something to do with it, I was sure of it—black men in bushes notwithstanding.

I had only a couple of days to figure out what had really happened here before the head of the Economics Department hauled me back to Cambridge.

It was high time I got started.

CHAPTER SEVEN

Raising the Dead

Forty minutes later, I was walking along Hillhouse Avenue, a broad, tree-lined street that my New Haven map indicated ran from the main Yale campus up to Science Hill. It was nearly ten o'clock, and the moon shone down through the skeletal limbs of maples and oaks as I walked along the deserted sidewalk, past a series of Victorian houses that loomed in ghostly silhouette.

I knew I was tempting fate, but Sergeant Heaney's visit had left me unnerved. He clearly considered Gary a suspect, and given Amanda's high profile, the sergeant's superiors would be demanding an early arrest to keep the media at bay. Under normal circumstances, I wouldn't have been so worried—Gary was a Dean of the university, and he hadn't gotten that far without honing his survival skills—but he was far too shell-shocked to defend himself now, and he also seemed to have made some powerful enemies in the Fisch brothers. Hovering in the back of my mind was another hapless potential suspect: Marcellus Tyler. I couldn't shake my fear that he would become a convenient scapegoat—who better to take the fall for the sexual murder of a white woman than a naive black boy? And I just couldn't let that happen on my watch. Had we been in Cambridge at that moment, I would have been working the phone to make sure that no one did anything stupid. But my Rolodex was useless in this town.

As I walked in solitude, I realized that this must have been what it was like for Amanda the night that she was killed. Shadows played across the leaf-strewn sidewalk, and the faint sounds of distant sirens and the rustling of leafless branches punctuated the hallowed, silent darkness. I wondered what she had been thinking about in those last, waning moments. Was she fretting about her career? Had she been wrestling with the outline of her next paper? Was she thinking of Gary? Or perhaps of someone else? What had she been feeling, just before it happened? I was certain that if I knew that, I'd know why someone believed she had to die. I glanced over my shoulder, by sheer force of will suppressing my misgivings about being out alone on a deserted New Haven street. I would have much preferred to be safely behind the wheel of a car, but Lily didn't have one, and Maggie's was back in Cambridge. I comforted myself with the thought that Amanda had probably known her attacker and that chances were she hadn't been done in by some mad serial rapist randomly roaming the city. Besides, I knew how to take care of myself.

The street signs were clearly visible in the translucent autumn air, and I turned from Hillhouse onto Sachem Street. I briefly considered consulting my map, but there was no point in advertising the fact that I was both alone *and* from out of town. If I was remembering it properly, the Resurrection Tabernacle Deliverance Church was about eight minutes away.

The brooding Gothic structures of Yale surrendered to urban desolation in the space of a block, stone giving way to wood, manicured lawns to angry tufts of grass, solemnity to menace. I recited the rules of urban engagement as I walked. *Never surrender the sidewalk. Make eye contact. Have a stone-cold stare. And don't try to be a hero.* I raised my head a notch higher. I'd passed invisibly through the nastiest neighborhoods of New York and Detroit, and I wasn't letting this place slow me down. A trio of black men in oversized down jackets approached me, their voices carrying clearly in the night air.

"You hear they brought Darryl in? Kept him overnight, too. I wish they *would* come after me for killin' that white bitch," one of the men said.

"Had no business comin' over here, anyway," his companion echoed. "White girl needed to stay on her side of the fence."

"I bet she came over here for a taste of dark meat."

"You see her picture? You ask me, a girl lookin' like that can come on over here anytime."

"Nigga, that's why your ass is gonna end up in jail."

The three passed me by without so much as a glance in my direction. Clearly, I was of no interest in a town obsessed with Amanda Fox.

Then I saw it, an illuminated cross marking a storefront in the next block—the Resurrection Tabernacle Deliverance Church. It was a parish of the type I'd seen hundreds of times: a two-story, narrow brick building, with a set of crumbling concrete stairs leading up to wooden double doors. On one side of the building was a deserted lot covered in waist-high weeds; on the other, a pawnshop.

I had been expecting bloodstains. But Monday's rain had washed the concrete nearly clean, and the deserted sidewalk where Amanda had died sparkled in the harsh glare of the floodlights now guarding the church. Almost fifty bouquets of flowers lay on the crumbling pavement, several small votive candles scattered among them. I bent down to read the note resting beside a large floral arrangement. *Amanda Fox, fallen angel,* it read. Someone had pasted a news article announcing the murder to the door of the church. *"When will the violence end?"* was scrawled across it in bright red letters. A pink flyer announced that a vigil was being held that evening at The Women's Table in front of Sterling Library. It was a very respectable outpouring of sympathy—far more than I had expected for a right-wing Yalie in a neighborhood of what I assumed to be liberal blacks. I crouched down, touching the unyielding ice cold pavement with my fingertips. Closing my eyes, I fought back an unexpected prickling of tears. Nobody deserved her fate.

A rustling sound behind me had me up on my feet in a matter of seconds, my heart in my throat. I had my trusty vial of pepper spray half out of my pocket when I realized that the noise was coming from the abandoned lot next to the church. I shuddered involuntarily. Probably rats, I reasoned. Then I heard a more familiar noise, and drew closer. It sounded like . . . mewling. Distressed mewling.

I walked the few steps to the edge of the lot and peered into the darkness. My ear wasn't deceiving me—somewhere in there was a cat with some kind of problem. I eyed the tall thicket suspiciously. A dark street in New Haven I could handle, but this was asking too much. I weighed the alternatives for a few more moments as the piteous wailing continued, and then, with the face of my own cat, Keynes, before me—and visions of killer rodents shoved firmly out of mind—I waded a few steps into the underbrush and clucked softly. The whimpering grew more insistent.

"Okay," I called out, whacking the vegetation before me with my handbag, "I'm coming in now." I shouted random phrases as I plowed through the brush—as if any vermin living in that jungle would be fazed by the presence of a cat-loving priss. Finally, bending over gingerly, I parted the weeds and uncovered the source of all the drama: a small black-and-white cat looked up impatiently at me. As I leaned closer, I could see that its foot was entangled in a mass of jagged, rusted cans that must have been discarded in the vacant lot years ago.

"Hold still, you," I said gently, almost laughing at the cat's indignant expression. As its foot came free, it squealed in frustration, and then, with a glimmer, it disappeared into the brush. I turned to leave and almost fell face forward as I stumbled over a large object half buried in the foliage under my feet.

Closer investigation revealed that it was a knife.

A huge knife, almost a foot long, from what I could see. It had a dark leather or vinyl handle. And while it was too dark to be sure, the handle looked stained. With what could have been blood.

I started to reach for it, then came to my senses and recoiled. It could be the murder weapon. Or it could be random urban detritus. Either way, having my fingerprints on it wasn't going to be helpful. I fumbled in my pocket for a tissue, a glove, or a scrap of paper.

That was when I heard the footsteps. Someone was coming down the sidewalk in front of the church. And he was moving fast.

Before I could duck down into the undergrowth, a black silhouette appeared at the edge of the abandoned lot, not ten feet away from me. A tall figure, dressed in what looked like a black down jacket and jeans, was staring right at me. Then it started moving toward me with slow but inexorable steps. I squinted into the darkness, looking for its eyes.

But where there should have been a face, there was a skull.

In my short life, I've been mugged three times. I never thought I'd be grateful for being victimized, but those episodes have left me with highly developed defensive instincts, and they took over as the distance between us closed. I faked to the left and then sprinted right. If I made it back to the sidewalk, I could outrun almost anyone. *Just don't let him get hold of you.* Apparently, the ghoul hadn't expected company any more than I had, because my amateurish evasion tactics actually worked. I cleared the weeds in seconds, and raced down the sidewalk as if the devil himself were after me.

I knew I shouldn't waste energy looking over my shoulder, but I couldn't help it. Yes, he was chasing me. And he was gaining ground quickly. The contours of the skeleton's head glowed evilly in the beams of the streetlights, and I could hear him cursing to himself as he came after me.

Why the hell are these sidewalks so deserted? Shock and fear had initially silenced me, but I needed help. I screamed out, the sharp night air burning in my chest. *Where is everybody?* I'd wanted to know what Amanda had been feeling that night. Now I knew.

I was out of breath and close to a frenzy when I rounded a corner and ran smack into a pair of strong arms that immediately wrapped around me like a vise.

"No!" I screeched, struggling to break free. This couldn't be happening.

"Hold up, woman," commanded a deep male voice. "You're screaming loud enough to raise the dead."

I looked up to find my face just inches away from a pair of truly extraordinary brown eyes that were looking down at me with a mixture of concern and censure.

"What's the problem here?" The arms released me, and then reached out again as I felt my knees folding.

"There's a man. Behind me. With a skull for a face." I whirled to find an empty sidewalk. He was gone.

"Are you all right?" My savior was a dark-skinned black man who looked to be in his mid-thirties. He was no more than two inches taller than I and he was completely bald, but he had the compact, powerful build of a wrestler or a boxer.

"I'm not crazy," I said rapidly, responding to the puzzled expression on his face. "A man was chasing me. He was wearing black, except for some kind of white skull on his head."

"I doubt it was a skull," he said grimly. "Sounds like the boy was trying to rob you. Or worse. We just had a bad incident in this neighborhood."

The man wasn't wearing a coat, and I could see his muscular arms flex underneath his white cotton T-shirt, as if they were itching to take on all comers. This display of strength I found immediately comforting.

I shook my head. "I don't know what he was doing. But thank God you happened along."

"What's a lady like you doing out here at this time of night, anyway?" He was looking me over, and had clearly concluded that I wasn't up to the task of being out on the street past 8 P.M.

"I was over at the church," I said a little defensively. "The one where that woman was stabbed."

"What were you doing *there?*" he asked sharply.

I took a step back, surprised at his tone. "Why do you care?"

"Because it's my church."

I knew that little black neighborhood churches tended to have fiercely loyal memberships—they had to, in order to survive—but this was a bit much. His proprietary expression demanded that I explain why I had set foot on what he clearly considered hallowed ground. Well, I had no intention of giving him that satisfaction. "You must be very pious," I drawled sarcastically, rolling my eyes.

"You could say so. I'm Russell Jackson. Assistant Minister of the Resurrection Tabernacle Deliverance Church."

Oh.

Before I could reply, a thin man dressed in a torn jacket wandered toward us, weaving slightly as he came. "Y'all got any money? Y'all got like five dollars?"

"My brother, you need to be at the shelter. It's going below freezing tonight." The reverend pulled a small laminated card from his pants pocket and gave it to the man. "The address is on this card."

He looked the reverend and me over, and concluded that cash wouldn't be forthcoming. "Well, thanks, man," he said dubiously. We watched silently as the man shuffled slowly down the sidewalk.

"Will he really go?" I asked.

Reverend Russell shook his head. "I'd walk with him and make him go, but we have to get you home."

"I can get myself home. You go with him. I'll be fine," I insisted.

He frowned. "After what just happened, I really think you need an escort. Whoever chased you could still be around."

I saw him stuggling to do right by both me and the homeless man, and decided to take the decision out of his hands. "Just point me toward the Yale campus. I'll run the whole way. I swear."

"All right. It's three blocks that way. I'd walk in the middle of the street if I were you."

I nodded my thanks and watched as he ran a few steps to catch up with the homeless man.

I'd known a lot of ministers in my day. And not one of them had arms like that.

"Did I wake you up, Rafe?"

"No, child, I just got back from the station. Maggie told me you're out of town. Are you all right?"

Sergeant Detective Raphael Griffin of the Harvard police force was fast becoming my father-confessor, as well as my landlady's boyfriend. We'd worked together on a murder case a few weeks back, and since then I'd come to treasure his lilting West Indian voice, his sensible advice, and his incredible pecan pie. I'd called him the minute I arrived back in Lily's room.

"I'm fine. But there's a lot going on down here." I rapidly filled him in on Amanda's death, Gary Fox, Marcellus Tyler, my discovery of the knife, and my subsequent pursuit.

He listened quietly, then asked one question. "Child, why are you doing this? Haven't you had enough murderin' and chasin' to do you for a while?"

"Of course I have, Rafe," I said with a sigh. "I'm not down here thrill-seeking. Gary is a friend. His wife has been killed, and now his name and his freedom could be on the line. If I'm right, and they think he's the prime suspect, then who else is going to help him?"

"He's got family, doesn't he?"

"No, he doesn't. No brothers or sisters, and his parents are dead. His friends are all he's got."

"What about this black boy? Maybe they're about to arrest *him*, and this Gary's got nothin' to worry about."

"I'm sure that Marcellus didn't do it."

Skepticism rumbled low in Rafe's throat. "Now, why are you so sure of that? You don't even know the boy."

"It's a hunch. No more than that. But you must have times when your gut just tells you that someone isn't guilty."

"Yes, child, I do. But I've been at this about thirty years longer than you. And right now my gut's tellin' me that you oughtta stay outta this and get your behind back to Harvard. It sounds to me like you're feelin' guilty about your boyfriend *here* and tryin' to make up for it by defending that black boy *there*—"

"Rafe! You think I've turned into a race crusader just to atone for dating a white man? I told you—this isn't about race. It's about helping a friend."

"Still and all, I know Magnolia's been pretty hard on you lately."

"I can handle Maggie. And I would never try to

help this kid if I had any reason to believe he was guilty, whether that makes me a traitor to the race or not. You have to know that. Look, Marcellus is a big kid—he's a football player. And whoever was chasing me tonight was about half his size. So it couldn't have been him. Now, will you help me?"

"Of course, child."

"So what do you think I should do next?"

"First thing you have to do is call that detective—Heaney, was that his name?—and tell him about that knife. Because the mon in the mask is probably out there lookin' for it right now. Hang up and call him, then call me back and we'll talk some more."

I couldn't help smiling as I dialed the number of the New Haven cops. I'd only been in town for six hours, and already I'd been chased by someone desperate to cover his tracks.

With any luck, it meant that I was onto something.

CHAPTER EIGHT

Gone Fishin'

Royal blue sweatshirts. Navy coffee mugs. Indigo windbreakers and sapphire boxer shorts. The only shade of blue that I find consistently appealing is the robin's-egg hue of a Tiffany's box, but on the main floor of the Yale Co-op, dark blue is the only game in town.

It was nine o'clock Wednesday morning, and I was in search of a comb, moisturizer, and mascara, all items that I had left in Cambridge in my mad dash to New Haven the day before. But before tackling the cosmetics aisle, I headed to the second-story book department in search of a newspaper stand. As I expected, the local papers were full of stories about Amanda and Gary. COP CONFESSES: NO LEADS IN PROF MURDER, screamed *The New Haven Register. The Yale*

Daily News carried the sober headline CAMPUS MUR-
DER INVESTIGATION STILL UNDERWAY. I quickly
perused the stories, but there was no new information. The police department seemed to have
clammed up tight after the lurid stories of the first
day, and most of the coverage was a rehash of what
had been in the papers the day before.

I was last in line at the only cash register that
appeared to be open in the entire store when I
glanced up and saw Jared Fisch heading toward me,
a pair of socks in his hand.

Since when did millionaires shop for accessories
at the Yale Co-op? And how could I get him to talk
to me about Amanda Fox? I was next up at the register. The moment called for desperate measures.

As the cashier cheerfully called out, "May I help
you?" I decided to go for it. I placed my items on the
counter and started fumbling through my backpack.

"That'll be ten dollars and fifty-nine cents," the
woman announced.

Ignoring my overstuffed billfold, I continued rif-
fling through my bag. "Shoot!" I wailed. "I left my
wallet at home." I made a show of searching through
my coat pocket. "I think I have about fifty cents," I
said sheepishly to the cashier.

The woman's smile faded. "Then I'm afraid you'll
have to put those items back."

"Don't worry," a voice drawled behind me. "I've
got it."

Yes.

I turned, a grateful expression artfully arranged on my face. "That's *so* nice of you. I'm really sorry. I must have been rushing this morning. I'll repay you as soon as I can run home."

"Don't worry," he repeated. "My treat."

"Well, at least let me buy you a cup of coffee," I cajoled. "Fifty cents would cover that, right?"

He grinned at me. "Fine." I waited while he paid for his purchase. Then we passed through a pair of glass doors and onto Chapel Street. Three ancient churches regarded us watchfully from across the street, their steeples luminous in the frosty gray air.

"I know you," young Fisch said, turning to me.

"I don't think so," I replied quickly. "I'm new in town."

"You're the girl in the dress."

"What?"

"Yale Art Gallery. Monday night. You were standing in the hallway when Max and I went by. Short black dress and incredible shoes."

I felt a flush creeping into my cheeks. "You've got some memory."

"Well, it was some dress." He smiled sleepily at me.

"So where does one go to get a good, cheap cup of coffee in this town?"

"Atticus," he pronounced. "Shall we?"

Five minutes later, we were installed at a small

table on the ground floor of an exceptionally well-stocked bookstore. Given the whir of an espresso machine, the classical music playing softly in the background, and the murmurs of patrons still lingering over their morning pastries, Jared and I had to lean toward each other to conduct a real conversation. This seemed to bother him not at all.

"So what brings you to New Haven?" he asked after ordering coffees for both of us.

"I'm visiting a friend. I'm a professor up at Harvard," I elaborated as he smiled expectantly at me. "How about you? With that accent, you can't be a New Haven native."

"Savannah. Born and bred."

"You're kidding! My father grew up there. My Grandma Chase is still there—she lives on Victory Drive."

"Well, shut my mouth. It's about time I met somebody who really knows what they're talking about when they mention Savannah. If I get one more knucklehead acting like they know the town just because they read *that book*, I'm gonna kill myself. Like the place didn't exist before some Yankee journalist discovered it. So how long since you been back there?" His accent was thickening with every word. I took this as a good sign.

"Too long. I haven't seen Grandma and had a decent plate of grits in almost five years."

"Shame on you. You need to get down there, and

when you do, look me up. I'll take you *and* Grandma to Coley's—that place has the best bar-be-cue south of Memphis."

The timing seemed propitious to take the conversation in the direction I wanted it to go. I leaned closer. "It's so sad about that professor who died, isn't it? I think you said on Monday night that you were naming a chair in her honor?"

"Yes, Amanda and I were good friends. She was a great girl. And *gorgeous*."

"How did you know her?"

"Max—my brother—introduced us. He met her at some conservative retreat weekend, and they bonded over the flat tax or something." He snorted under his breath.

"What?"

"Ah, it's nothing. Just that she and Max were all buddy-buddy up until a month or so ago, and then all of a sudden, they weren't speaking. And now this."

I remembered Max's expression when Jared had announced that the Fisch chair would be endowed in Amanda's name. So what was her connection to these two? One was dogging her husband and the other one had developed a sudden dislike for her.

"Listen, I don't believe in discussing one beautiful woman when there's another one sitting right in front of me. What I want to know," Jared said, leaning closer, "is who you're visiting in New Haven, and whether I should be worried."

Dante Rosario wouldn't be at all pleased if I embarked on a flirtation with this guy to shake loose the information that I needed. Which made it all the more delicious. "I don't think you have any cause for concern," I answered, smiling. "My friend Lily isn't the possessive type."

He grinned at me. "You gonna to be in town for a while?"

"At least a couple of days."

"Great. Because my band is playing a set at Toad's Place tomorrow night. I'd like you to be my guest."

"You have a band?"

"Yeah, I play blues guitar, and we get a little something goin' every now and then."

"Well, thanks. I'd like that." I riffled through the loose change at the bottom of my backpack and deposited fifty cents on the table.

"Don't insult me. I'm paying for this. And by the way, the next time you decide you want to spend time with me, all you have to do is ask. That lost wallet thing is cute, but it's one of the oldest tricks in the book." I looked down and saw that my billfold was clearly visible in the folds of my backpack. "I'll see you tomorrow evenin', Professor." And then he was gone.

Grandma would have said Jared Fisch was the type that could charm the skin off a snake. She also would have said that he was the type you had to keep an eye on.

• • •

"Is this a two-shot, Bobby?"

"Yeah, a two-shot of you and the guest on camera two, then we move to a close-up for the intro on camera one."

"Then can you remember to cue me over to camera one this time, please?"

It was ten minutes after I'd left Atticus Bookstore, and I was standing in the darkened studio of WYBS, watching Giselle Storrs rehearse for her weekly television show. A set of headphones sat in place of last night's headband, and she crossed her legs as she frowned into the darkness.

"I'm thinking of a thirty-second intro. Does that sound right to you?"

"Yeah, if you want to lose your audience," a disembodied male voice replied sharply.

"Just make sure my chyron doesn't block my face, okay?"

"Jane, *you* don't get a chyron, the guest does."

"I told you, it's Giselle!"

"What*ever*. We need the studio in five for Lockhart's show, so let's move it."

"These gear-heads think they own the world just because they get to play with someone else's equipment once a week. Honestly," Giselle huffed as she joined me in the shadowed studio. "Last week the idiot had me looking into the wrong camera for twenty seconds!"

"You really take this seriously, don't you?" I said mildly as we retired to the station's dilapidated "green room" and settled in on a threadbare plaid sofa.

"Of course! I'm planning to move to New York as soon as I get the hell out of here. I've already lost a lot of time. I kept telling my father that Cornell and Penn have better journalism programs than Yale, but he's so stubborn. *This is the family school*, he says. Bullshit." She paused to take a breath. "So how do you think Gary is holding up?"

I shrugged. "I guess he's doing as well as anyone could expect. It was nice of you to stop by yesterday."

"Are you kidding? I just wish he'd let me stay longer. We hang out together all the time."

"Amanda didn't mind?"

Giselle snorted derisively. "Like she was ever around. She was too busy speechifying to notice whether I was there or not. Such an *intellectual*."

"Were you at her speech at the Political Union last week?"

"Yeah, she made all of us in her Con Law seminar attend. Otherwise, I wouldn't be caught dead with those debate geeks. *Not* my crowd."

"Gary said that she pissed a lot of people off that night."

"She was always pissing people off. But, yeah, the rad-fems were really mad that night and they're still screaming about it. She started off saying that feminists are just women whose dates didn't call the next morning, and it went on from there."

Women whose dates didn't call the next morning. You had to give the girl credit. She knew exactly what to say to get noticed.

"She was totally in your face," Giselle continued. "I'll never forget the time she went after that black guy on *Crossfire*."

"Which black guy was that?"

"What's-his-name. He lives here in New Haven. Reverend Samson, Sanders, something like that."

"Leroy Saunders?"

"Yeah, that's him. She basically humiliated the guy on national television." Giselle laughed to herself. "I've never seen a grown man look so much like he was about to cry on the air."

"How long ago was this?"

"I guess a month ago or so. Sometime in October. I remember I taped it because Gary said I could improve my on-camera technique by watching Amanda—like I really want to come across as a ball-buster like her."

"You don't still have the tape, do you?"

"Sure. It's in my locker here. I have a bunch of them that I need to erase."

"Do you mind if I watch it?"

"Of course not! Watch it all you like. We've got about a million VCRs around here, if you want to see it right now."

I did.

Moments later, Giselle and I were perched on top of a couple of worn black leather stools in an empty office while the opening images of *Crossfire* flickered on a large-screen TV.

"We can fast-forward through the intro and the first segment. I think I remember the part that gets really good." Giselle expertly wielded the remote control as images of the standard talking heads flashed by. Suddenly, the screen was lit up by a flash of blond hair, and I saw a fuzzy version of Amanda flit by. "Here we go. This is it."

I hadn't seen Amanda Fox for at least three years, since she never seemed to be around when I passed through town to visit Gary, and I didn't make a habit of watching the political talk shows—our kitchen-table discussions satiated my need to debate any and all current topics, and were far more satisfying than talking back to a TV screen. So, despite myself, I inhaled sharply when her face came into focus.

She really was beautiful.

She was wearing a lime green dress that gave her skin and long blond hair a golden glow, and her blue eyes seemed to be twice as big as I remembered. A coquettish smile flickered across her face as she settled into her chair, and I found myself grudgingly respectful: clearly, she was a master at working the audience.

"Look at how *skinny* she is," Giselle breathed enviously. "Like a model."

That much I did remember. She'd always left me feeling ten pounds overweight. Which reminded me that I had to find a gym if I was going to stay here long.

"The topic of our last segment is affirmative action," barked one of the show's co-hosts. "Do we change it? Or get rid of it altogether?" The commentator turned to an overweight, leonine black man in his early fifties with wavy, heavily laquered hair. His chest puffed up as the camera zeroed in on him. "Reverend Leroy Saunders: you say . . . ?"

"Of course we cannot get rid of it," Saunders began.

"You know how Amanda stayed so thin, right?" Giselle interjected. I glanced at her and she mockingly stuck her index finger down her throat.

"Amanda was bulimic?"

"In a *big* way."

"Justice demands that we black people receive retribution—" Saunders was saying.

"Hold it right there," Amanda said abruptly. "I can't listen to any more of this. Do you honestly expect us to believe that preferential treatment is *justice?*"

"See how she just interrupts people? I would never let one of my guests get away with that," Giselle murmured.

"Anyone with any sense of decency, not to mention half a brain, has to believe that the legacy of the civil rights movement was supposed to be to create true equality, not to create new forms of discrimination."

"Don't you dare try to tell *me* about the legacy of the civil rights movement," Saunders began. "You weren't even born when I was out on the front line—"

"Oh, I know. You were there when Martin Luther King was shot, right? You had his blood on your shirt, right? And you're the only one who can speak for him? Well, you're wrong, Reverend. Martin Luther King was no saint, given his adulterous behavior, but he would be rolling in his grave if he could see what you've done with his mantle."

The reverend's face darkened into an expression that could only be described as murderous. "It's white people like you that make me—"

"Make you what?" Amanda taunted. "Make you stop and *think?*"

"Damn," Giselle murmured. "That was low."

We watched the remainder of the segment in silence, and then I said my goodbyes. I couldn't get Reverend Leroy's expression out of my head as I started for Calhoun. We had every right to be furious. I'd defended affirmative action to Amanda on numerous occasions, and she'd tried just as hard to humiliate me. Just not on national television.

He didn't look like the type that took too kindly to being one-upped. Least of all by someone like Amanda Fox.

CHAPTER NINE

The Thin Blue Line

Stationed at the periphery of the city in the midst of a desolate residential neighborhood, the headquarters of the New Haven police department is an edifice scaled for maximum deterrence: the soot gray concrete facade stretches eight stories skyward, its wings extending protectively across a long city block. Prominent signs proclaim the need to report any criminal activity at once, and the urge to repent becomes almost irresistible in the face of the looming black iron gates surrounding the building. I climbed the broad cement stairs toward the main entrance accordingly cowed. It was eleven-thirty Wednesday morning, and I was there to pay a call on Sergeant Detective Timothy Heaney. He had left an urgent message with Lily asking me to stop by the station as soon as possible, and I assumed that he wanted to talk about the knife I'd discovered the night before.

The building's interior turned out to be as drab as its exterior, but far more congenial: photographs of the mayor and a long parade of police chiefs brightened the beige cinder-block walls, and the baritone laughter of three uniformed cops at the glassed-in reception desk echoed playfully off the walls. One of the officers made a phone call, then directed me to Heaney's office on the third floor of the building. After stepping out of a tiny elevator with blood-red walls, I followed a series of brown signs into the Investigative Services room, which was carpeted in gray and filled with rows of battered brown wooden desks. The room was lined on either side with small offices, and at that moment every available space was filled with white men, most of them wearing suits or sport coats, and all of them speaking at full volume.

"Whatta you got?" a young blond man was asking a thin, shabbily dressed old man seated before him. "Is Marco workin' that area right now?"

"No. Nobody's talking," a stout, florid redhead in uniform said glumly into a telephone. "Uh-huh. I'll get on it."

"That's not LaShawn's M.O.," a third cop said to his companion, shaking his head adamantly. "He uses a box-cutter."

The desk attendant escorted me to an office near the back of the room, and waited politely to catch Heaney's eye.

"Sun-dried tomatoes?" I could hear Heaney's voice through the partially closed door. "What kind of yuppie crap is Sal serving up down there? Just get the usual, will you? Two large pies with pepperoni, sausage, and peppers." I saw a paper menu travel across his desk toward a young man in uniform. "And tell them to make it fast. The teams are all meeting here at twelve hundred hours. And tell Rose we need more coffee."

"I still don't see why we don't just hold 'em a while longer." The man in uniform, a lanky blond, had paused in the doorway. "It hasn't even been twenty-four hours. And they fit the description."

"Every black male between eighteen and fifty fits the description, Donahoe. We've questioned them, and now we're releasing them. You got it? Come in, Miss Chase," Heaney commanded soberly as the man departed.

"So, did you find it?" I asked eagerly.

His eyes narrowed as I settled into the metal chair in front of his desk.

"The knife," I prodded. "I assume you went back and searched the lot again last night, right?"

He nodded slowly. "Yeah, Miss Chase, we searched the lot again. But there wasn't any knife there."

"The guy must have doubled back and taken it before you got there. Did you find *anything* useful?"

"No, we didn't. We found bupkus." He sighed irritably. "And we spent the better part of the night there. I knew we released the crime scene too early—if I'd kept my men there another twenty-four hours, this wouldn't have happened."

"I think I remember what the knife looked like—" I began.

"Before we talk about that, why don't you tell me why you're in New Haven, Miss Chase?"

I looked at him in genuine surprise. "I told you last night, I'm here to comfort my friend Gary."

Heaney leaned toward me across the desk. "Right, you said that. But you seem to have a knack for turning up when there's a dead body around, Miss Chase."

"How did you know about—did you run a background check on me?"

"I make it my business to understand all the strangers who pass through my town, Miss Chase. And I'd like to know what you're doing in New Haven."

I stared at him incredulously. "I repeat. I'm a friend of Gary's."

"Uh-huh. The two of you must be very good friends for you to be giving him so much time. And *comfort.*"

"We are," I said tersely. "I've known both him and Amanda for over ten years."

"You and the wife were good friends, too?"

"Not really. Listen, Heaney, if you did more than a half-assed check on me, you would already know that I just helped *solve* a murder up in Cambridge, not *commit* one. Why are you wasting your time questioning me?"

"Just covering all the bases, Professor."

"Well, five people can confirm my whereabouts on Sunday night. Although you of all people ought to know that I arrived in town Monday morning. I was speeding because Gary had just called and told me about Amanda, and I was desperate to get to him." *Now, how far do you want to take this?*

To my amazement, Heaney's glare dissolved into a semblance of a smile. Apparently, I'd passed his little quiz. Although I suspected he'd never seriously considered me a suspect. He was just amusing himself by jerking my chain.

No wonder Gary was worried.

"So, have you found her hand?" I asked, leaning toward him. It was high time for a counter-attack. "Has it turned up, or did the guy keep it as a souvenir?"

"The son of a bitch stuffed it in her pocket," he said quietly.

It wasn't until that moment that I actually looked at him, and what I saw caused me to stop baiting him. Dark circles rimmed his eyes, and there was an expression of genuine anger on his face. This man was exhausted. And frustrated. And he was furious about what had been done to Amanda Fox.

"You've had a long night, haven't you?" I said.

"Yes, Professor, I have," he said flatly. "When I'm running an investigation like this one, I don't sleep until I feel I have the case under control."

I leaned back in my chair. "And you're having a problem getting this under control, aren't you?"

He surreptitiously rubbed his eyes. "What are you talking about?"

"I mean, if you're out doing a background check on *me*, you've got to be desperate."

A smile flickered across his face. "We're not desperate. But we can't afford any slipups."

"So, then, this wasn't some random street crime," I said eagerly.

"I never said that."

"You don't have to! I heard your officers out there, interviewing the usual suspects, and I can tell by your face that you've got nothing."

"You don't know that."

"I figure you've got to be thinking that it was someone she knew—not a random loon—or I wouldn't be here. And that's going to make your job a lot harder."

He stared at me. "No wonder the Harvard cops told me to keep an eye on you, Professor."

"So what do you want to know, Sergeant?"

"Everything that you know about Amanda Fox."

"That's a short conversation. We went to college together, I was a distant acquaintance of hers, then she married Gary and moved to New Haven, and I really hadn't talked to her since."

"Did you like her, Professor?"

I paused. "To be honest? No. She was very beautiful and very rich, and she didn't have a lot of time for people like me."

"Meaning—"

"Meaning that I'm black, I grew up in Detroit, and I'm a Democrat. Three strikes and you're out. I think she was afraid she might catch something from me."

To my amazement, he actually grinned at me. "I know the type. I grew up here, and I still get steamed when these private-school kids from Hopkins Grammar or these suburban types from Branford and Woodbridge come in to catch a show at the Schubert and then can't get out fast enough. *New Haven is too dangerous.' 'There's no safe place to park.'* Gimme a break. So what else?"

"I really don't know anything more. I told you, she wasn't my friend. Gary is my friend."

"So tell me about the husband."

"He's a terrific guy. A brilliant historian. A popular professor. And he wouldn't hurt a fly."

"Who says he would?"

"Come on. Spouses are always prime suspects in a case like this. But you need to know that Gary adored her. He was always talking about how well her career was going, how she was having amazing success, and how proud he was of her."

"Was he the jealous type?"

"What do you mean?"

"She was a good-looking woman. She got a lot of attention. Did that bother him?"

I shook my head. "Gary is on a fast track at Yale, Sergeant. He'd have no reason to begrudge Amanda her success."

"Did they ever argue?" he asked coyly. I was sure he already knew the answer to that question.

"Doesn't every couple? I'm not aware that they ever had more than the typical marital spat. I'm sorry I can't be more helpful. But I really only saw Gary once a year—at The Game—and when we talked on the phone, it wasn't about Amanda. Shouldn't you be talking to her friends to find out what was going on with her right before she died?"

"Don't think I haven't," he sighed in frustration. "But the blue-bloods are stonewalling me."

"The blue-bloods?"

"You know, the professors. Especially the ones at the Law School. No one over there will talk to us without a lawyer present. And that'll take weeks to set up. And the university people we *do* talk to are no help, anyway. They won't volunteer anything. All they do is respond to direct questions with 'yes' and 'no.' That gets us nowhere."

"At least you've got the members of the church where she was found. They've got to be more helpful."

"Are you kidding me? Forty people in that choir, but no one heard or saw a thing that night."

"So what are you going to do?"

"Keep working the case, that's what. If we don't crack a case like this in the first forty-eight hours, seventy-two hours *max*, we usually don't solve it. Ever. We have to get a handle on what happened, figure out who did it, even if we can't prove it. Otherwise the trail goes cold. I just wish this tabloid thing hadn't happened."

I looked at him quizzically.

"Some New York paper just offered a fifty-thousand-dollar reward for information leading to an arrest," he explained. "Every nut within a hundred-mile radius will be on the phone, tying up the lines and wasting our time."

"Let me help you," I said impulsively. "Hear me out," I continued, as he tried to interrupt. "I can get to the professors. I'm one of them, they'll talk to me. And I can get to the church folks. Because I'm one of them, too."

"No way," Heaney was shaking his head adamantly. "You'll just get in the way. And it's too dangerous."

"Hey. You said you needed to crack this thing in seventy-two hours. By my watch, that means you've got less than twenty-four left. I'd think you'd want all the help you can get."

"Stay out of it, Professor Chase."

"You can't stop me from asking questions, Sergeant."

"You ever heard of obstruction of justice? I'll have you cooling your heels in jail if I hear that you're interfering in this investigation."

Any benign feelings that I might have been developing toward him promptly evaporated. "Are you finished with your questions, Officer? Because if you are, then I've got work to do."

"Just stay out of trouble, Professor."

I started for the door, then turned back. "By the way. What's a sergeant detective doing riding around town writing speeding tickets? Last I heard, that's a job for a uniformed cop."

He grinned at me. "I was on my way to the murder scene when you raced by. Normally, I don't have time to stop bad drivers. But for you, I made an exception."

Fine, I thought as I left his office. *Then just keep on making them.*

CHAPTER TEN

A Yale Education

I left the New Haven police station and headed directly for Yale Law School. Heaney might be having a hard time with the blue-bloods, but I knew at least one of them who might be willing to talk.

A quick check of my campus map pointed me up Wall Street, toward Sterling Library and the massive stone complex that housed the Law School. The school's exterior was quintessential Yale: its outer walls were three stories high, lined with rows of leaded-glass windows, and topped by a series of turrets and chimneys. A stately tower rose from the behind the perimeter, looking for all the world like the cathedral at Chartres. From what I remembered from past visits, I was pretty sure that the entire Law

School was housed within these walls: classrooms, faculty offices, and student housing.

Passing through a pair of thick wooden doors, I was confronted by a large sign demanding PLEASE PRESENT YOUR YALE ID and a guard's desk. Without breaking stride, I breezed past, eyes resolutely on the floor; from what I could tell, the guard never looked up from his newspaper. Safely inside, I found myself in a wide hallway with stone walls and a high, arched ceiling. Wrought-iron grates, fleurs-de-lis, and mahogany panels lined the walls, and a row of black iron chandeliers cast a dim light; the overall effect was of entering an abbey. I resisted the urge to cross myself and walked further in. The solemnity of the hallway slowly diminished, dissipated by the chatter of the students flitting into classrooms and a series of gaily colored announcements that littered the walls on either side. A budding lawyer pointed me up a set of wide, shallow stairs to the third floor of the building, where she said I would find the office of Professor Reid Talbot.

A pale gray light suffused the landing midway up the staircase, shimmering through a set of stained-glass windows with engravings of elderly white men in various traditional judicial poses, some in white wigs and long black robes. As a group they looked solemn, judgmental, and the merest bit prissy. I smiled to myself as I turned the corner and headed toward the third floor, certain that their wizened faces must have frowned in horror at the generations of female law students who had passed under their noses, headed for glory. I wondered what they'd made of Amanda Fox.

Pausing at the top of the stairs, I saw the law library before me. My pace quickened. I couldn't resist it. As a political junkie, I just had to stand on the spot where Bill and Hillary first met. I coaxed the librarian into letting me have a look, and I wasn't disappointed: a two-story-high reading room with a wall of towering stained-glass windows beckoned. Leather-bound books lined the shelves on all four sides, and oil paintings of famous alumni and generous donors looked down benevolently from one wall, President Clinton prominent among them. That must have made Amanda *crazy*.

Turning down the hallway, I easily found Professor Talbot's office. Its arched wooden door was closed, however, and on it was a neatly typed sign that read: PROFESSOR TALBOT WILL BE HAPPY TO SPEAK WITH YOU IN THE AFTERNOON. PLEASE DO NOT DISTURB HIM IN THE MORNING, HOWEVER, SINCE HE WILL BE WRITING.

I glanced at my watch: 12:05 P.M. He was fair game.

I knocked on the door, and walked through as a low, cultured voice beckoned me in.

Talbot's office was exactly what one would imagine a senior Yale Law professor's to be: absurdly spacious, with a bay window overlooking a verdant courtyard, a brilliant red Oriental rug, and a heavy oak desk facing away from the window. Three framed diplomas graced the one wall. I turned to him accusingly as he scribbled a final sentence on a yellow legal pad and signed his name with a flourish.

"You didn't tell me that you graduated from Harvard Law School."

The professor looked up. "Yes, I have the best of both worlds: a Yale education and a Harvard degree." His sparkling blue eyes regarded me quizzically. "Now, how can I help you, Miss—?"

"Chase—Nikki Chase. We met Monday at the Art Gallery. I stopped by to talk with you about Amanda Fox."

He nodded in recognition, so I looked down and sighed softly for effect. "I remembered that you said you were a good friend of hers, and I've been thinking. Since the police have told Gary that her body won't be released for burial for at least a week—until they complete their autopsy—perhaps we should plan some sort of memorial service. Gary is so tired, I hate to trouble him with arrangements, and you seemed to have known her very well, so I thought perhaps you'd be willing to help." As I rambled on, I told myself this wasn't a complete lie; I *did* want to do something to help Gary deal with his grief.

"A memorial service," Talbot replied thoughtfully. "Yes. That's a splendid idea." He stood and crossed to the front of his desk. "I was just about to have some lunch, Professor Chase. Why don't you join me and we'll discuss it?"

"Only if you call me Nikki."

As we emerged onto Wall Street, my eyes traveled over the sweeping stone archway overhead, the intricate stonework of Sterling Library just before us, and a pile of dirty cotton suspended in midair.

Startled, I looked downward to see that the tuft of cotton was sitting atop a ratty, rolled-up brown carpet with legs.

"Yale—divest your tobacco holdings!" a voice cried. I realized that the apparition was a young man dressed as a cigarette. He was surrounded by four other people, all similarly attired.

"Really." Professor Talbot frowned as the man tried to press a brochure into his hand. "I remember when Yale used to admit *scholars*, not activists."

I followed the professor down the street, pushing myself to keep up with his surprisingly brisk pace. The carillon was playing again, and after a few bars I realized that it wasn't the usual hymn tolling out over the campus. I turned to Talbot. "Is that 'Louie, Louie'?"

The professor smiled faintly. "Yes. Professor Kent is playing today, and he's definitely partial to rock and roll. I myself prefer the classics—quite frankly, they're easier to handle."

"You're a carillonneur?"

"Yes. Anyone can join the Guild of Bellringers if they're willing to invest the time. I've been doing it

for a number of years now, every Saturday afternoon. Here's our destination."

He gestured toward a two-story white clapboard
house with black shutters. A discreet gold placard on
the door read MORY'S.

Stepping into the restaurant's foyer from the brisk
air felt like walking into a warm, if somewhat stuffy,
embrace: I found myself in a low, dark brown hallway that harbored the fragrance of old wood and old
men. We deposited our coats on hooks near the
door, and then followed a waiter in a blue jacket past
a series of small dining rooms into a large wood-
paneled room at the back of the building. Black-
and-white photos of young athletes covered the
walls; overhead, a vast array of oars hung horizon-
tally from the ceiling. YALE V. HARVARD, NEW
LONDON, CT, JUNE 22, 1934, read one.

"I'll bet there's some history here," I observed
dryly while glancing around at the room's wooden
tables, all of which appeared to be covered with
carvings.

"Yes, Mory's is one of Yale's oldest institutions. It's
a private club."

What a surprise. The place fairly screamed Ivy
League. The preponderance of blond hair and white
skin at the nearby tables made me certain that some
Yalies felt more welcome than others. Of course,
that may have resulted more from the menu than
from more sinister machinations. The special of the

day was shepherd's pie, and there were four varieties of "Mory's Famous Rarebits" on the menu, including Welsh and Yorkshire. If there was such a thing as WASP food, this had to be it. The waitress returned with a divided silver tray holding cottage cheese, some type of relish involving corn and bell peppers, and a truly unidentifiable condiment.

"What do you suppose that is?" I asked, gingerly raising the silver spoon that was immersed in it.

"Pickled watermelon rinds," Talbot said grinning. "A specialty of the house. So how is Gary managing?" he asked gravely after we placed our orders.

I frowned. "I think he's still in shock. I've known him for almost ten years, and Amanda was the only woman he's been close to in all that time. He really loved her. So you can imagine how he feels."

"Yes, disbelief is the first feeling. There are many worse ones to come," he said quietly. "I lost my wife five years ago. So I *can* imagine."

"I'm so sorry—"

"Well, then," he interrupted smoothly. "A memorial service for Amanda. Battel Chapel would be the appropriate place. I'll speak with the chaplain about dates, and you can speak with Gary about who should be invited."

"I assume Max and Jared Fisch will be on the list," I said casually.

Talbot frowned. "I would be very surprised if Gary wanted them there."

"Really? After the announcement that they're naming a chair after Amanda? I assumed they were close friends."

The professor hesitated, clearly not wanting to be a gossip, but also clearly wanting to say more. I decided to make it easier for him. "The reason I ask is because I really want to take the work off of Gary, and I'd hate to commit a faux pas by inviting the wrong people to this service."

"Then don't invite the Fisches," he said gravely, leaning closer to me. "I expect that it would cause some problems if you did."

"But if they don't get along with Gary, why did they honor Amanda with this chair?"

"Max thought quite a lot of Amanda. They shared a number of opinions about politics and education, and I believe that he was quite a vocal supporter of hers."

"Perhaps an inappropriately strong supporter?" I prodded, reading Talbot's expression.

"The Fisch brothers are not well liked here," the professor said carefully. "Despite their generosity. His patrician nose wrinkled ever so slightly.

"Really?" I prodded. "Why not?"

"Well." He hesitated. "They're hardly . . . the genuine article."

"And you are." I blurted the words without thinking.

He had the good grace to flush. "Yes, well, I suppose I am."

I focused on his features for the first time, and realized that he had the same equine head and lanky frame of the innumerable Boston Brahmins I'd run across at the Harvard Faculty Club. He probably *was* the genuine article.

"So are we talking *Mayflower?*" I teased.

"No," he said seriously. "My family was on the second ship to make the crossing. But we were talking about the Fisches," he continued. "The reception they received on Monday night was typical. Everyone is happy to take their money, but no one approves of the style in which it is given. So Max's favor was a mixed blessing for Amanda. She enjoyed the attention, but she was brilliant in her own right. She certainly didn't require his help to impress the Dean and the Law School faculty."

"His support actually undermined her, didn't it?" I said flatly.

He nodded. "Unfortunately, given her looks, some people drew the wrong conclusions."

A pretty blonde and her sugar daddy. It didn't surprise me that this was what "some people" assumed. In my experience, men were still all too happy to believe that a woman who progressed in a traditionally male profession did so only because of affirmative action or her willingness to sleep with her superiors. It's so much more palatable than accepting that the woman actually had talent and brains.

However, in rare cases, the assumptions were true. Especially when the woman turned up dead from a sexual assault. "Are you sure that the conclusions about her and Max were wrong?" I asked.

"If you knew Amanda, you shouldn't have to ask that question," Talbot said reprovingly.

Well, I did know her. And she seemed perfectly capable of cheating on her husband, if you asked me, but probably not with someone who looked like Max. "Was Jared as close to Amanda as his brother was?"

"If you asked Jared, he'd say they were even closer." I detected the merest hint of rancor in his tone.

"You make it sound like it was a contest."

"For the two of them, I think it was. From what I can see, whatever Max has, Jared immediately wants. A bit like a toddler in a playpen."

Was Amanda the prize in a sibling rivalry run amok? "So if it was a contest, who was winning?" I asked.

"I think it's fair to say that Jared was well ahead of his brother," Talbot said gravely.

"Talbot?" An imperious male voice interrupted our conversation, and I looked up to find a tall silver-haired man with ruddy skin towering over our table. "I thought that was you. I just told Linda to call you and tell you to come by my apartment at the Taft later today. This will save you a trip."

"It's nice to see you, Derek," the professor responded quietly. "But it's quite unfortunate that it has to be under these circumstances."

The icy blue eyes, the aquiline nose, the world-class haughtiness: this could only be Amanda's father, Derek Ingersol.

"Listen," he said, pulling an empty chair over from the adjoining table, "what the hell is going on up here? Why haven't they arrested someone by now? What are these police officers waiting for?"

"My understanding is that they're interviewing everyone who was close to Amanda to try to determine who might have done this," Talbot replied.

"Yes, my attorney actually received a call from some clerk asking when they could interview me. Of course I refused. A black boy has already confessed to being alone with her after class. How much more do they need?"

I cleared my throat sharply as Talbot shot me an apologetic glance. "Perhaps a little something like lack of evidence is slowing them down," I observed.

Ingersol shot an annoyed glance in my general direction. "And who are you?"

"I'm a friend of Gary's. I went to college with your daughter."

He snorted. "A lot of good that did. I send her to Harvard and all that happens is she meets a man and gets married. For that, I could have saved my money and sent her to Simmons. Right, Talbot?"

"Am I wrong, or was she about to become a tenured professor at the Law School?" I interjected.

Ingersol snorted contemptuously. "Of course, that would have lasted until she had her first child. She marries a *professor*, of all things, and then he can't even take care of her. I told her it was madness for her to come here. Do they have the death penalty in this state?"

"I believe not. Oh my, our meal has arrived. If you'll excuse us, Derek, I'd like to speak with you later," Talbot said firmly.

"Like father, like daughter," I muttered under my breath.

"She was his only child, and I think she spent her whole life trying to prove that she was as tough as he was," Talbot said gravely, as he watched Ingersol's departure.

That would explain a lot.

CHAPTER ELEVEN

An Afternoon Outing

Wednesday afternoon found me sitting on a somber gray stone bench in the Branford College courtyard, unsuccessfully fighting a wave of melancholy as the bells of the clock tower tolled three. The slight irritation of having to talk my way through a phalanx of reporters and Yale cops stationed at the entrance to the dormitory had actually almost driven me to tears, and I realized with growing horror that I was wildly homesick. The oppressive grayness and squalor of New Haven and the hulking cathedrals of Yale had seemed alternately romantic and edgy. But now I was finding them disorienting and vaguely irritating. The streets were too empty, the rain too persistent. And while I missed my fuzzy-headed cat, and Maggie's welcoming kitchen, and my beloved Harvard Square, I was fairly aching for Dante Rosario. I'd spent the last twenty-four hours turning over rocks and I wasn't even close to having any answers. And as much as I hated to admit it, Dante always asked the right questions to help me unravel my thoughts. I needed his relentless logic now more than ever. My fingertips strayed pensively over my lips and I smiled wryly to myself. His mind wasn't the only thing I was missing.

I rose abruptly, annoyed with myself. He had kept his conversations with Amanda to himself for two months, so he had no business knowing what I was doing now and no right to be privy to Gary's private anguish. I started quickly toward the door to Gary's entryway. This was no time for romantic longings. There was work to be done.

"Hold up, girl. I can save you a trip." Gary's friend Lance O'Brien emerged from the entryway just as I was reaching for the door handle. "He's not there."

I frowned. "Really? He asked me to meet him here at three o'clock."

"I know. He said to tell you that he got called to an emergency meeting with Detective Heaney."

"Is everything okay?"

"Who knows? He won't say." His brow furrowed. "I'm worried about him. He's not eating, you know. I've tried six ways to Sunday to get him to relax, and none of it's working."

"So what do we do?"

He shrugged. "I have no idea. But I've gotta pick up some stuff at my apartment and then beat it back to the Rep. It's opening night, you know. You want to hang with me?"

"You sure I'm not going to slow you down? You must have a million things to do."

"Are you kidding? I'm a nervous wreck. I could use the company. Come on."

I nodded agreement, and we started for the York Street gate. "So how did you end up becoming a set designer, anyway?" I asked as we ambled toward Chapel Street. "Were you artistic as a kid?"

He snorted. "Are you kidding me? Where I grew up, 'artist' was just another word for 'fag.' Which I am, of course, but that's another story."

He was grinning as he said it, and I smiled in complicity. The announcement that he was gay was not an entire shock, but the perfect pitch with which it was delivered was a nice surprise.

"So where did you grow up?" I asked.

"Upstate New York. A little town called Richfield."

"Is that near Rochester?"

"Girl, it's near *nothing!* Albany is two hours in one direction and Syracuse is two hours in the other, and in between is nothing but gas stations, auto body shops, 7-Elevens and five hundred shades of brown."

"Five hundred?" I raised my brows.

"Don't believe me? Here's a sample: the dun-colored aluminum siding of the Buff-O-Matic car wash; the tapioca exterior paint on the Gift Tepee; the moldy caramels on display at Sue's Sweet Shoppe; the sienna of the cornfields in September; and the tobacco stains on the teeth of the waitresses at the Midpoint Diner. Shall I go on?"

"Please don't."

"Yeah, those nice *Reader's Digest*–reading Rotarians didn't know *what* to make of me. I'm talking about people who think that wearing Dockers is a fashion statement. Our house was alongside this two-lane highway—Route 20—and I swear to God I seriously considered throwing myself in front of a car every other day."

I nodded in sympathy. As much as old folks and politicians may wax rhapsodic over small-town America, almost everyone I know who grew up there couldn't wait to get out. Not that I was much better: I'd grown up in a big city and had abandoned it just as quickly. That was one of the reasons I loved the college towns of the East Coast: like me, most people had run away from home and were hell-bent on recasting themselves in their own terms.

"So how did you escape?" I asked as we crossed Temple Street.

"Opera saved my life," he declared dramatically.

"Don Giovanni just reached out and touched you, eh?"

"I'm serious. The one saving grace of Otsego

County is that there's a summer arts festival—it's like Tanglewood, minus the yuppie bullshit. My mother started taking me to the Glimmerglass Opera when I was eight years old, and by the time I was fourteen, I had a summer job working in the props department."

"That sawdust is seductive, isn't it?" One of my friends is an actress at the American Repertory Theater in Cambridge, and I'd seen the same rapturous look on her face when she described her first starring role, which took place in a crumbling barn in West Texas but might as well have been on 42nd Street for the mythical stature it had attained.

"It wasn't just the sawdust." He smiled evilly. "Those big blond tenors didn't hurt. Anyway, I worked there every summer afterward, saving up money and learning the trade. My mother had a cow when I told her I'd actually gotten into Yale undergrad, but the scholarships came through, I stayed to attend the Drama School, and here we are."

I realized that we were now deep into what I supposed people would call the "real" New Haven: we had crossed the Green and were on a block of moderate-sized commercial buildings near downtown, half of which were empty. The black fumes from a municipal bus wafted over us as we turned onto Orange Street.

"So how did you meet Gary?"

"I was doing research for a play. *Richard III*. During a brief spell of madness, I actually thought I wanted to be a dramaturge, and I was spending all my time researching the mores of Elizabethan England, which was more fun than any man deserves. I interviewed Gary because someone told me he taught a course in British history, and we just got to be friends." Lance glanced up at a large apartment building with a sign proclaiming NINTH SQUARE CO-OPS. "This is me," he said.

"Why is it called 'Ninth Square'?" I asked as we passed through a set of glass doors.

"New Haven is like a ticktacktoe board. The major streets are laid out to form nine squares, and this one happened to be the last to receive any focus from the city fathers. But somebody got some government redevelopment money put into the neighborhood, so people like me can afford a roof over our heads." We took the elevator to the seventh floor, Lance growing more quiet as we went. Once we arrived at his apartment, he actually seemed tense. And alert. The way most people behaved when they were *outside* their homes.

"Is everything all right?"

"Yeah, sure. It's just that the police were here this morning, and one of the bastards left fingerprints all over my glassware," he said lightly.

"*What?*"

"They had a search warrant for my apartment." His voice dropped to a whisper. "And for all I know, they've bugged the place."

"What were they looking for?" I found myself whispering too.

"Who the hell knows?" He shrugged, a wry expression on his face. "Maybe a sheath for a hunting knife?"

"But you were out of town the night Amanda was killed." I forced myself to speak at normal volume.

"Well, obviously, they're covering their asses." He flopped into a chair. "Thanks to the Reverend Leroy, the media are swarming, and the New Haven cops can't appear to be partial to arresting a black suspect. You *do* remember a little case involving a black football player a while back?"

"Have you told Gary?"

"No. He's got enough on his mind without worrying about me. The poor thing still can't sleep without a sedative. And that lacrosse-titute—Jane, Giselle, whatever the hell her name is—can't even wait until Amanda's body is in the ground before throwing herself at him. Did you see all those flowers she sent? You've *got* to help me keep her away from him."

As he spoke, I watched his face. A sudden jolt of understanding hit me, and I wondered why it hadn't occurred to me before: Lance O'Brien was attracted to Gary Fox. Attracted enough to be jealous of Giselle Storrs.

So how had he felt about Amanda?

No wonder the cops were on his doorstep.

"I don't know about you, but I need some comic

relief." He glanced at his watch. "How do you feel about Ricki Lake?"

I vastly preferred Oprah, but I nodded my assent and he reached for the remote control. In seconds, the face of an overweight black man filled the screen, the camera's rays glinting off of a huge gold chain around his neck. I recognized him from the videotape I'd seen earlier that day: it was Reverend Leroy Saunders.

"And I'm standing here to tell you all right now— you white cops, you white reporters—there has been a grave injustice done." Saunders paused for emphasis. "A *grave* injustice. The arrest of Marcellus Tyler is a rush to justice. The police have no real evidence. I say, *no* real evidence."

"Oh my God," Lance breathed. "They did it! They nailed the kid."

My eyes were glued to the television set. Behind the reverend, I could make out the delicate filigree of stonework. This must be happening somewhere on the Yale campus. A press conference. In the background, I could faintly hear voices echoing the speaker's words. *No real evidence. Yes. A rush to justice.*

"And I'm standing here to tell you," Saunders continued, "that we have proof that there has been a cover-up. We will show that the New Haven police are in cahoots with Yale University to suppress evidence exonerating Marcellus Tyler and implicating another suspect. And if this evidence is not put forward, you mark my words: No justice, no peace. *No justice, no peace.*"

"I better call Gary," Lance murmured, and started toward a telephone at the far end of the living room. I swallowed hard, but couldn't cool the burning in my chest. Of course I was relieved for Gary. But I was sick about Marcellus Tyler.

The television shot shifted to a perky brunette reporter. "This is Dara Delaney, reporting live from the Sterling Library at Yale University, where Reverend Leroy Saunders is holding a press conference on this morning's arrest of Yale sophomore Marcellus Tyler in the brutal murder of Yale Professor Amanda Fox. Over to you, Rick."

Was the reverend serious? Did he really have something on the New Haven police?

"I can't reach Gary," Lance said, breaking my train of thought. "I'm going back over to Branford to wait for him. You wanna come?"

"No, thanks," I said quickly. "I just remembered I have an errand to run." Good thing Lance was as wired as I was. I needed to make a quick escape, and I was too distracted to think up a believable excuse.

Because I could spend time with Gary and Lance later.

But this could be my best chance to get up close and personal with the Reverend Leroy.

CHAPTER TWELVE

Touch the Money

By the time I arrived at the Cross Campus Plaza ten minutes later, Reverend Leroy's press conference had reached fever pitch. The reverend, delivering a masterful imitation of Al Sharpton, was standing with his arm around a frail black woman, who seemed to be cringing from his embrace.

"This fine woman raised Marcellus from the time he was a boy," he pronounced.

"Who's the lady?" I whispered to a bespectacled white man who was standing next to me scribbling notes onto a pad.

"That's the grandmother of the kid who was arrested."

Of course, I thought cynically. Trot out the relatives for a photo op. The reverend's arm was wrapped around the woman so tightly that there was no way the media could take her photograph without including him. And no way they could crop him out later. If you couldn't have the suspect, then have the suspect's grieving grandmother. Just be sure to touch the money.

"We will not rest until justice is done," Reverend Leroy was intoning. "Not just for Marcellus Tyler. But for Abner Louima. And Tawana Brawley. We saved O.J. from the rush to justice, and we'll save this boy, too."

"You've got to be kidding me," I muttered. "That's ridiculous."

"You think racial justice is ridiculous?"

I must have been talking more loudly than I realized. I turned to find the Reverend Russell Jackson staring at me, his eyes ablaze in righteous indignation. He was wearing a black sport coat, a black banded-collar shirt, and faded jeans, none of which could completely disguise his well-developed pecs.

"This boy is a fine student at a leading university, with a spotless record of behavior, who just happened to be in this woman's classroom on the night of her murder," he thundered. "But because he's black, he's been railroaded into prison, his reputation ruined, his freedom denied, and his very life at stake. And you think we're being ridiculous?" *What kind of black person are you?* was the clear subtext of his message.

"I don't disagree with you," I said calmly, stifling the urge to snap back. After all, he'd saved me the night before from something I didn't even want to contemplate. "I haven't heard anything other than circumstantial evidence of Marcellus's involvement, and it's impossible to believe that the cops have looked at all the other potential suspects, given how quickly they arrested him. Personally, I think he's innocent. My point was that lumping him in with Tawana Brawley and O. J. Simpson is completely unnecessary, and plays right into the hands of the people trying to reduce your credibility. Why tar him with that brush?"

"Because we believe that his civil rights have been violated just as brutally as theirs were."

"You really believe that?" I asked sharply.

Our eyes locked, then suddenly he winced and bent over. I saw that the cause of the commotion was a small black boy, who had barreled into him at a decent rate of speed and whose arms were now wrapped tightly around the man's right leg. The boy was grinning up playfully, and tugging ferociously on the man's pant leg.

"Wilbert Lucius Green! Now you *know* that is not proper behavior." Russell Jackson's voice was incredibly resonant, commanding, and deep. The boy immediately straightened up and hung his head sheepishly. "Sorry, Reverend."

"I beg your pardon?"

"I'm sorry, Reverend *Jackson*," the boy answered.

"That's better." The minister was looking down at the boy sternly. "Now, is there something you need?"

"Yes, sir," the boy said nervously. "Miss LaDonna sent me to ask when you be comin' back, 'cause she need to leave. In an hour, she said to tell you."

"Slow down and say that properly," the Reverend said calmly.

"She sent me to ask . . . you . . . when you be comin' . . ."

"When *you'd* be coming back," he prompted.

"When *you'd* be coming back, because she"—the boy paused—"because she *needs* to leave. In an hour."

The reverend smiled so broadly that I felt cheered myself, and the little boy looked positively blissful.

"Tell Miss LaDonna that I will return within an hour. And look both ways on the way back!" he called as the boy scampered off.

That was when I remembered it. I was positive that the *Herald* article had said so. "You're the one who found the body Sunday night, aren't you?"

The reverend shot me an appraising look. "That's right. You seem to know a lot about me, and I don't believe I caught your name."

"Nikki Chase." I proffered my hand.

"You're new in town." It was a statement, not a question.

I nodded. "I'm a friend of Amanda Fox's husband."

"What a surprise," he said, dropping my hand. I immediately realized my mistake, but it was too late to rectify it. The contempt on his face was clear. "I guess they *had* to fly you into town once they decided to pin this on a black man."

"Hey!" I said sharply. "I've already told you that I, too, think Marcellus is innocent. And don't accuse me of being a pawn in some white game against black people. You don't even know me."

He looked completely unfazed. "So you're visiting, eh? From where?"

"Cambridge. I'm a professor at Harvard."

He didn't even blink. "Enjoy your stay, Professor." He nodded curtly and turned away as Reverend Leroy bored in for the big finish.

"This man is an innocent victim of the system. A lamb led to the slaughter. But justice will prevail. I promise you, my friends. Justice will prevail."

Reverend Russell disappeared into the press of bodies as the crowd surged over the stairs leading up to Sterling Library. I moved slowly toward the podium, but realized that it would be hopeless to try to talk to anyone in this mayhem.

The Reverend Leroy must have hated Amanda for what she'd done to him on *Crossfire*. And the Reverend Russell was the person who had found her body. That seemed to me like more than just a coincidence, but I had no idea how I was going to get close enough to either one of them to learn more. That morning, I'd cockily assured Sergeant Detective Heaney that I could get access to the black community in New Haven. But the two reverends were clearly out of my reach. And I was running out of time.

There are two places that you can always go if you really want to know what's going on in the black community: a church or a beauty parlor. And this couldn't wait until Sunday morning.

I was suddenly overcome by the need for a shampoo and set.

The House of Beauty on Dixwell Avenue reminded me of the hair salon my mother used to take me to when I was growing up: a small glass storefront with a bright pink awning and a sign in the window reading BRAIDS, RELAXERS, PRESS-AND-CURL. I'd strategically chosen it from the five or so salons I had passed on my walk from the campus for its proximity to the Resurrection Tabernacle Deliverance Church. At a half block away, I was counting on at least one of Reverend Leroy's parishioners being a regular customer. As I entered, the sticky-sweet scent of hairspray and the faint burning smell of styling appliances wafted toward me. Both of the hairstylists standing behind large pink swivel chairs looked up quickly, and the one closest to me smiled.

"Hey," she said easily, her fingers still working furiously on the scalp of the woman in her chair. "You have an appointment?"

I shook my head. "I was hoping you could take me anyway."

"What are you having?"

"A wash and set."

The hairdresser waved me toward a trio of plastic-covered chairs on the far side of the room. "I'm Marva. Have a seat. It may be a while, but we'll get to you."

Perfect.

"This relaxer burning yet, Pearl?" Marva asked her elderly customer as I hung up my raincoat. Pearl's hair was coated with a white perm solution that I knew from lifelong experience had the potential to bring tears to your eyes if it stayed on the scalp for more than five minutes. But the longer it remained on, the straighter the hair would be.

"I can take it," Pearl replied with a slight grimace. "Keep working. I want it *bone straight*." She smiled wryly at me as I caught her eye. "My grand' is doin' the reading at the service tonight, and I gotta look proper for him. Otherwise, I wouldn't be in here today. All this rain, I'll be lucky to get home still lookin' decent."

I smiled in commiseration. "You must be proud of your grandson."

"Praise the Lord, yes. The reverend has just

turned that boy around. It's like he's a different child."

"Don't get her started on Reverend Russell." Marva rolled her eyes. "Otherwise, we'll be hearin' about it for the next hour."

"That man has *saved* those kids," Pearl said indignantly. "You remember what this block used to be like. Dealers just hangin' around like they owned the place. Gangs just waitin' for you to look at them cross-eyed. And look at it now."

"Pearl *loves* her some Reverend Russell," Marva teased.

"Well, he ain't too hard to look at," she said mischievously, winking at the young girl in the other hairstylist's chair. "Right, Charlayne?"

"You're talking about Russell Jackson?" I asked casually, settling into a vacant chair.

"Yeah!" Pearl answered, surprised. "You know him?"

"I just met him at a rally over at Yale. He was—"

"Oh Lord," Pearl interrupted. "That was the thing for that poor boy that got arrested, wasn't it?" She shook her head. "That's white folks for you. I just knew they were gonna go after one of us. And a *Yale* student at that. Lord have mercy."

"They'll be sorry," the second hairstylist said abruptly. Her voice was unusually deep, and her sudden pronouncement echoed in the small room like a prophecy.

"You wish, Phyllis," Marva scoffed. "They'll rail-road that boy the same way they done everybody else. You know these people don't give a damn about us. Come on, Pearl, let's go to the sink."

"Well, Reverend Leroy says we don't have to take it. Don't have to lay down and let them run all over us," Phyllis said. "Because you know if it had been a black girl killed, no one would give a damn. No headlines. No manhunt. No nothin'."

"I still think you should tell the po-lice what you saw, Phyllis," Pearl called from the shampoo bowl.

"Pearl!" Marva snapped. She quickly glanced at me.

"I'm not telling those pigs a damn thing," Phyllis said. "They'll just twist it around and use it against that boy."

"But if you saw—" Pearl began.

"Reverend Leroy said not to talk to any cops," Phyllis snapped. "He said to tell him if we saw or heard anything at choir practice, and he'd decide if they needed to know. I told him, and that's that."

"You need to pray on this, Phyllis," Pearl counseled loudly, over the sound of running water. "You know what the Good Book says: 'The truth shall set you free.'"

I was about to jump out of my skin. "It sounds pretty important," I said quietly, meeting Phyllis's eyes.

"Reverend Leroy knows what to do," she replied

evenly. "And this is the last time I tell you *anything*, Pearl."

"I still think that if you saw the person who stabbed that girl that you need to tell the po-lice," Pearl said indignantly. She rose majestically from her chair at the sink as the others stared at her in stunned silence.

"Dang, Pearl, we're not alone!" Marva hissed.

"Aw, she's all right," Pearl scoffed. "She's one of us, ain't she?"

"You better be right, you crazy old woman," Phyllis snapped. "Or else we're all in deep you-know-what."

"You don't have to worry about me," I said calmly. *Give it time.*

"See?" Pearl huffed.

"But I hope you're not gonna leave me hanging," I continued casually.

"Well, what happened is—" Pearl began.

"I'll tell her!" Phyllis cut her off. "It's *my* story. You just get on under that dryer." She turned to me. "I left choir practice early this past Sunday. I was coming down with a sore throat, and I wasn't good for anything, anyway, so I figured I'd just go on home. I came out the side door, and I heard a noise. Like a kind of grunting or something. So I came around to the front of the church. And I saw them."

"Who?"

"I saw somebody lying on the ground. And I saw

somebody else hunched over them. Holding a knife."

"Did you see the person's face? I mean, the person who had the knife."

She shook her head. "He had on some kind of Halloween mask or something."

A chill went down my spine. I was quite familiar with that mask.

"But it didn't fit too well," she continued. "I saw part of his face when he stood up." She looked over her shoulder, reassuring herself that no one else could overhear. "I saw part of his face," she repeated.

"And?" I prodded impatiently.

Her face twisted into an uncomfortable grimace. "And he was black."

CHAPTER THIRTEEN

In for a Penny

Gary Fox was aging before my very eyes.

I'd raced back from the beauty salon in time to meet him at Branford, my mind reeling from Phyllis's revelation. I needed time to sort it out, but at the moment, I owed Gary my undivided attention. We were perched on his sofa, sifting through brochures and trying to make the hundred small decisions that planning a funeral requires: the flowers, the music, the pallbearers. I couldn't get over how haggard he looked, and I was determined to help him through this. I'd gotten a message that morning from my department chairman: he had demanded a new draft of a paper I was working on for the AEA Conference, and reiterated his displeasure with my absence.

For a split second, I had considered beating it back to Cambridge. But Gary needed me. In for a penny, in for a pound.

"You really think just white orchids and some greenery?" he asked wearily.

"Absolutely," I said, feigning confidence. "An intense burst of one flower in one color will be classy and really striking. Mixed bouquets are passé now." At least, that's what Lily had said when I called to get her advice.

The shrill jangling of the telephone broke the silence as I checked flowers off our To Do list. We waited in silence for the ringing to stop. "They're nothing if not persistent," I commented. Ever since the announcement of Marcellus's arrest, the phone had been ringing off the hook with reporters looking for a quote from Gary.

"Do you believe in forgiveness, Nikki?" Gary asked abruptly. His eyes looked haunted.

I laid my hand gently on his forearm. "What is it?"

"We had that argument on Friday night, and then I was in meetings all day Saturday, and she was so busy Sunday, I just never—" He stopped, his voice dying away in his throat.

"You're afraid Amanda died angry with you."

"Yes. And I'm afraid she didn't know—how much I loved her." Tears were quietly streaming down his face now. I gathered him to me, and rocked him gently while he sobbed on my shoulder. "She knew, Gary. Of course she knew."

Eventually he quieted, and I released him. "Can I ask you something?" I questioned gently.

He nodded, and I looked away to give him a moment to regain his composure.

"Please don't take this the wrong way," I said carefully. "But why did you marry her? And why was it so sudden?"

Gary smiled ruefully. "I've been wondering how many years would go by before you screwed up the nerve to ask me that, Nikki." He reclined on the sofa. "To be honest? I wanted to marry her from the first day I ever saw her."

I tried, unsuccessfully, to avoid rolling my eyes.

"*Not* because of her looks," he said, correctly interpreting my expression. "Although I thought she was stunning. I wanted to marry her because she seemed more alive than anyone I'd ever met. She was just—" He paused reflectively. "She was aflame with intelligence, and passion. I would have done anything to be with her. To possess—what she had."

"But why did you keep it such a secret? And why did you marry her so *fast?*"

"You know what would've happened if anyone had known that I was having a romance with a student, Nikki. I mean, I wasn't her instructor, and I never wrote her a recommendation, but it still wouldn't have looked right. I didn't want to put you in the position of having to lie for me. But I know the way we announced our engagement hurt you, and I'm sorry about that." He paused. "But we had to marry fast. Because, to be honest, I was sure that if we didn't do it quickly, she'd change her mind. Her father was dead set against it, and he's . . . very persuasive, shall we say."

"So were you happy?"

A glimmer of tears welled up in his eyes again, and he nodded silently.

"So then what's with you and this Giselle?"

Gary looked down quickly and then back at me. "I'm not sure what you mean. We're friends."

"Is that what she thinks?"

He looked puzzled. "Of course. Why would she think anything else?"

I squeezed his arm affectionately. "You don't know your effect on women, Gary. I'm going to make some coffee. You want some?"

He nodded and I disappeared into the spare bedroom that had served as their study.

The room was dim, but I could see a pair of desks and an oversized mahogany bookcase. The urge to snoop was overwhelming. So after measuring coffee and water and coaxing the machine to start, I surveyed the top of the desk that clearly had been Amanda's: the one with the back issues of the *National Review* stacked neatly in one corner. I skimmed the surface quickly, encountering a pile of blue books, a sheaf of funding requests from the ominously named Freedom and Justice Foundation, and an airline schedule.

What was most striking was the utter lack of anything remotely personal. No photographs, no letters or scribbled phone messages from friends, no personal items on the neatly inscribed daily To Do list. Who was that guarded in their own home?

Perhaps Gary had already gone through everything and put away the painful reminders. Or Heaney and his boys had taken the material as part of their investigation. Or perhaps home wasn't where she kept what was really dear.

The burbling coffee machine abruptly fell silent. I had run out of time. Sometimes what you don't find is as important as what you do, I reminded myself. And at least my fruitless search had reminded me of something that I'd been meaning to ask Gary. I grabbed our coffees and started back to the living room.

Gary glanced up as I entered. "Was Amanda very athletic?" I asked casually, as I passed him a mug.

"Not really. She could eat anything and never gain a pound, so she didn't exercise much. Why?"

"I'm trying to understand how she ended up so far from Science Hill on Sunday evening. I walked around up there last night, and the place where she died is a good ten minutes away from the classroom building, in the *opposite* direction from the campus."

"You were up on Science Hill last night? After

what happened?" He leaned toward me, looking shocked. "Nikki, are you *crazy?*"

"Of course not. I just—" I worried that it was cruel to discuss my suspicions with Gary, given his fragile mental state. But he deserved to know. "I'm not sure that Marcellus Tyler did this. I think they may have the wrong person."

"What do you mean by *that?* Who else could it be?"

I felt terrible. I was clearly upsetting him. "I don't know, Gary. But something tells me that there's more to this than we know."

"Why would you say that?"

"Too many loose threads."

"Like what?"

"Like where her body was found. The Amanda I knew was no jock, and you just confirmed it. When you told me that she had been killed in a black neighborhood, I just assumed that it was because she'd been accosted on her way home from Science Hill, tried to outrun her attacker, and ended up being chased near that church. But if she wasn't particularly athletic, there's no way she would have gotten more than half a block before the killer caught up with her. Remember, he would have had the element of surprise on his side."

Gary was listening intently.

"The other thing is that when I went to the church last night, I realized that her body was found in the *opposite* direction from where she should have been if she was walking home."

"You said that before. But what does it mean?"

"I think it means that she didn't run frantically into that neighborhood. She was lured there. Or she voluntarily went there. She walked there after her class ended, and the killer was there waiting for her."

Gary sat quietly, absorbing the thought. "But why couldn't it have been this Marcellus who lured her over there?"

"It's possible. But Giselle said that she saw someone fitting his description *on her way home from class*. If that person was Marcellus, he would have been almost a mile away from where the murder occurred. It doesn't add up."

"So you think the killer is still out there?" He looked even more distressed.

I took his hand. "I don't know. That's what I want to find out."

"I think we should let the police handle it, Nikki. We don't know what we're dealing with here."

"Why don't you rest for a while?" I said briskly. "We have a long night in front of us."

"Stay out of it, Nikki. *Promise* me. I just can't—I can't lose anyone else."

"I'll be careful. I swear, Gary. Now get some rest."

"This discussion isn't over," he said. "But I'm tired. You'll stay, right?" I nodded my assent as he disappeared into their bedroom, then checked my watch. Five minutes, and I'd continue my search of their suite. Gary should be asleep by then.

Four and a half minutes later, a key turned in the front door.

"Hello?" I called out, startled.

"Dorm crew," a young male voice called. The door swung open and a slight, sandy-haired boy appeared, mop and bucket in tow. "I'm here to clean the bathroom," he explained.

"Come on in." I smiled in commiseration. I'd taken a similar job as an undergraduate to earn some extra money, and I knew what his afternoons must be like. I'd lasted exactly a week, resigning in haste after my first encounter with a four-man suite and the aftermath of a drinking binge that had clearly ended badly.

Given his presence, I immediately decided to postpone my search. After all, if this kid was in their suite on a regular basis, he must know something about Amanda Fox.

"Terrible about Amanda, isn't it?" I said, leaning companionably against the bathroom doorjamb as he set to scrubbing the sink.

"Yeah. She was nice."

"Was she usually here when you came by?"

"Not really. I'd see her a few times a month. She was really busy, you know. Traveled a lot. But when she *was* here alone, she really liked to talk."

"Really? About what?" I asked.

"I'm a Political Science major, so we had a lot in common. She was smart, and she used to crack me up, the way she'd rag on people. She had a great sense of humor." He laughed as he wrung the mop into his bucket.

"Did she seem . . . lonely?" It was just a hunch. But the Amanda I knew wouldn't have spent time talking to what she would have described as a pimply freshman unless she was truly desperate for company.

For the first time, the boy's eyes met mine. "Yeah. I guess you could say that. Whenever she was here, I'd always end up being late on my rounds, because she—you know, I could tell she really didn't want me to leave."

"I guess she never talked about personal things, huh?" I said lightly. "Strictly politics?"

He smiled. "Yeah. For her, that *was* personal." The boy glanced down as he gathered up his cleaning supplies.

"Hey, you forgot to take the trash," I called after him as he started for the front door.

"I don't do the trash anymore. Dean Fox asked me not to. He said he prefers to take care of it himself."

"Really? When did that start?"

"I guess about three weeks ago." The boy shrugged. "Guess he likes his privacy."

I frowned at the door as he closed it gently behind him.

A lonely wife and a husband suddenly concerned with privacy.

I didn't like the sound of that.

"So do you think I should tell Heaney?" I demanded.

"Child, you have to."

Six o'clock Wednesday evening found me on the phone with Rafe Griffin. Gary had slept for almost two hours, and Giselle Storrs had appeared just as he was waking up. I'd taken that as my cue to head back to Lily's and decide on my next move.

"But if I tell him that an eyewitness saw a black man at the murder scene, isn't it game over for Marcellus Tyler?"

"If you don't tell him, you'll end up in jail for obstructin' justice."

"But it still doesn't prove that Marcellus did it, Rafe. I told you, the guy who chased me was a lot smaller than him."

"I'm not sayin' that it implicates the boy. I'm just sayin' it's an important piece of information."

"But say for the sake of argument that it wasn't Marcellus, and I tell the cops. Doesn't that put this lady's life in danger? I mean, she saw the killer at close range."

Rafe snorted derisively. "This 'lady' managed to see someone gettin' killed and didn't even bother to report it to the police. From what I read, that poor girl was layin' there in the street for a couple of hours before anyone found her."

"Yeah, I guess Phyllis's instinct for self-preservation will keep her out of trouble. But what if she's lying?"

"If she said she saw a *white* mon, I might think she was lyin'. But she's got no reason to lie about seein' a black mon, if she's as loyal to Reverend Leroy as you say." He clucked disgustedly into the phone. "Can you believe that mon, tellin' all those church people not to talk to the police?"

I glanced at my watch. I was meeting Lily for dinner in five minutes. "One other thing, Rafe. I poked around in Amanda's room today—I thought I might find something that would tell me whether anything strange was going on just before she died. But it's strange. I couldn't find anything personal anywhere in plain sight. You know, no notes to herself, no phone messages, no letters, nothing."

"Maybe she was really tidy. Or maybe the husband put it all away."

"Maybe. The other weird thing is that Gary all of a sudden wants to empty his own trash. What do you think that's all about?"

"I had a friend who got like that. Real private, all of a sudden."

"And?"

"And I think you need to ask your friend how good his marriage was."

The trouble was, I already had.

CHAPTER FOURTEEN

A Moving Target

Wednesday evening found me in the control booth of the Yale Repertory Theater, high above the rear of the auditorium. The perch provided a commanding view of the stage and the backs of the heads of a sold-out crowd for the opening night of *Macbeth*. Lance had invited me to sit with him ("stage manager's prerogative," he'd said), and the atmosphere of controlled chaos was making me even more anxious to get on with my investigation.

"Did you find that chair?" he snapped into a pair of headphones, while flipping rapidly through an oversized manuscript—which he called "the prompt book"—balanced on the console in front of him. There was a brief pause, and then he barked, "Tell her there's no way we're doing that. I told her yesterday, she's wearing that shawl. I ought to wrap it around her neck," he muttered to himself. He jumped out of his chair and I scrambled to get out of his path as he stepped over a tangle of cables under his seat and headed for the stairs leading up to a catwalk high over the audience.

"Are you sure I'm not in your way?" I asked for the third time.

"No, you're fine. Don't mind me. I can never sit still until the curtain is up."

"He just thinks we can't hit a moving target," called a thin, blond girl with an armful of what appeared to be brown wool hooded cloaks.

Having watched Lance in action for the past two hours, I knew that he was incredibly wound up about something. But whether the cause of his agitation was Amanda's death was still open for discussion. Certainly, the stresses of opening night would be enough to make even a normally calm person manic: Lady Macbeth had turned up forty minutes late following a fight with her boyfriend, the fog machine had gone on the fritz at seven-thirty with an eight o'clock curtain, and there were numerous New York and Boston critics in the very first row. Lance had handled these and many other problems in rapid succession, but I could see his hands shaking as he settled in at the control booth.

"Okay, people. Curtain up in five-four-three-two-one," Lance intoned.

I'll never forget that performance. The actors, the sets and the lighting were all as exquisite as one would expect from the Yale Rep. But it was the portrait of a marriage that I still can't get out of my head. I'm sure that my growing certainty that there was more to the union of Gary and Amanda than met the eye was making me uncharacteristically cynical. That, and my ongoing battle of wills with Dante. But as the play unfolded, I found myself ruminating on "power couples" and the various ways in which they can destroy each other, and becoming quite certain that I was destined to be a professional success and a romantic failure. If I was lucky. If I didn't beat it back to Cambridge soon, I'd strike out on both counts.

"What's the matter?" Lance whispered anxiously to me at intermission. "You look positively *despondent*. Do you hate it?"

"No, it's wonderful! It really is."

"The lights were too dim in Scene One, and if that idiot down there isn't careful, that scrim is going to end up in the lap of the critic from the *Courant*. Jerry!" he shouted into his headphones. "Get that thing tied down. Now!"

"Take a pill, Lancelot," drawled a bearded man at the console next to ours. "What's with you tonight, anyway?"

"Nothing," Lance snapped. "Mac, I told you, get those house lights dimmed. We're already two minutes behind."

"Just what we need. A stage manager with PMS," the bearded man muttered. "You're *such* a Virgo."

"The pace up here is unbelievable," I said lightly. "But at least they've made an arrest in Amanda's murder. That's got to make you feel better."

Lance frowned but kept his eyes on the console before him. "Sure. Right. Of course it does."

Okay, so I wasn't even being subtle. But why was he so stressed? If I hadn't just been told that Amanda's killer was a black man, I would have added Lance to the list of suspects. He was certainly anxious about something. I knew I had Amanda Fox on the brain, but as I watched his face during the hand-washing scene in Act Three, he looked as if he was about to jump out of his skin.

It wasn't until the curtain call that it occurred to me. When one of the actors stepped too close to the footlights, and the line of foundation below his hairline became evident.

A white man wearing makeup could easily appear to be black.

And what man had easier access to a disguise than one who worked at the Yale Rep?

Forty minutes later, Gary, Giselle, and I turned onto York Street, headed for the Beinecke Rare Book Library. Apparently, the media horde had abruptly decided that Gary was old news, because we walked unaccosted through the rain-soaked streets for the first time since Monday afternoon.

"I've never heard of a theater gala being held in a library," I commented. "I thought they'd go for a more dramatic space."

"You haven't seen this library," Gary said, smiling faintly.

"Are you sure you're up for this?" I said, putting my hand gently on his arm.

"Of course he is," Giselle interjected. "And even if he isn't, he still needs to make an appearance. It puts on a strong front."

"Jane—I mean Giselle," Gary corrected himself as she glared at him, "believes that my career requires that I be here."

"I told you—people are going to think you have something to hide if you stay holed up in your room. You have to let them see you. They need to see some angst." Giselle paused as Gary mockingly shook his head. "You *do* want to be President, don't you?" she said sharply. "Then you have to keep these people feeling good about you."

A forty-year-old political wife couldn't have made the case any better. With a flourish, she swept open the glass door leading to the library foyer. "Remember—keep your head up."

We were immediately plunged into a soaring, five-story atrium at the center of which was an immense rectangular glass case filled with thousands of leather-bound books, a tower of Babel that stretched all the way to the ceiling. The red and brown spines of the books seemed to shimmer in their glass sanctuary, and the very light seemed animated.

"You weren't kidding," I said, turning to Gary.

"It's an amazing space, isn't it? There are over eight hundred thousand books in storage here, including the original Gutenberg Bible." Gary turned to Giselle. "We have to show Nikki around, and prove to her that Harvard doesn't have a lock on great libraries."

"This room has such a magical glow," I commented as we started up a broad flight of stairs. Its warmth had restored the good humor that had faded in the midst of Giselle's coldly calculating strategy session.

"That's because the walls of the building are made of translucent marble, which filters the light like no other surface I've seen. You should see it in the daytime." Gary looked over his shoulder at me. "The legend is that because the family that donated the funds for the building made its fortune in Green Stamps, the building is intended to look like a book of them. You'll see what I mean when we leave."

"Tour's over, Gary," Giselle announced as we reached the top of the stairs and were confronted by a well-dressed throng nibbling hors d'oeuvres and sipping champagne. "It's show time." She extracted a piece of lint from his sleeve and broke into a toothy Nancy Reagan grin.

Gary rolled his eyes at me as he glanced over her head, and I relaxed a bit. He obviously found her amusing, and he needed all the help he could get.

As we moved into the crowd, we were immediately immersed in theater chat: *"It never broke down in rehearsals. Only at performances"* . . . *"Her last production was a disaster too. She's got one more shot, then she'll be history"* . . . *"The Banquo was marvelous, but I found Malvolio's interpretation lacking in . . ."*

"Gary, darling!" A silver-haired woman in a blue knit suit placed her hand on his arm, smiling as he dutifully kissed her cheek. "It's so good to see you. And of course, we're so sorry about Amanda."

"President's wife," Giselle whispered *sotto voce*.

"Thank you, Priscilla," Gary was saying. "That means a lot."

"Courtney!" she called out. "Look who's here!"

A younger blonde pressed through the crowd and proffered her cheek for a kiss. "I was going to call you! How splendid that you're here. And I heard that they made an arrest. You must be so relieved. How we're going to miss her."

The space between Gary and me grew larger as word of his arrival spread quickly through the crowd. There were profuse offers of sympathy, voluble apologies for not having called, cursory remarks about how lovely Amanda was and how they'd all miss her on campus and on TV. Then the remarks turned to the culprit and his capture.

"So is it true that this boy was stalking her?" . . . *"I heard that he became absolutely enraged when she rejected his advances."* . . . *"They're just like wild animals."* . . . *"Can you imagine that he was a* Yale *student? I guess we have affirmative action to thank for that one."*

"This is rich," said a voice behind me. "These are the same people who up until yesterday were snubbing Gary because they thought *he* did it."

I turned to find Lance O'Brien standing behind me, still wearing his trademark overalls.

"All I know is that if I hear the phrase 'they're just like wild animals' again, there are going to be tufts of blond hair all over this floor," I growled.

Gary glanced up from the gaggle surrounding him and noticed Lance's arrival. I watched the look that passed between them: Lance was silently pleading for admission to the circle. Gary smiled and imperceptibly beckoned to him.

"Lance," Giselle interceded as he started toward Gary, "I'm sure there are some other people here that are just dying to talk to you." She lowered her voice. "And Gary needs to speak with the Provost as soon as he's done with Mrs. Danforth. Why don't we all give him some room to do that?" She shot me a look, expecting my complicity. I frowned at her.

"And in any case, he can't possibly be seen with the likes of me," Lance snapped. "How did he ever, ever survive without you, Jane?"

"Lance," I interrupted. "I would love it if you would introduce me to the set designer. I thought that using those box springs instead of a scrim during the witches' scene was really inspired."

"Yes, please show her around," Giselle sniffed.

"You see what she's like? You see how she treats me?" he growled as we headed for the bar at the far end of the room. "Like I'm some little nuisance to be taken off her hands."

"I wouldn't worry about it," I said in an effort to be pragmatic. "She's harmless, and Gary needs all the support he can get right now."

Lance visibly brightened as his friends from the Rep began to surround him, offering their congratulations. That was when I saw the Fisches. Max was holding court with a small circle of thirtysomething women who were clearly feigning interest in whatever it was he was saying. I pegged them as either gold diggers who hoped to snare him or Yale development officers who didn't want to let his checkbook out of their collective sights. At his side was younger brother Jared, sipping what appeared to be a martini—and looking at Gary with an expression of startling animosity.

I crossed the room and casually approached him. "You must not have enjoyed the performance, Mr. Fisch."

"Oh, I enjoyed the play just fine. But there's another performance going on that isn't so entertaining."

"Really? What's that?"

"The return of the prodigal son." He nodded in Gary's direction. "Two days ago, no one would touch him with a ten-foot pole. Now he's suddenly the victim, the star of the show."

"That's what I said to Bob Livingston last week!" Max suddenly bellowed to his audience. "These welfare queens have taken enough of our money. Half of 'em are driving Cadillacs, and the other half are pregnant."

As much as I wanted to know why Jared was so obsessed with Gary, I couldn't let Max's remark go by. So what if he hadn't been talking to me?

"Did it ever occur to you that maybe this whole 'welfare queen' concept is just a myth concocted by conservatives to excuse their selfishness toward poor people? Exactly how many welfare recipients do you personally know who are driving around in luxury cars?"

Max's mouth dropped open. "Didn't your supervisor tell you that waitresses aren't supposed to talk to the guests?" he asked, as the chorus line of young women stared at me.

"I'm not a waitress. I'm a Harvard professor. And I'm sick of hearing rich people talk about how much we coddle the poor. You know, the average welfare recipient only gets three dollars and sixty cents per meal. Think about that the next time you hit the '21' Club."

Max stared at me. Then he started to chuckle and winked at the woman standing next to him. "She'll get over that after a few days in New Haven." He looked me straight in the eye. "It's like my daddy always says: a conservative is just a bleeding-heart liberal who's been mugged and seen the light."

"That's funny," I said, smiling brightly. "My daddy always says that a liberal is just an arrogant conservative who's been *arrested* and seen the light."

Jared grinned broadly as he took my arm and turned me away from Max. "I like a girl who'll pick a fight in the middle of a party. You remind me of my Great-aunt Wilhelmina. But you'd best watch out."

"Why? What happened to her?"

"She's six feet under. She got popped in a barroom brawl. Like my daddy always says: 'A headstrong woman and a chattering hen always come to some bad end.'"

"Your daddy is a big talker, isn't he?" I drawled.

Max glared at us as Jared laughed. "Let's get out of here. Are you on your own, or is your friend with you?"

"I'm with—" I began. A loud male voice from a few yards away interrupted me.

"She's not even in the ground yet, and you're already out socializing?"

I found the source of the indignation very easily: Derek Ingersol was standing nose to nose with Gary. The matrons looked appalled.

"Not that its any of your business, Derek, but one of my closest friends was a part of this production. And I'm here to show my support."

"Could damn well have done that by just going to the performance and going back home. I always knew you had no class."

"Hold it right there," Gary said. He seemed to rise to his full height as he glared at Ingersol. "I loved your daughter more than life itself. And I don't have to prove it to you, or to anyone else."

"Really, Derek," a voice said firmly. Reid Talbot had materialized behind Gary, and had his hand on Gary's shoulder. "This is hardly the place for this conversation."

Ingersol harrumphed and then turned away. The silence was broken by the dulcet tones of the President's wife. "Did anyone see the performance of Bohème on PBS last night? It was quite extraordinary."

The tension dissolved in a flood of murmurs, and Gary slowly but visibly relaxed.

"Don't mind him," Professor Talbot said comfortingly to Gary. "I had quite a long talk with him this afternoon, and he's just a bit upset about the provisions of the life insurance policy for Amanda. Apparently, you're the only beneficiary, and he feels betrayed. This is just his way of channeling his grief."

"Thank you, Reid," a blond woman whispered as

she clasped the professor's arm. "Derek really should mind the Dewar's, shouldn't he?" She turned to Gary. "And you, poor lamb. Let's get you something to eat."

That was my cue to leave. Gary was clearly safe in the well-manicured hands of the Yale doyens, and Giselle wasn't going to let me near him anyway. As for Jared Fisch, I'd have ample time to flirt with him the following evening after his gig at Toad's Place.

But an eyewitness had said that Amanda's killer was a black man. Which had given me an overwhelming urge to pay a call on Marcellus Tyler.

CHAPTER FIFTEEN

Fitting the Description

Ten o'clock Wednesday evening found me walking through a maddeningly steady downpour toward the New Haven police station. The expressions on the faces of my few fellow pedestrians ran a very narrow gamut from vaguely annoyed to downright angry. It seemed the entire town was on edge, and whether it was the weather, the arrest of a black Yale student, or causes unknown that had led to this collective vexation, it was making me anxious. The sight of police headquarters did nothing to mitigate the feeling: the building was even more forbidding by night than by day. The fluorescent streetlights lining the sidewalk outside cast an accusatory glow on passersby, and the wet, deserted staircase leading inside offered no solace to an apprehensive visitor. I folded my umbrella as I reached the main entrance, belatedly realizing that I had no idea how I was going to talk my way into the holding cell to see Marcellus Tyler.

It turned out to be simpler than I thought.

"His lawyer?" The cop at the sign-in desk looked me over skeptically.

"That's right," I said briskly, glasses in hand. I assumed my most judicial pose. "I flew in the minute his grandmother retained me to assist in his representation. My driver will be picking me up in twenty minutes, so how can we expedite this?"

My investment banker days in Manhattan taught me that hauteur is the key to opening virtually any door.

"Can I see some ID?" he asked, his expression already more accommodating.

I slid him my driver's license, shamed yet delighted at the ease with which the lie slid off my tongue. What on earth would looking at my license prove?

"I'll be just a second," the cop said as I glanced at my watch with mock impatience.

"What*ever*."

Two minutes later, he ushered me through a set of large steel doors and down a long corridor lined with small holding cells on either side. Marcellus Tyler's was at the very end, in a darkened corner.

"All yours, counselor."

Marcellus stood up quickly as I approached the

bars of his cell, an anxious expression on his face.

"I'm Nikki Chase," I said, preempting his question. "I'm an old friend of Amanda's."

"The cop said you're a lawyer?" the boy asked, as the officer disappeared back down the corridor. "I know my grandmother was trying to find somebody—"

I quickly shook my head. "I'm really sorry. I needed a story to get me in here, Marcellus. I wanted to see how you were doing."

I winced as he sighed in disappointment. It hadn't occurred to me that he might think I really was there to represent him. Poor kid. I looked up to find him eyeing me suspiciously. "So then what's this about? You're the one who was with Dean Fox that day, aren't you?"

"Yes. I've known both of them for a very long time." I swung my purse off my shoulder and let it lie on the floor. "I really admire you for going to see him. That couldn't have been easy."

"If you're the Dean's friend, what the hell are you doing here? Trying to set me up?"

I held my hand up to stop him. "You've got me all wrong, Marcellus. I'm just trying to understand this thing. I want to know who's trying to stick this on you."

"Yeah, right. Why do you care?"

"Well, for one thing, as you can see, I'm black. And I know that the nearest black man without an alibi is frequently the one who ends up imprisoned. Because he 'fits the description.'" I came closer to the bars. "I don't think you did it. I think you were in the wrong place at the wrong time. And I'd love to know who *did* kill her." I paused again and met his gaze. "Come on, Marcellus. What do you have to lose?"

He shrugged silently.

"So let's start this again. Why did you go to see Gary Monday morning?"

"It was the least I could do for her," he said quietly. His voice was curiously soft, given his large stature, and suddenly it seemed to be all he could do to keep his head up and his eyes focused on me.

"Please, sit down," I said. "This has been a really long day for you."

He looked directly at me then, and the fear and sorrow and exhaustion that I saw in his large brown eyes almost broke my heart. He seemed to be in shock, and with good reason: three days ago, he was a budding Yale football star. Now he was just another black kid at the mercy of the criminal justice system.

"Are your folks in town yet?"

He sat down heavily on the scarred wooden bench in his cell. "My grandmother is. She took the train up from the city. My mom's been dead since I was three, and my dad . . ." His voice trailed off.

"So when did they say you might be able to get out of here?"

"I go to court tomorrow. For the arraignment. I guess that's when they set bail. Not that I'll be able to pay it, anyway." He buried his head in his hands. "The cops said if I can't, they'll be moving me to some other jail, out on Whalley Ave.—some state jail." Even though I couldn't see his face, I could hear the fear in his voice.

"I'm sure that there will be a lot of people who will want to help with your bail," I said, trying to comfort him. "There was a press conference earlier today, so a lot of folks know what's happened. It'll be all right."

He shook his head. "No it won't. I'm dead meat at Ray Tomkins House."

"Who's he?"

"It's not a he. Ray Tomkins House is where the coach's office is. They're already saying I may not be allowed to play in The Game. If I had just walked her home the way I wanted to, none of this would have happened. None of it."

"Why didn't she let you do that, Marcellus? I mean, she can't have wanted to walk alone at that hour."

"She said she had to organize some papers, and that I should go ahead. . . ." his voice trailed off.

"But you must have insisted," I prodded him gently. "You seem like the type who would have waited if she needed more time."

"She didn't want me to wait." He said it flatly, and with no small amount of anger. "She made me go."

"Why, Marcellus?" I said softly.

He sat in silence.

"It was because you had an argument, wasn't it?" I was making this up as I went along, but his face was completely transparent, so I wasn't finding it particularly difficult. "You can trust me," I said, as he looked at me wordlessly. "I don't believe you did anything wrong, and I really want to find the person who killed Amanda. I've known her a long time," I repeated, as his eyes searched mine.

"Yeah," he said finally. "We had an argument. I had sent her something—just a little stupid thing, but I thought she might like it—and she said I shouldn't have. She kept trying to give it back to me."

"What was it?"

"Just a little charm for a bracelet she had. A silver football." His sheepishness was utterly endearing. I'd had similar conversations with my little brother, Eric, a million times. *Girls.*

"So what happened to the charm?" I asked the question while pondering for the millionth time why it was that Amanda had been so adept at attracting the attention of any male within a hundred-yard radius. It was truly amazing to me that a nineteen-year-old black boy had found a thirty-year-old right-wing bottle blonde so irresistible.

"I wouldn't take it back. I really wanted her to have it, after all she did for me. So I left it on the table in the classroom at Klein, and I took off."

He looked at me in utter misery. "I just took off."

Despite the day's developments, my gut kept telling me the same thing: this boy was no killer. "Marcellus, you have to stop beating yourself up," I said. "You had no way of knowing—"

"What are *you* doing here?" a male voice thundered.

I'd been so absorbed in the conversation that I hadn't heard the footsteps. But I knew without turning around that the Reverend Russell Jackson had just entered the hallway.

"I hope you haven't been talking to this woman for long, son," he said, striding purposefully down the corridor.

"I told you, man, I don't want to see you anymore," Marcellus said sharply.

Russell Jackson inhaled audibly. "Son, you need help right now—"

"Stop calling me son, and stop using me. I told you once, and I'm not saying it again." Marcellus was glaring at the reverend as if he would have happily strangled him. What had happened to the alliance between them?

"I thought you had asked for their help," I said to Marcellus.

"No. I told them I didn't want anything to do with them. Then my grandmother tells me that they staged some rally this afternoon. And they all came down here tonight. I told you, you're not using me.

And I meant it," he said, turning to Reverend Russell. "Now step off."

"Marcellus—" Russell began.

"I'm out," Marcellus interrupted. "I'm tired and they're taking me to court in the morning. So good night."

I met the boy's eyes. "I meant what I said, Marcellus. Stop blaming yourself. I don't think you could have prevented this. I think it was planned well in advance, and that there's no way you could have stopped it."

Both of them stared at me.

"I'll come back and see you again later, if that's okay," I continued. Marcellus nodded, his eyes searching mine.

"Good night, Reverend," I said, brushing past him.

"I'll be back tomorrow," Reverend Russell said to Marcellus. "I want to talk to you some more." Then he strode down the corridor after me.

"What kind of game are you playing?" he demanded.

"You should talk, Reverend," I hissed as we passed the guard at the reception desk.

"What did you mean 'this was planned'?" he persisted as I headed for the door.

"Just what I said." I turned to face him. "I don't think he did it. But someone sure as hell wants to make it look like he did."

"How do I know that you're not here to lull that boy into a false sense of security so that he'll tell you something that you can run back to the police with?"

"Why would I do that?"

"You wouldn't be the first Uncle Tom to pass through here, Professor."

"Hold it right there. That kid doesn't even want you here, and you have the nerve to insult me? Why are you even here?"

"Because he may not know it yet, but he needs us. He and his grandmother have no idea how badly they're about to be treated. They have no idea how important it is that the media be watching. But we've been through this before, and we know how to protect him."

I snorted. "Right, all you want to do is to *protect* him. That's why Reverend Leroy spends all his time prancing around onstage, playing for the cameras, polishing his image as the savior of the downtrodden. How is that going to flush out the real killer?"

"What's that supposed to mean?"

"Exactly what I said. We both know Marcellus didn't do it. Doesn't that beg the question of who did, Reverend?"

He regarded me silently, and then unexpectedly, his face broke into a grin. For a brief moment, I felt as blissful as Wilbert Green, the little boy who had barreled into the Reverend Russell earlier that day at the press conference.

"You've got a point, Professor." He glanced over his shoulder. "Where are you going right now?"

"Back to campus."

"I'd like to walk you, if you don't mind."

I started to turn left as we headed out of the station, but he took my arm and firmly steered me the other way. "I know a shortcut," he said.

"So you've lived in New Haven awhile," I commented as we swung onto the sidewalk. A teenaged kid wearing huge baggy jeans and a Tommy Hilfiger jacket brushed past us, speaking urgently into a cell phone.

"Yes, I came here for Yale undergrad almost fifteen years ago, and once I got back from the U.K. on my Rhodes scholarship, I never left," Russell said, surveying the streetscape. "I don't think I could live anywhere else at this point."

"Really?" I attempted, unsuccessfully, to hide my incredulity.

"Don't look so shocked. I wrote my master's thesis about the impact of social networks on violence in young black men, and I felt there was no better place than New Haven to put it into practice."

"What does that mean—social networks?"

"It means that when black boys have institutions like the church, a sports league, a community center, some kind of network, that they are less than half as likely to commit an act of violence."

"Is that why you're a minister?"

He smiled. "It's not the only reason. But it helped me answer the call."

"So how did someone like you hook up with Reverend Leroy?"

"You say that like you think he's disreputable."

"I read about his request for the parishioner's W-2 forms. And his Mercedes."

Russell smiled ruefully. "Leroy can get a bit carried away. But he's a good man. I always tell people that if you took everything about black folks—our passion for justice, our spirituality, our anger and our suffering—and put it in a pot, and boiled it for an hour, what would be left is Leroy."

I had to laugh.

"I still have to figure out a way to get through to that boy." Russell said abruptly.

"Why?" I asked a bit impatiently. "Why does he need *you* so badly?"

"Because I know these cops. I'm down here almost every week. Do you know how many boys from my church were tossed last week? *Three.* All fine boys, not troublemakers—I'm talking about kids from good families."

"What do you mean—'tossed'?"

"It means searched without cause. Thrown to the ground, humiliated, brought into the station house and in one case held overnight. Without cause. I've spent hours trying to tell these cops who the good kids are, who's dealing, and who's causing trouble.

Even showed them pictures. But let them see a black face and they start busting heads."

Out of the darkness, a black man materialized, dressed in a stocking cap and a well-worn wool peacoat. "Yo, Rev! What's the word?"

"The word is stay inside, my brother. You don't need to be out in this rain."

"I hear you, man. But can't you make it stop? Ain't that one of your powers?"

Reverend Russell shook his head, laughing, and the man joined in.

As I watched the reverend cajole the man into spending the night in a nearby shelter, I found myself channeling the voice of Maggie Dailey. *He's handsome, a Rhodes Scholar, a defender of the downtrodden.* And *he's black. Girl, what are you waitin' for?*

For once, I didn't disagree.

CHAPTER SIXTEEN

Black and Blue

It was exactly eleven o'clock Wednesday night when the collective vexation of the denizens of New Haven boiled over into something more dangerous. I know this because Russell Jackson and I had just entered Old Campus through an arched stone gateway on the eastern perimeter, and the clock there dutifully proclaimed the hour. Our conversation had become more and more heated, as I refused to elaborate on why I thought Amanda's murder had been planned. But the words died in our throats as we were brought to a full stop by what was going on in the usually placid quadrangle.

All hell was breaking loose.

A large wooden platform had been erected near

the statue of President Woolsey, lit by licking flames from eight or nine large metal drums and the piercing light of several television cameras. The Reverend Leroy Saunders was standing on the platform, using a bullhorn to address a crowd of what looked like five hundred people, most of whom looked too old to be Yale students. While center of the crowd was largely black, I noticed that there was an ever-growing ring of young white men encircling them. Gradually it dawned on me that Reverend Leroy was only *trying* to address the crowd. The crowd, in the meantime, seemed more intent on yelling racial epithets, shoving, and throwing small projectiles. An angry hum, like a swarm of bees, punctuated the shouting.

"I say it again. The New Haven Police Chief, Patrick Fitzgerald, should step down. Immediately. There is no *justice* in this town. Therefore, there shall be no *peace.*"

A young black man leaped to the podium and shouldered the reverend aside. "Word to your mother!" he shouted. "These white folks have stepped on us long enough! We're gonna turn this place *out!*"

A cluster of other young blacks roared their approval. A white man next to me took the opportunity to shout, "You niggers are crazy!"

I turned to the Reverend Russell in fury. "Is this what you call helping Marcellus? Starting a riot that makes it look like we blacks have no respect for the law? What the hell are you all thinking?"

Without answering, he plunged into the crowd and started toward Reverend Leroy.

The howls of the crowd intensified, as if a year's worth, a lifetime's worth, of frustration had suddenly found an outlet. "Turn it out!" a harsh voice called. I heard the spiny crackle of breaking glass.

Who started it? That's what they would ask later. *Who started it?* Reverend Leroy, I could have answered. The cops who decided to arrest Marcellus Tyler. The black man who threw the first bottle. The white man who threw the first punch. But we all knew who really started this. The son of a bitch who had killed Amanda Fox.

I ducked as the head of the black man in front of me abruptly disappeared. I looked over to see him doubled over on the ground, clutching his abdomen, screaming. A white man stood over him holding a baseball bat. "That's for Amanda Fox," the man sneered.

Within seconds, Old Campus dissolved into a series of nightmare images: the white man who had been standing next to me being kicked mercilessly by a black man; the face of the black man on the ground turning blood red under the fists of two white boys; the leaded-glass windows of Phelps Hall shattering under an onslaught of jagged rocks and broken beer bottles.

A lifetime went by before the cops moved in. But they were nothing if not efficient. I heard a soft whisper, then smelled a sharp, painful odor. Tear gas. A sickening crack was followed by the sight of a billy club being drawn back from a skull. A wall of blue helmets and plastic riot shields moved inexorably forward, and a scramble began as people ducked out of the way, disappearing into the darkness beyond the stone arches of the quadrangle. What remained was a much smaller, much more subdued crowd of what appeared to be mostly Yale students from the surrounding dormitories. Shock was writ large on their faces. Shock, and fear.

I spotted a familiar head of silver hair at the periphery of the crowd, and headed directly toward it. I really wanted a word with Officer Timothy Heaney.

"So, you made your deadline," I said coldly to the back of his head. "The PR department must be *so* proud."

Heaney turned toward me, startled, and I came closer. "Just three days after the crime is committed, you've got a nice, scary-looking suspect behind bars, and the citizenry can sleep well again. At least, once the riots are put down. Great work, Detective."

Heaney refused to meet my eyes.

"That kid is going to be scarred for life by this—" I continued.

"Listen," he interrupted soberly. "You don't have

all the facts, and you have no idea what kind of pressure we're operating under."

"Oh, you don't have to tell me, Officer," I said sarcastically. "When a white girl is in trouble—let alone dead—the whole world goes insane trying to help."

"You honestly believe that I wouldn't be busting my ass just as much if Amanda Fox had been black?"

"*You* might. But you aren't the only one calling the shots here."

Heaney's jaw tightened. I'd clearly struck a nerve. "The police chief, the mayor, even the governor, for pete's sake—" I continued. "They all want this wrapped up as quickly as possible. It only takes one hothead to launch a rush to justice. And you see what the result is."

The frustration on the policeman's face was completely transparent.

"You have to admit that this was awfully quick," I pressed him. "We both know arresting Marcellus was a hell of a lot more acceptable than going after one of the blue-bloods."

"I *really* hate it when people play the race card." He shot a contemptuous look toward the now deserted podium. "I'm not interested in black and white. I'm interested in guilt and innocence, and the one has nothing to do with the other."

"Then we need to talk, Heaney. Because there are plenty of people who could've wanted that girl dead other than Marcellus Tyler."

A young white man in a slicker jostled hard against us. "Move on, fella," Heaney said sharply. Then he turned to me. "You got some information, spill it. Otherwise, I've got work to do."

"Yeah, I have some information. You want to hear it?"

He collared a passing uniformed cop who was pushing a handcuffed rioter. "Joey, tell the teams I've gotta finish up here, and I'll meet them at oh-one hundred hours." He turned back to me. "You've got five minutes."

The rain resumed in earnest as we sat down on the stone stairs of Welch Hall and I started to fill him in on what I'd overheard at the beauty salon. I put my umbrella up; Heaney, ever macho, refused to even pull up the hood of his slicker, instead keeping half an eye on the shattered glass on the pavement below us.

"So she said she saw a black guy," he said quietly, looking pleased. "That's great. The case against Tyler is even stronger."

"How do you know that it wasn't a white person made up to look black?" I said quickly.

He rolled his eyes. "Jesus Christ, Professor."

"Well, how do you know?"

"I don't. But after thirty years on the force, I can tell you one thing: whatever you might see in the movies, when all the evidence points toward one particular guy having committed a crime, nine times out of ten he really did it."

"Don't condescend to me, Heaney. Both Gary and Amanda were surrounded by people who had unusually strong attachments to them. Romantic attachments. And that's a fine motive for murder."

"Tell me more."

"Well, Gary's little sidekick Giselle Storrs, has a huge crush on him, and she was in the same classroom as Amanda and Marcellus that night. And Jared Fisch hates Gary with a passion. Isn't it possible that he was crazy about Amanda and snapped when she rejected him?"

"It's possible." He started to get up, then sank back to the step as one of his men wrestled a laggard rioter to the pavement. "I've gotta get going soon."

"Fine. Just one more thing. Giselle Storrs is lying about that man that she claims to have seen in the bushes."

Now I had his attention.

"I walked the route myself," I continued, "and there's no way that the man she saw—if she saw someone at all—was the man who killed Amanda. The timing doesn't work. She says she saw someone hiding on her way home from class. But Amanda was killed fifteen minutes away from the route Giselle should have taken if she was walking back to campus. Besides, does Giselle really seem like the type who's observant enough to see anything more than five inches away from her nose, unless it's her own reflection?"

Heaney snorted in agreement. Then he looked straight at me. "You're right," he said.

"*What?*"

"I said, you're right. I don't disagree that there are plenty of loose ends here."

"So are you still working this case?" I whispered.

He looked me over carefully, as if taking my measure. "You're just going to keep trying to wear me down on this, aren't you?"

I nodded. "You can count on it."

"Well, as tired of you as I am, Professor, I appreciate your giving me that information," he said gruffly. "So I'll tell you something. But it's not for public consumption." He leaned toward me. "I'm still working the case. *Me*—not the rest of the teams."

It didn't give me a lot of hope for Marcellus, but it was better than nothing. "Then I'll call you if I find out anything you need to know," I said as he stood up.

"I've got a feeling I don't have any choice." Heaney grimaced, then disappeared into the night.

I watched pensively as he left. I knew I was right about at least some of the local cops having an inherent bias against Marcellus Tyler because he was black. But wasn't I just as bad? My refusal to believe that a black man had killed Amanda was just as deep-rooted. And I'd instinctively kept Lance O'Brien's name out of the conversation—even though in my mind he was a prime suspect—because I knew that a gay man would be almost as easy to scapegoat as Marcellus had been. So what did that make me?

A bad detective, I concluded as I rose from the damp stone stairs. I needed to keep my political beliefs from clouding my judgment.

I was sure that Amanda Fox would have agreed.

It was well past midnight when I arrived back at Lily's. The storm had increased in intensity, and rain lashed against the windows, eliciting rattles of protest. A lamp glowed softly in the living room, but the bedroom light was extinguished, and I assumed that Lil was asleep. I wanted to tell her about the riot—to give her the scoop before she read it in the papers tomorrow. I was completely wired, and there was no way I could sleep. But I doubted her hospitality extended to being awakened out of a sound sleep at this hour. I sighed, peeled off my jacket and quietly set about making a pot of coffee. Five minutes passed before I noticed the note taped to the telephone: *"A guy named Dante Rosario called three times tonight. Wants you to call him as soon as you get back."*

My mind calmly contemplated the possible consequences of returning his call while my heart performed a series of somersaults. As I stared indecisively at the telephone, it rang.

"Hello," I whispered. "Lily Cho's line."

"This is *way* too much, even for you," commented an achingly familiar voice. Dante Rosario never had been the type to wait around for the phone to ring.

"So what took you so long?" I baited, perching on the arm of the sofa.

"Your alarming ability to cover your tracks, that's what. Maggie wouldn't crack, but Jess finally told Ted where you were, and he told me. You need to come home, now."

"Excuse me? Before you start the caveman act, let's get one thing straight. This is none of your business. I'll be back when I'm finished down here, and not a nanosecond before."

"You have no idea what you're dealing with, Nik. It could get dangerous."

Tell me about it. "That's why I'm here, Rosario. Because things are not as they should be." A gust of wind set the windowpanes rattling in violent agreement, and I could hear the rain pounding on the pavement outside.

"Why are you so determined to go looking for trouble? You're down there alone, you've got no air cover—"

"I'm hardly alone," I interrupted. "Gary's here."

"Oh, great. Like he could help if things start to get crazy. He sure as hell didn't protect his wife."

"What's *that* supposed to mean?"

"Come on, Nik. What's that guy weigh? Ninety-six pounds or so? Amanda said that—"

"You know what? I could care less what Amanda said about Gary. She'd say *anything* if she thought it was what you wanted to hear. That was her stock-in-trade."

"That's not fair. You couldn't be more wrong about her, Nik," he said firmly.

"Oh, of course I'm wrong. To you, she's Saint Amanda of the family values. Never mind that an innocent black kid is being accused of her murder, and all her white society friends down here can't wait to put the noose around his neck." I could hear my voice cracking, and covered it with a cough.

"You want to talk about it?"

"No, I don't want to *talk* about it," I snapped. "You can't understand how I feel. These smug white matrons have just had their worst fears confirmed; they're all so certain that every black man they pass on the street is thinking about robbing them or killing them. And this yahoo minister, Reverend Leroy, is holding himself out as the spokesman for the entire black race when he's clearly just out for himself. And of course, any reasonable black person gets dismissed by both sides as being 'inauthentic.' Meanwhile the cops are sitting around with their feet up, crowing over how quickly they were able to railroad a nineteen-year-old kid. So no, I don't want to talk about it. I'm sick of these people!" I paused to take a breath.

"What can I do to help?" he asked simply.

"Nothing. I have to deal with this myself." I wanted to say more—I wanted to tell him about how off-kilter this whole experience was making me feel. About how much this town reminded me of Detroit. And how Russell's commitment to it was making me feel guilty about my own abrupt abandonment of my home town. I wanted to confide how jarring it was to be reminded about how disconnected my existence in Cambridge was from the black community—and how sad and scared it made me to see how quickly a black boy could be yanked from his sheltered campus life into the maw of an urban jail. But how could he possibly understand any of that?

"You're not in this alone, Juliet," Dante replied gently, as if he was reading my mind. "You think I don't understand? I do. But—I'm not going to try to convince you of that tonight. You sound completely worn out. Why don't you try to get some sleep?"

I shook my head, even though he couldn't see me. It was time to get back to business. "I'm nowhere *near* sleep. I've got to finish the next draft of my paper for the AEA Conference. Professor Irvin wants it on his desk first thing tomorrow morning."

"How's it going with him?"

"Terribly. He's determined to make me pay for what I did to his best friend, and he's threatening to yank me from the conference agenda if I don't finish this paper by next Monday."

"Is there anything I can do?"

"No. I just have to work."

"I get the hint. I'll let you go. But one last question. You're not walking around there alone at night, are you?"

"Well, gee, Pop, since you took the car keys after I broke my curfew last week, I have no choice but to walk."

"Very funny," he muttered. "I ought to—"

"Ought to what? Stop lecturing me?"

"Hardly. But what I'm contemplating can't be managed long distance."

"Then I guess it's an idle threat."

"I wouldn't count on that, Juliet."

I hung up the phone and lay back on the sofa, listening to the steady drumming of the rain on the pavement outside.

He had actually sounded concerned about me.

I had to get out of town more often.

CHAPTER SEVENTEEN

DWM

"I'm off to the DWMs."

It was Thursday morning, and Gary Fox and I were finishing breakfast in the Branford dining room. I was on my third cup of coffee, having stayed up all night working on my AEA paper, and it took a moment for his voice to penetrate my foggy brain. I raised my brow quizzically.

"Dead White Males," he elaborated with a wry smile. "Otherwise known as History of European Thought, nine A.M. section."

"You sure you're up to doing this?" I asked.

He nodded. It'll take my mind off things. I'll see you this afternoon."

I lingered over my coffee as the dining room

emptied out, musing about what I should do next. On impulse, I decided to stop by the Yale Rep to see Lance O'Brien. I'd promised myself the night before that I would revisit my assumptions about his innocence. When you were investigating the murder of Amanda Fox, of all people, political correctness was particularly inappropriate. Lance's behavior the night before had made it clear that his attachment to Gary was intense. I wanted to know just how far it went.

Looking upward as I emerged into the Branford courtyard, I realized that my time in New Haven had significantly deepened my appreciation for the nuances of gray. That morning, the sky was smoky white, punctuated by puffs of charcoal gray clouds scattered randomly across the horizon, an aerial archipelago. Sunshine would have seemed superficial and a bit trite in comparison.

Five minutes later I was entering the Yale Rep. Lance had told me that the small redbrick building on Chapel Street had originally been a church, and now that the theater was deserted, I could see the original pitched roof and the outline of the former nave. The stage was empty except for a man in dusty jeans and a work shirt who seemed to be in the midst of repairing a chair.

"Excuse me," I called. "I'm looking for Lance O'Brien."

"Downstairs," he barked.

I took that as permission to go exploring. Following a set of scruffy tiled stairs to the basement of the building, I passed through a large, eerily empty auditorium and approached a door marked SMOKING ROOM. Behind it was a small space with exposed brick and the stagnant odor of countless *après*-performance smokes. But no Lance.

I backtracked and turned down a narrow hallway with five doors on either side.

"Hello?" I called out. My voice echoed off the closed doors, and I realized that something about this place was getting me spooked. *Where was everybody?* "Lance?"

Methodically, I worked my way down the corridor, knocking on doors, but finding only tiny, empty rooms furnished with dressing tables and small stools. Finally, I opened the door of the last dressing room, and there was Lance O'Brien.

He was hanging from the ceiling. With a noose around his neck.

Timothy Heaney arrived at the Yale Rep in what seemed like a matter of seconds after I called 911, and he disappeared into the dressing room without so much as a word.

"What the hell happened?" he growled when he emerged minutes later.

"I found him hanging from the ceiling, and I pulled him down because I thought he might still be alive. I tried CPR, but I never got him to breathe. I'm pretty sure he was already dead when I found him."

Heaney was staring at me, and I knew what he was thinking.

"You had better not be planning to ask me if *I* had anything to do with this," I said. "I came over here to talk to Lance about his relationship with Gary, and I found him just like that."

"So you two were friends?"

"He's Gary's friend. I just met him earlier this week. We spent a little time together this week, and like I said, I was here because I knew they were very close, and I was trying to figure out how close."

"Did you touch anything else?"

"Yeah," I replied. "This."

I held up a white sheet of paper that I'd found on the dressing table.

Dear Gary,

There's no point in going on this way, and so it has to end. I've loved you since the day we met. I know you won't believe me, but I'm sorry that I killed her. It shouldn't have come to this. I know you can't forgive me. I can't forgive myself.

The note rambled on for about a page, and then abruptly ended.

"What do you think?" I asked.

"Weirdest fucking case I've ever seen," Heaney muttered under his breath.

"So I was right about that makeup."

Heaney looked at me uncomprehendingly.

"The eyewitness said the killer was black. But as I said to you, a white person wearing makeup could have *looked* black at night. Lance must have used it to throw people off the track."

Heaney was shaking his head.

"He could have!" I insisted.

"Maybe. But I don't like this." He gestured to the note.

"What do you mean? You think it's ungrammatical?" I drawled sarcastically.

"No, Professor. I mean it's *typed*."

I nodded grudgingly. "You're right. It could be fake."

"We're checking the guy's alibi for Sunday night. But I don't like the looks of this."

"So what happens now?" I demanded. "When are you going to release Marcellus Tyler?"

"Whoa!"

"Look, either way, Marcellus has to be innocent. Either this *is* a confession, or someone set O'Brien up to make it *look* like a confession. But either way, Marcellus was under lock and key when this happened, so he can't have been involved."

Heaney held firm. "Could have been one of his supporters. You saw the people out there last night."

"Fine. But it couldn't have been *him*."

"We'll see what the chief and the DA think."

"But at a minimum, this *has* to mean that Amanda Fox wasn't killed by some deranged stranger, doesn't it?"

At that, Heaney nodded his head with sobering finality. "One death may be a random tragedy," he said. "But two means that someone has a plan."

Three o'clock Thursday afternoon found me in a tiny dorm room in Timothy Dwight, a redbrick College on the outskirts of the campus. Giselle Storrs had offered her room as a refuge for Gary from the ravenous media horde that had resurfaced once news of Lance's suicide emerged. Against my advice, he'd accepted her offer.

"Did you end the relationship with him, Dean Fox? How long had the two of you been lovers?" The words wafted up from the grassy quadrangle below Giselle's window.

Another reporter with a New York accent shouted up "Dean Fox! Did the love triangle anger your wife?"

"When are the cops going to get rid of those guys?" I snapped, peering through a pair of chintz floral curtains. My commitment to First Amendment rights was waning by the second.

"As soon as they eject the crowd in the hallway is my guess," Giselle said calmly. She was surprisingly unruffled, given the stunning news and the cacophony from the courtyard. Gary, on the other hand, appeared to be in shock.

"What am I going to do?" he moaned quietly. He'd repeated the phrase every few minutes ever since I'd broken the news of Lance's death to him two hours ago.

"You want some advice?" Giselle said coolly. "Talk to them."

I quickly shook my head. "He's in no shape to do that."

Gary looked at Giselle. "*Talk to them?* Why should I?"

"Because they're going to run a story tonight, whether you talk to them or not. The lead can be 'Yale Dean Fox Involved in Gay Murder-Suicide' or it can be 'Yale Murderer Confesses.' That's up to you."

"If he talks to them, everything he says will get twisted," I protested. "How do you answer the question 'So, are you still gay?' It's like 'Have you stopped beating your wife?'"

"Nikki, this is PR 101," Giselle snorted derisively. "If you don't give the press a story, they'll make one up. I'll talk you through it," she said, turning to Gary. "We could do it right here, right now. All you have to do is go down to the courtyard and start talking with one of the guys, and the rest will follow. It'll be an informal press conference, and you can stop whenever you feel like it."

"I'm not going to turn the courtyard into a circus," Gary said firmly. "There are students studying here."

"So we'll do it in the dining hall—it'll be deserted right now. Come *on*, Gary," Giselle urged. "I'll be with you. I'll stand right next to you."

"Oh, *that'll* help his case. His wife isn't even dead a week, and he's holding a press conference with *you?*"

"Well, of course you'd be there too, Nikki. What better image could he have when some gay guy has just told the world he was in love with Gary than being surrounded by women? Plus, I'm his student, which reminds people that he's a dedicated educator, not some pervert."

"Giselle!" Gary and I both said sharply. "I don't appreciate those kinds of comments," Gary continued. "Lance was my best friend. Don't ever let me hear you refer to him or any other gay man as a 'pervert' again."

"Fine," she said dismissively. "But are you going to do it?"

I shrugged in resignation as Gary's eyes met mine. This entire experience had been completely surreal. What more harm could be done?

"Okay," Gary said with a sigh. "Let's do it."

Fifteen minutes later we were surrounded by a veritable multimedia cavalcade: journalists from radio, print, broadcast, cable, and the Internet were arrayed around the well-worn wooden tables in the TD dining hall, watching expectantly as Gary ceremoniously cleared his throat.

"Lance O'Brien, a very dear friend of mine and my wife's, passed away today. I am shocked by his death, and I will miss him terribly," he began.

"Was he your lover?" a male voice called out.

"Amanda Fox was my lover," Gary answered sharply. "You denigrate the memories of both of these fine people by asking such questions. The three of us were all very close."

Giselle nodded her approval.

"But your wife wrote several articles condemning gay and lesbian lifestyles," another reporter interjected. "So how could she have liked Mr. O'Brien?"

Gary ignored the question and stuck doggedly to his notes. "Having lost my wife and one of my best friends in the space of a week is a grief thankfully beyond the understanding of most people. I can only appeal to the citizens of New Haven to honor Amanda and Lance by stopping the violence that has been an unfortunate result of Amanda's death."

"The cops say O'Brien confessed to killing your wife. And you're *sorry* to hear that he's dead?" a reporter interrupted.

"Lance was deeply troubled," Gary responded. "I had no idea how much until today. And there is still some question about the authenticity of the note that was found with his—his body."

"Are you saying that O'Brien *didn't* kill her?" the reporter pressed.

"I really can't say any more. You'll have to speak with the police about that."

I watched Giselle's face as the questions continued. She looked flushed, happy, and completely in control, and I realized that as of that moment she had achieved everything she seemed to want. Her two rivals for Gary's affection had been neatly disposed of, and now she was alone with him, sharing the stage with no one else.

She looked very innocent in her plaid Catholic schoolgirl skirt, smiling sweetly at the cameras. But I ignored the facade.

I knew from personal experience that willful little preppie girls could be perfectly lethal.

CHAPTER EIGHTEEN

Behind God's Back

"They had *best* be releasing that boy now. These white folks. I knew all along they were pure evil. Some—some *funny* man kills that girl and they go blamin' it on one of us."

Pearl Johnson's vocabulary obviously didn't include any of the current derisive appellations for homosexuals. For a moment, I thought she was accusing Lance O'Brien of being a comedian.

"They going to release that man now, Reverend Russell?"

"I would expect so, Wilbert." The minister laid a comforting hand on the little boy's head.

It was five o'clock Thursday afternoon, and I was standing in the basement of the Resurrection Tabernacle Deliverance Church, the only stationary object in a maelstrom of activity. In one corner a group of very young children was busily erecting a church out of building blocks. In another, a slightly older group was playing a raucous game of musical chairs to the strains of the Wu Tang Clan. A steady stream of ten-year-olds was flowing back and forth through an open door, carrying shovels, wooden boards and pails of dirt. Apparently, the door led to a small garden behind the church.

"Slow down, Ashley," Russell Jackson called as a little girl with pigtails raced by with a rake in her hand.

"I'd best get on out there and see what these children are gettin' into," Pearl declared, heading for the door.

"This is amazing, Russell," I said. "How many kids come here every day?"

"Who are you?" Wilbert piped up.

"Wilbert, that is not how we address adults. And we don't interrupt, either," the reverend said sternly.

"Sorry, Reverend Russell," the boy murmured.

Wilbert and I chatted amiably for a moment while Russell rescued a small boy who had managed to wedge himself inside a cardboard box. "We have about fifty kids who come here regularly after school," he finally answered as we strolled the length of the room. "We rely on parents and other parishioners to help us out, so that we can provide the service for free. Nice to see you, Beverly." He simultaneously smiled at a middle-aged woman with a toddler on her lap and picked up a crumpled piece of construction paper from the floor. "These are the girls I wanted you to meet. We call this program 'SOS'—Save Our Selves."

His arm swept toward a group of about ten teenagers arrayed in a semicircle of metal folding chairs in a corner of the room. Two of them were visibly pregnant. I inhaled slowly, considering the best way to get started.

The call I'd received from the reverend early that morning had caught me off guard, given that we hadn't parted on the best terms the night before. I thought he might be calling to continue pressing me about my comment about Marcellus, but he'd asked me to meet a group of young women at his church to talk about Harvard, why I had left my job on Wall Street, and what it was like being a professor. "They don't meet many black women like you," he'd said.

I'd immediately said yes to his request, but now that I was here, I was stymied. My job was to give them hope about what a young black girl could grow up to be without coming across like a Pollyanna or a handkerchief head. The expressions of boredom and skepticism on their faces didn't give me much confidence.

"I don't want this session to be me lecturing you," I said as Russell departed. "So let me tell you a little about myself, and then I want you to talk to me about whatever you want, okay?" My opening gambit was met with stone-faced stares. "I grew up in Detroit—"

"*You're* from Detroit?" a tall girl said skeptically. Her eyes openly registered her opinion of my chemically relaxed hair, my red miniskirt, and my Ivy League diplomas. *White girl.*

"Yes, I'm from Detroit," I said firmly. "From the *city.* Not the suburbs. I was the first person from my high school to ever go to Harvard," I continued. "And it was a lady from my church who helped me get there."

"Why'd you want to go to some school like that, anyway?" the tall girl challenged.

"Because I thought it was the best. And I think all of us as black people need to push ourselves to achieve the best."

"How come you didn't go to a black school? Or wasn't that good enough for you?" she shot back.

I paused to consider her question. "To be honest, sometimes I wish I had."

The girl looked surprised.

"I don't have the deep ties and friendships in the black community that I would have had if I had gone to a black school, and I regret that. But as a high school senior, I wanted to be a CEO. Or the president of a college. Or a Supreme Court Justice. And to do it, I felt I needed to learn how to excel in a white environment. That's not to say that you can't succeed in life by attending a black college. I just didn't happen to take that path." I leaned forward for emphasis. "The main thing is that you choose a path and follow it. And don't let anybody distract you or undermine your confidence. Which they *will* try to do."

I met the eyes of the tall girl, and to my surprise, she grudgingly smiled. The rest of the girls subtly relaxed, and I exhaled. We were off.

An hour later, I looked up and realized that the basement was nearly deserted. While we'd been talking, the smaller kids had gradually dispersed. I said my goodbyes to the girls and then lingered as they trailed up the rickety stairs to the front door.

Perhaps it was the conversation I'd just had with the girls about growing up in Detroit, going to church twice a week with my family. Or maybe it was the faint scent of frying onions wafting down from the kitchen upstairs, which smelled exactly like my favorite aunt's famous liver and onions. But something about this place was making me incredibly homesick, and to my surprise, I wasn't ready to leave. I drifted slowly up the stairs, past a series of sepia pictures of Jesus and the saints, the voices of women growing louder as I climbed.

"*Now folks are gonna be showin' up here any minute, so remember: no eatin' while you're servin' people. I'm talking to* you, *Darius! . . . Is the sweet tea made? . . . Where did Pearl go with those pies?*"

I dawdled in the small entry foyer and soaked in the familiar cadence of hardworking churchwomen getting ready for a potluck supper. That was when I heard the other voices.

The sound of men talking loudly drew me toward a pair of scarred wooden doors. One was ajar, and I could see that this was the main entrance to the church's sanctuary. The Reverends Leroy and Russell were standing at the front of the fifteen-row chapel, near the altar, flanked by two large black men.

"It has to be *big*," Reverend Leroy was saying. "I'm talking coverage on all three networks. *National* news."

"I hear you," echoed one of the men. "*National.*"

"After what happened last night?" Russell Jackson was shaking his head. "Too risky. We can't control these folks."

"That's the whole point," Leroy snapped. "We need to let these people *know* that we can't be controlled. Let them *know* what happens when an innocent black boy is kept behind bars, even after new evidence emerges. Even after a white man has *confessed* to the crime."

"All right, man, it's just us now," the other men said. "You need to save that for the press conference."

"What we *need* to do is get in their faces," the first man said. "All up *in* their faces."

"I think a march is too risky," Russell repeated.

"Especially tomorrow night. There's a big football game Saturday, and there'll be all kinds of folks in the street. You know how many people ended up in the hospital last night? Twenty-five."

"And whose fault is that?" Leroy thundered. "The white cops who refuse to talk to us. I'm not lettin' some white-boy football game get in the way of justice."

"Amen," said the first man.

"Leroy, you're pushing your luck," Russell began. "We don't have a permit, we know the cops will be all over us—"

"Man, I'm tired of you!" the first man exploded. "You so busy living behind God's back, acting all righteous and shit, that you can't see what's really going on here. These white people got to know. *They can't treat us like this.*"

Reverend Leroy nodded in agreement, and turned to the second man. "Brother Martin, you put out the word. Nine o'clock tomorrow night, we go."

"Brother Martin" signaled to the first man, and they started down the aisle. I stepped behind the door and watched them as they left the church. Then I turned back to my listening post.

The Reverends Leroy and Russell were now sitting in the first pew. "You know you really don't need to go this far," Russell said quietly.

"Yes, I do," Reverend Leroy responded. He put his hand on Russell's shoulder. "It's working, isn't it?"

Russell was silent.

"Hey, nobody's suspecting anything, are they?"

"No, they don't. But it's enough. I think we should cool it now."

It was all I could do to stay where I was. I leaned forward, straining to hear.

Reverend Leroy was shaking his head adamantly. "They'll be so busy running around trying to keep the peace, they won't have time to put the shit together."

"Innocent people are getting hurt, Leroy." Russell said it so quietly that it took a moment for his words to register.

"That may be," Reverend Leroy responded as he rose heavily to his feet. "But what else can we do?"

I watched as they walked through a door at the back of the church. Then I started back toward the campus, ruminating. Two secretive reverends, two vindictive brothers, a deceased gay man, and a preppie blond cheerleader—any of whom could've conceivably wanted Amanda Fox dead. There was only one way that I was going to figure out who killed her.

I was going to have to get inside her head. And fast.

And since her home had been stripped of any useful personal effects, a visit to her office seemed to be in order.

• • •

Yale Law School was shrouded in mist when I approached it in search of Amanda Fox. It was twilight on a day when the sun had never really risen, and the compound loomed like a wraith before me. I regarded the building impatiently. Amanda was as elusive as the wisps of fog curling around its turrets, and I could almost hear her mocking me. Was she so very complicated? Or was I just missing something obvious?

I found her office on the deserted second floor of the building, and jimmied the lock with my Harvard ID card. It was smaller than I'd expected, but far more charming: her desk faced a stone fireplace flanked by bookcases, and the ashes in the grate indicated that the fireplace actually worked. Slinging my backpack onto her chair, I surveyed the top of her desk. Here were the personal mementos that I'd been expecting to find at her apartment: a coffee mug from *Politically Incorrect*, a large button reading DOLE/KEMP, her press pass from the last Republican convention, and a framed copy of an article on her from *The New Yorker*. So why didn't she keep this stuff at home with Gary?

I made a cursory sweep of her bookcase: mostly law texts and history books, with a few random biographies. She was partial to Paul Johnson and William F. Buckley, not a huge surprise given her propensity for conservatism. The collected works of Gary Fox were clustered in a prominent place at the end of one of the rows.

Next to the bookcase was a low file cabinet, and to my relief, it was unlocked. I riffled quickly through the top drawer, which held files on the various courses that she'd taught. I assumed that Heaney had already done a thorough check of who had been given bad grades, and what had become of them, so I spent almost no time on them. The second drawer began with the background material for her recent law review articles: "Twenty-Five Years Beyond Roe v. Wade: The New Case Against Abortion." "The Death of Lesbian Chic: Why Custody Should Be Denied to Parents in Same-Sex Relationships." "Proposition 209: Why Affirmative Action Is Reverse Discrimination." These were followed by pieces she'd written for the *National Review* and *Commentary* that were even more conservative than the scholarly articles, if that was possible. It still amazed me that a thirty-year-old woman had held the political views of a sixty-year-old man, right down to ceding control of her own body to the same government that she distrusted to spend her tax dollars. *Whatever.*

As I stood up, I brushed against the wall, and a small grate, which looked like the cover to the heating vent, tumbled to the floor. As I stooped to replace it, I realized that it covered a small cubbyhole in the wall. Wedged into the space was a thick manila file. "Fisch or Foul?" read the white tab at the top of the folder.

Inside were clippings on the Fisch family. Some were recent articles, others were old photographs. A couple had handwritten notations on them. Several had come from the *Savannah Morning News*, and almost all focused on Max and Jared's "daddy," Maxwell Senior. Quickly scanning the file, I found a photocopy of the *Who's Who* entry on Maxwell and more than a few business stories, Yale press releases, and articles on contributions to the university made by the Fisch father. I sat on the floor and skimmed the longest of the articles. It was from an obscure Georgian business weekly, and it detailed Max the First's rise from a dirt farm in Due West, South Carolina, to prominence in the business world via the timely establishment of a paper mill in Savannah at age nineteen. He had been an average student, enjoyed occasional visits to the racetrack and had at one point trained as an amateur boxer. I wondered if the editors of *Town & Country* were aware of the truly plebeian roots of one of their favorite dynasties. The more recent facts mentioned in the article were more in keeping with the Fisch reputation: "Maxwell Fisch, Sr., became a senior fellow at the Hoover Institute after serving as the ambassador to Barbados under the Reagan Administration. . . ."

Amanda had some indecipherable handwritten notes in the margin of the article. One appeared to read "Start something?" and referred to a passage about Max Sr.'s business ventures in his mid-thirties.

Another read "boxing, average student to ambassador, college philanthropist." A particularly cryptic scrawl seemed to say "check with J."

Leaning against the file cabinet, I pondered what she had been up to. Why had she hidden this folder? "Fisch or Foul?" indeed.

I glanced at my watch. Seven o'clock. I was meeting Jared Fisch in an hour. Perfect opportunity to try to find out what Amanda had been up to. In the meantime, I had to get through the rest of her office. Her desk, oversized and wooden, beckoned. The shallow top drawer held the expected collection of pens and pencils, which were uniformly scarred with teeth marks. The bottom drawer was a jumble of takeout menus, paper napkins, plastic utensils, and a small bundle of neatly stacked letters. Fan mail? Hate mail? Whatever it was, it looked personal. I plucked the first one off of the pile and carefully slid the missive out of its envelope.

I prefer to know a woman by the taste of her, and so I will lead with my tongue, read the first line. I closed my eyes and looked again. Yes, that was really what it said.

I begin with your breasts, milky white, and redden them with my desire.

I've never been one for peeping through bedroom keyholes, but in the name of my investigative duties, I felt honor-bound to read on. Suffice it to say, the author was both imaginative and inexhaustible, and I was ready for a good smoke by the time I was finished.

Laying the letter aside, I reached for the next one in the stack. As it turned out, there were fifteen of these soft-porn epistles, all clearly written by the same person. I reclined in Amanda's chair and studied them again. The pages were creased, as if the notes had been re-read several times. One had a small stain, as if water had splashed against it.

I knew Gary Fox pretty well, and I couldn't see him as an author of purple prose. Besides, it wasn't his handwriting.

Amanda Fox had a lover. Or maybe a stalker. The question was who.

"Professor Chase?" I glanced up to find Reid Talbot standing in the door of Amanda's office, regarding me with a quizzical expression.

"Professor Talbot!" I smiled cheerfully as I slipped the letter I'd been holding back into its envelope. "How are you? Gary asked me to come by and start cleaning out Amanda's office. We agreed it would be too painful for him. Besides, the media's all over him today. I guess you heard about the suicide of his friend."

I was talking so fast and saying so much that I was sure he'd suspect something, but nothing registered on Talbot's face. He just nodded soberly. "The press can't seem to focus on the real tragedy here. A wonderful woman has died, and instead of focusing on her legacy, they're trying to titillate their readers with sex tales."

I glanced at the open drawer that contained the cache of letters. There *was* a sex tale here—it just hadn't been told. "How very true," I responded.

"I mean, no one has even reported on the clinic."

"What clinic?" I asked idly, my mind already running through the list of names of the men who could have written those letters. *Jared Fisch? Or maybe Max?* Jared seemed more the type to dash off a billet-doux. But he also seemed more subtle than this.

"She thought of the whole idea and approached them herself," Talbot was saying. "She didn't speak about it much, but she was passionate about giving young children a chance to succeed. She just didn't think that the government should get so involved. It's terribly ironic that of all places, *that* was where she was killed."

His last words snapped me back to attention. "What did you say?"

The professor looked at me in gentle reproof. "I was saying that it's a terrible irony that she was killed right where she had been working so hard to establish some sense of hope."

"What are you talking about?"

"The clinic that Amanda had just established, where she had arranged for her students to tutor the children after school and encourage them to think about pursuing careers in law."

"Where was this?"

"I'm surprised that she didn't tell you about it. I guess she wanted to keep it under wraps until it was more established. I really hope that they'll continue the program, now that she's gone."

"Where was it?" I repeated, forcibly resisting the urge to scream the words.

"Didn't I say?" the professor asked rhetorically. "At the Resurrection Church. The church where her body was found."

CHAPTER NINETEEN

Dressed to Shill

When I need to deceive someone, I always wear pastels.

A black woman in dark colors immediately puts people on guard, but the sight of one in lighter tones conjures up images of Sunday school and iced tea on the porch and housekeepers dressed in crisp white linens.

When I arrived at Toad's Place on Thursday night to meet Jared Fisch, I was wearing pale pink.

Not from head to toe, of course. That would have been too obvious. I figured a curvy pink sweater and a beige mini-skirt would be the perfect combination of innocence and sin to loosen his tongue. And I'd brought Lily along with me, just in case.

"Tell me again, what do you want me to do?" she asked, as we slipped through the narrow entrance of Toad's Place, a club across the street from Sterling Library.

"Distract him," I murmured as we fell in at the end of the ticket line. "Talk to him, flatter him, hang on his every word, the basic treatment. I know you know how to do that."

"Right. I've seen *How to Marry a Millionaire* at least twice," she cracked. Lil was wearing a sweater and slacks in one of those gray-green-brown shades that can only be found off-the-rack at Armani, and she looked perfectly capable of bringing a mogul to heel.

"Just get him talking, okay? I'll do the rest."

"Professor!" a voice drawled. "Don't insult me by standing in line."

I turned to find Jared Fisch grinning at me. "I've got your comp right here," he said, waving a ticket.

"I hope you don't mind. I brought my friend Lily." I steered her out of line as Jared smiled appreciatively.

"Not at all," he said, extending an arm to each of us. "I shall be a thorn between two roses. This way, ladies."

We walked abreast through a pair of double doors into an immense room with exposed brick walls and a hardwood floor. I breathed in the odor of stale beer and cigarette smoke as Jared steered us toward a large, darkened stage, where a trio of men with various types of facial hair were warming up their instruments.

"Two women already, and the night ain't even started good yet," called out the one with the goatee. The one with the mustache just shook his head.

"Ignore these heathens," Jared said grandly. "Front-row seats. Enjoy the show."

An hour later, he was looking at me accusingly. "You were *sleeping!* Right through the last set. I saw it with my own two eyes!" He turned to Lily. "Back me up here."

"I told you, I was up all night working on a paper," I pleaded.

"What is she, like a sophomore in college or something?" Jared asked Lily. "Is there a final tomorrow?"

"Come on, cut her some slack. She lives in Cambridge, for God's sake. You know there's no night life up there," Lily teased. "Maybe a cigarette will revive her."

Jared obligingly proffered a pack of Dunhill's and a silver lighter, and in minutes the three of us were sprawled across the deserted stage, smoking reflectively.

"So how long have you been at this? Your music, I mean," I asked, forcing myself to stop yawning.

"Since I was fifteen. I used to hang out at this blues club on River Street in Savannah until all hours, waiting to get a chance to play. Got my hide tanned more than once for staying out all night."

"So when are you cutting an album?" Lily asked, sitting up. She leaned against a giant gray speaker. "You were really good."

Jared snorted derisively. "That'll be the day. My daddy would pitch a major fit. A son of his, playing 'nigger music' in public? I don't think so." He shot me an apologetic grin.

"That sounds like something your *grandfather* might have said," I retorted. "You Fisch are incredibly retro."

"Yeah, well, Daddy is strictly old school. And Max is just as bad. Neither one of them wants a musician in the family. Too distracting. Got to stay focused."

"On what?"

"On making money, darlin'. And making the world safe for all the good girls and boys."

"Is that why you're trying to force us all to go to church?" Lily said dryly.

"That was Max's idea. 'We have to have a legacy,' he says. 'The Annenbergs have their media foundation. The Whitneys have their museums. This is what we'll be known for.'"

My bleary brain was spinning through the file in Amanda's office. The one on the Fisch family. Why was she keeping clippings on them, anyway?

"Wake up over there, Professor," Jared teased. "Have some more nicotine."

He fumbled in his pocket, and as he extracted a pack of cigarettes, the contents of his pocket flew into the air. Loose coins, crumpled sales receipts, and the silver lighter cascaded across his lap. A small object rolled across the floor and came to rest a few feet away from me.

I stared at it, then blinked. Suddenly, I wasn't the least bit sleepy.

A small silver football was shining up at me. It looked like a charm for a bracelet. A charm for Amanda Fox's bracelet, to be exact.

Marcellus Tyler had told me that he'd tried to give Amanda a small gift on the night she was killed. A charm shaped like a football, he'd said. So what the hell was it doing in Jared Fisch's pocket?

He retrieved it casually as I pried my eyes from the floor.

"That's a beautiful piece," I said breezily. "I used to wear a charm bracelet in college. They're kind of sweet."

Jared smiled sleepily at me. "I bought this for my mother yesterday. She's coming up for the game this weekend, and it's her kind of thing. She loves baubles." The charm disappeared into his pocket.

"So where was I?" he said, turning to Lily.

That was what I wanted to know.

Fleurs-de-lis on the ceiling, gargoyles protruding from the walls, and a faux Madonna beaming down over the circulation desk. Sterling Library was a paean to the gods of knowledge, and Lily had dragged me there to pay homage on our way home from Toad's Place. She was working on a paper herself, and needed to retrieve several books from the stacks as a prelude to her own all-nighter.

Severe lack of sleep was beginning to make me faint, so she pointed me toward a small reading room adjacent to the library's main entrance, which turned out to be the perfect place for me to catch a nap. Lined with golden maple bookshelves and carpeted in forest green, the Linoma & Brothers Room's most inviting feature by far was the twenty oversized emerald leather-upholstered chairs that lined its perimeter. They faced away from the center, toward the bookshelves, and each was deep enough to constitute both chair and ottoman. When I arrived, they were all occupied by studying undergraduates, but thankfully, one was packing up to leave. Within two minutes, I had claimed his chair and was out cold.

When I opened my eyes, at first I thought I was dreaming.

Dante Rosario was sitting on the floor at my feet, his back resting against the bookcase. He was wearing a navy blue sweater and reading a large, tan, leather-bound book, and he looked perfectly delicious.

"What are you doing here?" I whispered groggily.

"Finally!" he said, grinning at me. "Despite the presence of all these impressionable young minds, I was about to resort to desperate measures to wake you up."

The student in the adjacent chair shot us an annoyed look, and Dante's smile broadened. "I'm sorry. We're disturbing you," he said to the young man. "May I have a word in private with you, Professor Chase?" He took my hand and drew me into a deserted alcove just beyond the reading room.

Ten minutes later we emerged in disheveled, breathless companionship. More than one student shot us a knowing glance as I gathered up my abandoned backpack.

"You're going to get me kicked off of this campus," I murmured.

"Are you kidding? These kids should be happy to know that you're never too old to participate in the time-honored tradition of making out in the library. Besides, it's not like it's finals or anything."

"What's in the bags?" I asked as we walked toward the main entrance. He was carrying a small black duffel and a brown paper lunch bag.

"I figured you could use a few more clothes. Knowing you, you're getting tired of wearing the same outfits, and you probably didn't pack for this long a stay. Plus, I brought you a piece of Maggie's apple pie; I figured you must be homesick for it by now."

"Oh my God," I said slowly. "You're—you're acting like a—a *boyfriend*."

"I know. Scary, isn't it?"

In a big way.

"Nikki?" Lily had emerged from the entrance to

the stacks with three books in her arms; she was regarding us with a shrewd grin that jolted me back to reality. Falling into Rosario's arms was foolish on so many levels that it didn't even bear discussing. And I had work to do.

"So, I'll catch up with you . . . later," Lily said after my hasty introduction, and promptly disappeared.

"You shouldn't have come," I said sharply as we descended the library's stone staircase.

"Are you kidding? After the reception you just gave me?"

"That was an impulse."

"Which you should keep following."

"Not a chance." I stumbled slightly as my foot overshot the last of the stairs. God, I *had* to get some sleep. Dante's arm shot out to steady me, and lingered around my waist.

"Sure about that, Juliet?"

"Positive." I detached his arm firmly and looked up at him. "But now that you're here, you can tell me everything you know about Amanda Fox. Since the two of you were such good pals." He'd said he talked to her a week before she died. Maybe he *did* know something.

His hand brushed my cheek as he straightened the collar of my jacket. "We could talk about that. Among other things. But first, let's get you home."

We started across Cross-Campus Plaza for Calhoun. "So where are you staying tonight?" I asked pointedly.

"A little bed and breakfast a couple of blocks from here. The Three Chimneys Inn. It's your kind of place—chintz as far as the eye can see, a four-poster bed, and a fireplace."

"Sounds delightful." Actually, it *did* sound delightful, especially after a couple of nights on Lily's sofa.

"I'd be happy to give you the grand tour," he said, grinning.

"I think not." We'd reached the Calhoun gate, and I was fumbling for the key Lily had given me when I felt his lips brush my cheek.

"Sleep well, Juliet."

"*What?*" I pulled away from him.

"You're dead on your feet, Nik. Get some sleep, and we'll talk tomorrow morning."

"Stop treating me like a two-year-old!" I said impatiently. "I know when I need rest. And if you do know something, I need to know it *now.*"

He was already walking away from me. "I'll call you tomorrow."

"You don't have my number!" I shouted, exasperated.

The trouble was, we both knew that he did.

CHAPTER TWENTY

Forty Days and Forty Nights

"Rain, drizzle, and fog, forty degrees. That's right. Rain, drizzle, and fog, forty degrees."

The radio weatherman sounded morbidly pleased with the utter lack of appeal in his forecast. It was Day 5 of nearly continuous rain, and Noah sightings had been reported.

"I swear, it really doesn't rain here every day," Lily called out unconvincingly as she emerged from her bedroom Friday morning. "Hey, that looks great on you."

I was sporting black leggings and a cropped red shirt that Lily had loaned me for a trip to the gym. I was brimming with energy after finally getting some sleep, and she'd agreed to get me in for a workout to burn off the innumerable slices of pizza I'd consumed during the week.

"Here's the jacket that goes with it," she said, tossing me a red windbreaker from the hall closet. "And here's my ID. Flash it fast, and you may actually pass for Korean."

"Tell me again—where am I meeting you afterward?" I asked.

"In the lobby of HGS—the Hall of Graduate Studies. We'll grab lunch at Commons."

Eight minutes later, I crossed Tower Parkway and paused on the threshold of the Payne Whitney Gymnasium, a structure literally designed to be a temple to athleticism. The building's exterior was like a Gothic cathedral, and its eight-story entry foyer felt like the narthex at Notre Dame. I crossed the slate floor, my eyes gradually adjusting to the dim lighting, and surveyed the bulletin board next to the reception desk. I'd just missed a step class, and was in no mood for a session on the weight-lifting machines. I brightened as I scanned the building directory and saw that there was a boxing studio. *Perfect*. I'd taken the sport up earlier that fall after a close encounter with a thug, and I was really loving it. And after my encounter with Rosario the night before, I had a lot of nervous energy to work off.

A dangerously creaky elevator took me to the ninth floor of the gym, and I followed my nose to a sweat-soaked room at the end of the hall. A smile spread across my face as I scanned the space: a jumble of jump ropes, well-worn boxing gloves, and rolls of gauze. And in the midst of it all, pummeling a shabby brown leather punching bag, was Marcellus Tyler.

I watched him in silence for a moment as he executed a perfect series of hook-hook-jab combinations with a strength and grace that was mesmerizing. If this building was about body worship, here was an appropriate shrine.

"You must be seeing the D.A.'s face in that bag," I said casually, beginning to wind a gauze strip around my knuckles.

Marcellus looked up, startled, and then smiled shyly.

"So have they dropped the charges?" I smiled in return.

"No. But I'm out on bail. One million dollars."

"That's *insanely* steep. But at least you're out. What's the problem?" I asked, as his expression darkened.

"Nothing. I just wish I had been able to pay it myself. I ended up letting Reverend Leroy and his people take care of it. They've given me a lawyer and everything."

"Why do you dislike them so much?" I asked, genuinely curious.

He shook his head. "I don't believe in taking charity. Even from other black folks. But there was nothing else I could do. I can't take my grandmother's last

dime. Like that would have been enough, anyway."
He grabbed a towel from the floor and mopped his
brow. "So you're still in town?"

"There's a memorial service for Amanda on Sunday. I'll be here at least until then." I selected a battered red glove from the pile in the corner and
pulled it onto my left hand. "I still can't believe she's
really gone."

"I know. I wish I could do something. Her husband isn't going to want me around at that service,
but I sure wish I could do something."

"You really liked her, didn't you?"

"She was the best professor I ever had!" he
answered animatedly. "She was like—I'll never forget
the time she made me stay after class for a forty-five-
minute lecture on—what did she call it? *Reticence.* I
thought she was going to flunk me out or something,
and she turns to me and says, 'You're really pissing me
off.'" He laughed at the memory. "So I'm thinking,
'*What* did this lady say?' And she says, 'I read your first
paper, and you're busted. You have all these great
ideas, and you're sitting on your butt in class not saying anything. You'll never get anywhere in this world
if you don't speak up and prove that you're smart.
Even if you offend people, say something—*anything.*
Just let them know you were *here.*' She made me swear
I would talk at least once every session. And I could
tell that was when people really started to respect me.
I'll never forget that. *Just let them know you were here.*"

"Amanda did that?" *For a black student?*

He must have read my expression. "I know everybody thought she was a racist because of what she said on TV. But she did a hell of a lot more for me than all those 'liberal' professors I had, who just assumed I was some C-minus student here to win football games. She treated me like a person, not some big black kid from the ghetto."

"Was that why you tried to give her that charm? The little football?"

"Yeah," he said sheepishly. "But like I said, she wouldn't take it."

So how the hell had it ended up in Jared Fisch's pocket? And who had written those mash notes to Amanda?

"Do you have a girlfriend?" I hadn't intended to voice the thought, and I backpedaled as he stared at me. "Don't take that the wrong way," I said hastily. "I'm not making a pass at you. I was just curious."

He looked down and smiled. "No. I don't. Between hitting the books and practice, I've got no time."

"Heartbreaker," I teased. I didn't care what Gary and Heaney said. I'd never believe that this kid was a murderer. "Speaking of having no time, you'd better get back to your workout. The Game's tomorrow, isn't it?"

I was hard at work on my right uppercut, Marcellus having departed a half hour before, when a familiar voice interrupted my strokes.

"In this corner, wearing an incredibly becoming red-and-black ensemble, the reigning champ, Nikki "That's Not Sweat, It's Perspiration" Chase!"

"If I were you, I'd retreat to my corner, Rosario," I growled. "I'm no Mike Tyson, but I do bite."

His eyes glittered at me. "Yes, I seem to remember that."

"So are you ready to talk, or am I going to have to beat the truth out of you?" I asked, only half joking.

"I wouldn't mind going a couple of rounds with you," he said, grinning. "But I won't press for it now, since you've clearly regained your strength. So let's talk."

"Not here," I said, nodding toward two boys coming through the narrow doorway. "But I've got the perfect place."

The Grove Street Cemetery is a stone's throw from the gym, smack in the middle of Yale's campus. That morning the misty graveyard was strangely peaceful, its crumbled head- and footstones and gravel pathways covered in damp brown leaves. The turrets and chimneys of the surrounding buildings were visible among the bare tree limbs, and the hallowed silence was broken only by birdsongs and the soft hiss of an occasional car passing on the adjacent street.

"What I want to know is how you keep finding me," I said as we walked along the main pathway. "Do you have a tracking device stuck to my bag or something?"

"Nope." Dante laughed. "I just close my eyes and think like Nikki."

"You are *completely* full of it. Why are you here, anyway?"

"Because you need a sidekick. A Watson. A Robin."

"A Butt-Head?" I arched my brow.

"Seriously, Nik. Tell me where you are on this. Maybe I can help."

I considered it for a moment, then shrugged resignedly. I *did* need someone to talk to, and for the moment, he actually seemed sincere. "All right. Let's sit." We settled onto a low stone bench alongside the footpath. "This is a little complicated. But the way I see it, there are three categories of suspects here. First are the people who may have killed Amanda because they had a crush on Gary and wanted him for themselves."

"There's more than one person with a crush on *Gary?*"

I laughed at his expression. "I know you find this impossible to believe, but some people actually find him attractive."

"I assume you're talking about the gay guy they found dead a couple of days ago. And who confessed to the crime, from what I read."

"Right. Lance O'Brien."

"So why don't you believe his confession, Nik?"

"Because it was typed, for one thing. Also, Heaney

told me this morning that Lance had an airtight alibi for Sunday night. He was down in New York looking for costumes for *Macbeth*, and at the time of the murder, he was in a bar in the West Village. Plenty of witnesses."

Dante sat forward. "So your killer is pretty sloppy. Planting a confession that flimsy was worse than just leaving the body there."

I nodded. "Whoever it is, they're in a panic."

"What I'd like to know is why someone offed Lance O'Brien. Figure that out, and you've got your murderer."

"Well, I can think of one person who definitely wanted him out of the way: Giselle Storrs. She's obviously infatuated with Gary, and she couldn't stand Lance. She was in Amanda's class the night she was killed. *And* she fingered Marcellus Tyler with her black-man-in-the-bushes story, which I still think is pure fiction. Motive and opportunity—and anyone has the means to come up with a knife."

"The only way she would perceive Lance as a rival is if Gary were actually interested in him," Dante said pointedly.

"Come on, Gary's not gay."

"Sure about that?"

I paused to consider the thought. "Yes," I said decisively. "But that doesn't mean that Giselle isn't nutty enough to have done it anyway."

"So why aren't the cops on her?"

"Because she's cute, blond, and fourth-generation Yale, that's why."

Dante snorted. "I'm sure that's not the only reason. Maybe she has an alibi, Nik."

"Doubtful."

"So what's your second group?"

"People in love with *Amanda*."

"Now *that* should be a long list."

I glared at him, but refused to be baited. "Actually, it's not. I'm coming up with two names: Max and Jared Fisch."

"Are they a part of—"

"Yes. *The* Fisch family. Savannah, big money, big mouths. The brothers are real rivals."

"I remember Amanda telling me about them."

"What did she say?" I demanded. "Did she talk about being involved with one of them?"

He shook his head. "She talked about doing research on them."

"Research?" My mind went back to the file in her office. "Did she say what for?"

"She was writing an article. For *Vanity Fair*, I think."

"Probably a puff piece. Max was a big supporter of hers."

Dante shook his head again. "I don't think so. I got the impression that they weren't going to be happy with the outcome."

My radar pricked up. "Really? Exactly what did she say?"

"She said she'd heard some things about the father that she was checking out."

"Like what?"

"Sorry, Nik. I don't know. I just remember her saying that he wasn't what people thought he was, and that the family wasn't going to like it."

"So maybe they're category three, then," I muttered.

"Which is?"

"Which is people who wanted her dead for some reason other than unrequited love. Like maybe this article she was writing."

"You really think someone would kill her over a magazine article?"

"Sure, if it had information in it that would cause embarrassment. Or make someone lose money. Why not?"

Dante looked skeptical. "Who else is in category three?"

"The Reverend Leroy. He's suppressing evidence in this case, and I overheard him talking about needing to keep the media and the cops focused on Marcellus Tyler. *And* I just found out that Amanda was starting some legal clinic at his church. Maybe she uncovered something that he wanted kept secret."

"So he stabbed her outside his own church? Unlikely."

I leaned against the bench and nodded appreciatively. "Excellent point."

"I think it's more likely that someone wanted to make it *look* like he was involved," Dante continued. "Think about it. All this racial unrest is a great red herring. It keeps the media attention focused and distracts the cops, so no one has time to explore other avenues."

"So what do you think, Rosario?"

"I think you're missing a suspect."

"Who?"

"You know who, Nik." Our eyes met squarely.

"Not possible," I shook my head adamantly. "Gary loved her. He's absolutely devastated." Of course I had my doubts about Gary. But I was keeping them to myself.

"Just listen to me for a minute," Dante insisted. "Has he ever spoken to you about their marriage?"

"Sure. And don't tell me that they argued sometimes. I know all about that. But who doesn't? They sounded basically happy to me."

"Then he didn't tell you about the divorce."

I stared at him, speechless.

"The last time I spoke to Amanda, she said they were seriously considering it."

I thought about the letters in Amanda's drawer. Was she leaving him for their author?

"But, then, what was Gary's motive?" I asked, playing for time while I considered this new information. "If they were discussing separating, and they both agreed on it, why would he bother to hurt her?"

"You don't need me to answer that question, Nik."

Jealousy. Revenge. Spite. The motives flitted through my head as I rejected them one by one and shook my head again. "You're wrong. He would never do that. You know him, for God's sake. You know he's not capable of murder."

Dante shrugged casually. "Maybe. So then, who-dunit, Agatha?"

"I'm thinking Giselle," I replied pensively. "But I don't know how to prove it. And I'm running out of time." I glanced at my watch. "I better get going. I have a conference call with Professor Irvin in half an hour."

"I still can't get over how you jump through hoops for that man," Dante commented as we started back along the footpath.

"Look—he's gunning for me, and I can't hand him any more ammunition."

"You're worrying too much, Nik. Just because he's the acting chairman doesn't mean he controls your destiny."

"That's easy for you to say. Your department chairman thinks you walk on water."

"You want me to rough him up a bit?"

"You are *such* an alpha male, Rosario," I responded distractedly. *Did Giselle have an alibi?* I needed to talk to Heaney. I'd asked him that question earlier and he hadn't responded. And I had to figure out who had written those letters to Amanda. I was deep in brooding when I suddenly felt myself falling. Seconds later, Dante and I were entangled in a pile of sodden leaves beside the pathway.

It took me a moment to figure out how we got there. "You tripped me!" I breathed incredulously.

"I had to get your attention *somehow*, Juliet."

His lips were inches away from mine, and I swallowed hard. "You've got it, you Republican brute. Now what are you going to do with it?"

"I thought you'd never ask."

CHAPTER TWENTY-ONE

Friend or Faux?

The eve of The Game is always a carnival in Cambridge, and despite the previous night's riot, the atmosphere in New Haven proved to be no different: the campus and its surrounding streets were gradually filling up with boisterous visiting Harvard undergrads and returning Yale alums, all of whom were oblivious to the undercurrent of tension that lingered among their hosts. Against all odds, it had actually stopped raining, and by that evening a full moon bathed the campus in an ethereal glow. It was turning into a great night for a party.

"I told you it was a mistake," Gary Fox hissed.

"And I told you we had no other choice," Giselle Storrs snapped back.

At Gary's request, I'd agreed to start off the evening at an open house in the Master's Residence at Branford College. But I hadn't been able to get a word in edgewise since the topic of yesterday's press conference had arisen.

"Did you see the headline in the *Daily News* today?" Gary continued, waving away a waiter bearing the obligatory glass of sherry. "*Friend or Faux? Dean Fox 'Outs' His Deceased Best Buddy.*"

"Come on, Gary. Lance O'Brien was hardly in the closet. The word 'flaming' comes to mind," Giselle replied calmly. "And just imagine what it might have said if you *hadn't* talked to them." Taking a sip from a crystal champagne flute, she coolly surveyed the crowd. "This story is going to be dead in another twenty-four hours. Trust me. What you need to be thinking about is how to quickly get your name in the paper on a topic wholly unrelated to this murder. Do you have any great research findings you're sitting on?"

What a little Amanda she was, I thought idly. Twenty-something years old and a stone-cold—

"You agree with me, right, Nikki?" Giselle interrupted my train of thought. "It's time for people to be reminded that Gary is a brilliant scholar and a prominent Dean, not a pawn in some *Melrose Place* fantasy of Lance O'Brien's."

I bit my tongue and smiled brightly at her. If I wanted to know about her alibi for Sunday night, I was going to have to play nice. "She has a point, Gary." I turned to Giselle. "But I've been wondering how all of this has affected *you*, Giselle. With all the police questioning, it must be really difficult keeping up with your coursework."

"It hasn't been that bad." She shrugged.

"Really?" I said casually. "I would have thought the cops would be all over you, since you were with Amanda right before she died."

"Sure, I was in her class. So were twenty other people," she said, a shade too quickly.

"Right, but *you* were the only one who saw someone hiding in the bushes afterward." *Take it slow*, I cautioned myself.

"I guess I'm just more observant than most people."

"I'm just surprised that you didn't call the police right that minute. I mean, right after you saw the guy. If he was *hiding*, didn't it seem like something that they should know about?"

There it was again. The little glance that Giselle exchanged with Gary every time the topic of Sunday evening came up.

"I—I did think about it. But then I thought, maybe I imagined it. It happened really quickly, you know."

"You must have nerves of steel," I pressed. "If I saw someone hiding in the bushes that late at night, I would have needed to talk to somebody, even if I didn't call the cops. Weren't you scared?"

The question hung in the air between us, and she involuntarily glanced at Gary again. I followed her gaze and looked at him quizzically, waiting.

"Sure, I was nervous—" she began.

"Don't," Gary said quietly.

"Gary!" Giselle's tone was full of warning.

"It's all right," he said firmly. Then he turned to me. "We need to talk." Leaving Giselle in the Master's library, we ducked into a small anteroom off the foyer.

"Giselle didn't see a man in the bushes Sunday night," Gary said without preamble. "The only man she saw that night was me."

Of course I had seen it coming. But his words still hit me like a blow to the face. "I assume she 'saw' you in the biblical sense," I said angrily. No wonder he'd been acting so guilty. He'd been with another woman the very night Amanda was killed.

Gary nodded slowly. "Yes. I didn't want to tell you, for obvious reasons."

"So why are you telling me now?" I demanded.

The sadness was becoming a permanent fixture on his face. "Because it struck me when Lance died. Life is too short to keep lying," he said simply.

"So what time did Giselle show up at your place that night?"

He shook his head. "We couldn't meet at Branford. Amanda might have turned up. So I went to her room. Around eleven."

"It wasn't the first time, was it?" I felt obligated to ask the question, although I already knew what his answer would be.

"No. We'd been—together—several times before."

"You're crazy, Gary. You know your career will be over if this comes out," I said quietly.

He shrugged resignedly. "That's what Lance kept saying. He kept pushing me to end it. If it makes any difference, I'm planning to."

It didn't.

"Is this why you and Amanda were going to divorce?"

He stared at me. "How did you know about that?"

"A friend told me." But he hadn't mentioned that a twenty-year old student was the other woman.

Gary shook his head. "Giselle's not the reason we were separating. Babies were the reason we were separating." He actually rolled his eyes. "Amanda was desperate for one. I was very happy being child-less, but it meant everything to her, so I agreed to try. And then it turned out that I—I'm unable to—" he faltered.

"You're infertile," I said flatly.

"Yes. And I guess that was illustrative of a larger problem between us. I couldn't give her what she wanted. So we were in the process of separating."

I wanted to say I was sorry, that I felt badly for him. But at that moment, I really didn't. He'd clearly made a habit of sleeping with undergraduates—starting with Amanda. And he'd been lying to me all week about his marriage. "You're sure it was around eleven o'clock Sunday night when you saw Giselle?" I pressed on, refusing to surrender to my disillusionment. There'd be time for that later.

"I'm pretty sure it was eleven. Why?" He read my expression. "Oh, come on, Nikki. Giselle had nothing to do with Amanda's death."

"How do you know? You just provided her with an alibi for Sunday night, but Amanda would have been dead already by the time you met up with Giselle. So who's to say she wasn't involved?"

"Please don't, Nikki. Don't go after her because you're disappointed with me. She would never do something like that. Lance confessed to killing Amanda, and now it's over. Let it go."

Our eyes met and he was the first to look away. "Do you hate me now?" he asked.

I exhaled slowly. "I don't know what I think right now, Gary."

He smiled at me with a forced jocularity that pained me more than his previous air of resignation. "You want to grab a coffee?"

I shook my head. "I've got to go. I'm meeting someone at Xando's in five minutes."

I watched Gary reenter the party and launch into a desultory conversation with a silver-haired man in a suit. He had no idea what he was dealing with. To me, Giselle seemed perfectly capable of murder. She could have easily decided to get rid of Lance because he'd been pushing Gary to end their affair.

Still, there was something bothering me even more.

If Gary Fox would lie about being with Giselle, what else would he lie about?

The corner of Park and Elm Streets was fragrant with the scent of roasting java beans. The aroma sped my pace toward Xando's, the coffee house where I'd agreed to meet Dante at nine that evening. But ten steps away from the front door I was stopped dead in my tracks.

Reverend Leroy was on the march.

Coming down Broadway, flanked on all sides by police vehicles, was a large group of black people carrying hand-lettered signs and chanting. The blaring horns of impatient motorists punctuated their refrain: "Ain't gonna stop till the charges are dropped!" Reverend Leroy was at the front of the crowd, his arms linked with two older ladies.

"What the hell is this?" scoffed a young white man next to me on the sidewalk. I shot him a look and realized that he was wearing a crimson T-shirt proclaiming "YUCK FALE."

"It's some black thing," his companion replied. "Let's hit The Doodle for a burger." The two of them turned and disappeared into the crowd.

I watched as Reverend Leroy brought the crowd

to a halt at a traffic island just in front of a large Gothic structure that actually appeared to be a church. The piercing white light of television cameras immediately illuminated the darkness.

"We are here tonight for *just*-ice," Reverend Leroy intoned. "And justice shall be done!"

Eyeing the crowd, I could see that the marchers weren't just people from the Resurrection Church. Several of them were wearing clothing with Yale insignia, and one banner read HARVARD BLACK STUDENTS' ALLIANCE IN SUPPORT OF JUSTICE. I moved closer.

"Despite the fact that a white man has *confessed* to this crime, the New Haven police refuse to drop the charges against an innocent boy, Marcellus Tyler. Instead, they put a million-dollar bail on his head," the reverend began.

"Tell it!" a voice came from the crowd.

"Tonight I'm announcing a boycott of all the white establishments in New Haven until these charges are *dropped!* Until our concerns are taken seriously, our dollars will not be available!"

The crowd roared its approval.

"Thanks for coming by yesterday," a voice echoed behind me. I turned to find Russell Jackson smiling down on me.

"No problem. It was fun." I gestured toward the assembly. "You got a good turnout."

"It wasn't hard."

"So why didn't you tell me that Amanda Fox had a program at your church?"

He shrugged. "I assumed you knew. She was setting up a mentoring program for kids interested in the law. Yale students would come by after school once a week to talk about different careers and educational requirements."

"I'm amazed that she would do something like that, given how conservative she was."

"I know. When she came by offering to help out the first time, I thought she was joking. Then I thought it was a publicity stunt."

"And now?"

"I think she was sincere. She never told anyone that she was doing it. She put a lot of time into it, and the kids really liked the first couple of sessions."

"Was that why she was over by your church that night? The night she was killed?"

He shook his head. "No. The program was on Tuesday afternoons. I don't know what she was doing over there that night."

Sadness flickered across his face, and I instinctively laid my hand on his arm. "It must have been hard on you to find her there. I mean, it must have been a shock."

His eyes met mine and I could see that despite the street-preacher facade, my words were true. It *had* been a shock. And he hadn't fully recovered.

"Are you going to be all right?" I asked impulsively.

He shook himself slightly. "Sure. But I better get back." He turned toward the street, then paused. "You going to be in town for a while longer, Professor?"

"Yeah. Big game tomorrow, remember?"

He smiled. "Then maybe I'll see you."

"I think that's a safe bet."

I watched him as he walked away. *Really* nice guy.

"Who was *that?*" Dante Rosario had suddenly materialized before me.

"Russell Jackson. He's the minister at the church where Amanda's body was found."

"Is that the way you look at a 'yahoo' whom you also suspect of murder? Your word, not mine."

"What's with you? *He's* not the potentially murderous yahoo. His *boss* is. Russell is a terrific guy. The work he's doing in the community is absolutely incredible."

"Really?" Dante replied flatly.

"He's amazing. The kids adore him, and the parents think he's a saint."

"What do you think?"

"I think you're jealous, Rosario."

Our eyes met, and to my amazement, he wasn't smiling. "Should I be?"

A roar went up from Reverend Leroy's rally, and the column of marchers slowly resumed their procession. Russell was now at its head, one hand on the shoulder of a younger man and the other encircling the waist of a gray-haired lady. "Hey, Nikki!" he called to me over the din. "Why don't you join us?"

I looked not at Russell's face, but at the faces of the marchers. Angry, excited, frustrated, proud. Tired, but moving forward anyway. Demanding justice. How could I not be with them?

I made the choice instinctively, and we both knew that I was talking about more than just the march. I looked at Dante.

"I'm going," I said simply.

He nodded soberly. "I know."

CHAPTER TWENTY-TWO

Blues in the Night

As Friday night wore on and the full moon slid across the sky, I realized that the carnival atmosphere of the Yale campus was gradually becoming more menacing, like a carousel whirling too quickly, threatening to spin out of control. As I walked pensively through the shadows cast by the streetlights on High Street on my way home from the march for Marcellus Tyler, I saw a group of white guys hassling the homeless man who liked to hang out near the gates of Branford College. And despite the presence of New Haven and Yale cops stationed prominently at all of the major street corners, several boys from the march seemed determined to pick a fight with any random white person who happened along.

Everyone seemed to acknowledge that whatever was coming couldn't be contained by a couple of uniformed policemen.

I quickened my pace as I passed the gates of one of the secret societies. The building looked like a tomb: a black wrought-iron gate encircled a stone walkway leading up to a massive sepulcher with six stone pillars and a large black wooden door with a brass knocker, but no knob. I'd been told that this was Skull and Bones, the formerly all-male enclave of the Yale elite. I'd also heard rumors about the building's interior—friends had told tales of a banquet hall lined floor to ceiling with skulls and of a subterranean room holding a coffin. I'd dismissed the whole enterprise as a useless remnant of white male supremacy, but at that moment, the building was a tangible manifestation of my growing dread.

A pale figure appeared from behind the far corner of the building. It took a couple of seconds for my eyes to make out what it was in the dim light, and when I did, I still thought it was an apparition. Dressed almost entirely in black, Jared Fisch was skulking around in the darkness.

I stifled the impulse to call out to him, and instead stood in the shadow of the gate, considering my next move. He couldn't be outdoors this late at night just hanging out.

He must be waiting for someone.

As my eyes adjusted to the gloom, I realized that

he was wearing a tuxedo. He fumbled at his jacket pocket and retrieved his lighter. Seconds later, a soft hiss of flame touched the tip of what I assumed was a Dunhill.

"What the hell do you want?" growled a voice from the shadows behind him.

"Get out here, Max," Jared responded softly. "*Now.*"

Max Jr. appeared beside him, his own tuxedo looking decidedly the worse for wear. "You got five minutes, boy. Daddy wants us both in there."

"Fuck him," Jared hissed. "And I'm sick of you and your 'Bonesmen.' We have to talk about this announcement."

"So Daddy just announced the chair isn't going to be endowed in the honor of Amanda Fox. Why should that surprise you? After what she did?"

"I *never* ask you all for anything. But I need this. She was my friend," Jared pleaded.

"Which is why you're busy tryin' to destroy her husband, right?" Max scoffed.

"That son of a bitch was cheating on her. With some bimbo student. She didn't deserve to be humiliated that way. Especially given her condition."

"Well, she sure as hell planned to humiliate *us*. I told you the questions she was askin'. She was onto us, and she was gonna make big bucks off it."

"So she found out how Daddy made his money. You think anyone really gives a damn?"

"Of course they do! There's nothin' they'd like better than to make a spectacle of us. Can't you see the headlines?"

"Yeah. *Former Whorehouse Owner Endows Ethics Curriculum*. Big deal."

"Maybe not for you. You're goin' nowhere anyway. But Daddy would lose his chances at another ambassadorship."

"And you'd lose your Yale Corporation seat, which means more to you than your own dick," Jared sneered.

"Watch it, boy."

"You're happy she's dead, aren't you?"

"Yeah, I am. That black kid did us a big favor."

I stifled the urge to join in the conversation. This remark from a man trying to force other people to attend religious services.

"Although I figure you might have had something to do with it," Max continued. "Given how you were with her that night."

"How do you know that?" Jared's voice had lost some of its bravado.

"I know a lot of things, boy," Max needled. "I know you were up on Science Hill that night."

"So what. I went up there to walk her home. I did it every Sunday night."

"So how'd she end up dead, then?"

"Because she wouldn't come with me, that's how. She said she had to meet somebody, and she wasn't going straight home. And she wouldn't let me go with her."

"Is that when she gave you that stupid thing you've been carrying around?"

"It's a charm, Max. For a bracelet. She didn't give it to me. She asked me to hold onto it."

"Well, I'd ditch it if I were you. How you gonna explain it to the cops?"

"The cops have nothing to connect me to her, and they never will as long as you keep your mouth shut." Jared's voice regained its strength. "But I'm not kidding, Max. I want her to have that chair. Either she gets it, or I'll publish the article myself."

"Don't threaten me."

"It's no threat. It'd be the simplest thing in the world. I know where all the skeletons are buried. I'll happily dig 'em up."

"You'd turn on your own family just to protect that girl? She must have been one good—"

"For the last time, Max!" Jared interrupted. "I told you we weren't sleeping together. She was my *friend*. Which is a concept you clearly can't understand. So just understand this. You and Daddy give her that chair, or you go up in flames. Your choice."

Max turned on his heel and disappeared behind the building. Jared crushed the butt of his cigarette with his heel and then started toward me. I moved further into the shadows as he turned onto the street and loped off.

Then I headed for the pay phone across the street.

Timothy Heaney wasn't at his desk when I called, so I had to leave a message.

"Heaney, it's Nikki," I said, speaking rapidly. "I need to know something from Amanda's autopsy report, and I'm assuming you have it back by now." I glanced over my shoulder to make sure no random Fisch were in the vicinity. "I need to know if Amanda Fox was pregnant when she died."

When I walked away from Dante Rosario earlier that night, I'd had every intention of making it stick. Events, however, conspired against me. It was well past midnight and I was crossing one of the slate pathways of Cross-Campus Plaza, headed for Calhoun, when I heard it.

"You niggers need to go back to Africa," a voice barked.

"I told you to leave me alone," came the response. "Now get out of here."

In the grassy shadows of the plaza, a solitary figure was swaying unsteadily. It was a white man who looked to be in his mid-twenties—a very drunk white man. And he was shouting at Justine, one of the girls who lived across the hall from Lily. He lurched toward her and then paused, a disgusted expression on his face.

"Nigger," he spat.

"Get lost, asshole," she snapped.

"I don't think so." The man stepped out onto the pathway, blocking it.

"Leave me alone," she repeated. Her voice wavered slightly now.

I started toward them, but someone else got there first.

"What did you say?" Dante Rosario asked calmly.

The man was so drunk that apparently he couldn't figure out that repeating it wasn't the brightest idea. "Nigger," he muttered under his breath.

The blow that Dante delivered to his jaw was so swift and strong that it looked like the man was crumpling from a gust of wind.

"Get the hell out of here," he said coldly. The man rose to his feet, appeared to consider retaliating, and then thought better of it. Dante turned to Justine. "Are you all right?"

She nodded, staring at him. "Yeah. Thanks." She glanced over her shoulder. "What are you, like, Superman or something?"

Dante's laugh echoed across the quad. "No. I'm waiting for someone who's staying at Calhoun to get home. But do you need a walk back to your dorm?"

She shook her head. "I live right here. Thanks."

He was watching her leave when I arrived next to him. He turned, looking startled to see me. Then he frowned. "You'll never learn, will you?" he demanded. "Walking around at this hour, *alone*. Juliet, what are you thinking?"

I couldn't help smiling as I extended my hand. "Can't you tell?"

CHAPTER TWENTY-THREE

Boola Boola

"Now, don't gimme some little spoon shake, darlin'.
Is that how you all treat company down here?"

Maggie Dailey laughed as Lily doubled the helping of potato salad on the paper plate she was holding. It was a brilliant Saturday morning, an hour
before kick-off at the Harvard-Yale Game, and
despite a huge breakfast at the Copper Kitchen, we
were observing the time honored tradition of tailgating in the shadows of the Yale Bowl. The grassy
field sparkled in anticipation in the late-morning
sun, dotted with an assortment of station wagons,
Jeeps, and the occasional Rolls-Royce. Harvard
alumni sporting thick sweaters and crimson scarves,
and carrying bowls of chili—and in many cases their

progeny—wandered freely between the cars. The same scene was being reenacted on the other side of the stadium, except the color of choice there was Bulldog blue. The faint strains of the Yale fight song "Boola Boola" floated across the deserted field, and the air smelled of wood smoke, fallen leaves, and cinnamon.

"Hey, I'm not even supposed to *be* here," Lily laughed. "But I heard the food was better on this side." My housemates had arrived from Cambridge at the crack of dawn that morning, sustenance in tow. Maggie had prepared the pregame feast, and as usual had provided enough victuals to keep a small army on its feet: cold fried chicken, biscuits, potato salad, green salad, chicken gumbo, two cakes, and a pie. Lily was playing hostess by serving up overflowing plates to all of us.

"So where's Dante?" Maggie asked as she settled into a folding chair. "I made this coconut cake just for him."

"He'll be along later," I said quickly. "I think he's catching up on his sleep."

Maggie shot me a look that I resolutely ignored.

"I want to know what's in this thermos," Jess said, sipping from a red plastic cup. "I'm tasting apples and cinnamon, but I'm getting *really* buzzed."

"It's me brother's secret recipe," Rafe called from a folding chair at the foot of Maggie's red Cavalier. "He owns a bar on Tortola, and he calls this Caribbean

Apple Pie. You'd best be careful. It sneaks up on you."

"Drink up, sweetie," Ted said, his hand resting on Jess's shoulder. "It'll save me from actually having to go *shopping* with her after The Game," he whispered *sotto voce*.

"Just save some room, because we have to go to Mory's after the game and do cups," Lily said, laughing. I looked at her quizzically. "You drink out of these big silver trophy cups while the rest of the table sings to you, and the game is to see who finishes the cup," she explained. "It's a Yale tradition."

"I've done that!" Jess said. "Don't the drinks come in different colors, like red and green, or something? And you turn the cup over at the end to see if it's empty?"

"Exactly. You turn the cup out onto a white napkin, and if it leaves a ring, the person who drank last has to buy the next round."

"It takes the best minds in the country to think up these sophisticated Ivy League drinking games. Really impressive," drawled a sarcastic voice.

"Officer Heaney! I didn't figure you for the football type," I said as the policeman sauntered toward us.

"Are you kidding? I never miss The Game." Heaney was wearing a Yale sweatshirt and a Bulldog scarf, but still had his badge at his belt.

"You on duty?" I asked.

"I'm *always* on duty."

"There's someone I want you to meet. Rafe, this is Timothy Heaney, the officer I've been telling you about."

I felt the two of them take each other's measure as introductions were exchanged. Then, to my surprise, Heaney broke into a broad smile. "So *you're* the one I have to blame for getting this lady into the habit of interfering in official police business."

Rafe grinned back. "Guilty. As if I could stop her, mon."

"Okay, okay, that's enough." I lowered my voice. "Did you check out what we discussed last night?"

Heaney nodded and imperceptibly beckoned me to step away from the crowd a bit. "Rafe can hear this, can't he?" I whispered. "I mean, he's a cop." At Heaney's assent, Rafe and I followed him a few feet away.

"Your hunch was right," Heaney said quickly. "She was pregnant."

"Holy shit," I said softly.

"You wanna tell me why it matters so much?" Heaney asked.

"Because her husband was infertile, that's why."

Rafe whistled slowly, while Heaney looked at me with what appeared to be genuine appreciation. "So she was fooling around and it went too far," he concluded. "You think the husband found out and killed her?"

"No!" I said quickly. As disappointed as I was in

Gary, I still wasn't ready to believe he was a murderer. "But the fact that she was pregnant has to have something to do with this. Maybe the father-to-be wanted her to abort, and she refused."

"So he killed her?" Heaney looked thoughtful.

"Who are we lookin' at?" Rafe asked.

I could only think of three candidates for fatherhood. Jared Fisch. Max Fisch. And Marcellus Tyler.

The Yale Bowl is something like the Roman Coliseum: a towering stone edifice with a warren of tunnels underneath. Twenty minutes later, I was wandering through the bowels of the building, intent on finding Marcellus.

I'd read in the paper that morning that he wouldn't be playing in this game. His coach had apparently decided it would be too controversial to have an accused murderer out on the field. But I was willing to bet that he wouldn't be able to stay away from the stadium for the last contest of the season. I figured benched football players would generally be found in the vicinity of the locker room before game time, so that was where I was headed.

I found the locker room and planted myself in front of it. Ten minutes later, Marcellus appeared, looking absolutely despondent.

"Nikki?" he said uncertainly as I approached him.

"We need to talk about Amanda. Now. We can do it in front of your friends or not. You decide."

"But the game's about to start!" he protested.

I leaned toward him and spoke quietly. "We know she was pregnant, Marcellus. Soon we'll know who got her that way. And I'm guessing you'll want to talk before that happens."

He started away from the locker room so quickly that I had to scramble to keep up. He came to rest on a low wooden bench just outside the stadium. I chose to remain standing.

"Was it you?"

"No! I swear to God, it wasn't."

"There's no point in lying, Marcellus. They can test paternity very easily these days. And if she was pregnant by you, you start to look like a damn good murder suspect."

"It wasn't me," he repeated adamantly. "But I know who it was."

"How could you know that?" I demanded. "I thought you said yesterday that all you were was her student."

"Okay. It was more than that." He sighed. "You all just don't get it." He stood and paced uneasily. "She was like—she was like the best friend that I had here." He took a deep breath. "I don't know why, but she really liked me. She thought I could make it here. I grew up in Brooklyn. Not the chi-chi part. In Bed-Stuy. I know they took me in here because of this." He gestured at the stone walls of the stadium. "Because I know how to play ball. But she didn't care about that. She only cared about what I *thought*, not how I played."

"I know, I know," I said impatiently. "You told me that. She took you under her wing. But constitutional law wasn't all you talked about, was it?"

"No." He looked uncomfortable.

"I already know a lot of it, Marcellus. I know she wasn't very happy before she died. I know she had a lover."

"That son of a bitch," he said quietly.

"Who are you talking about? Dammit, Marcellus," I said impatiently, as he hesitated. "Do you *want* to be in jail? I'm trying to help you out here."

"Russell Jackson," he said abruptly.

I recoiled from him as if he'd hit me. *"What?"*

"That's right. Reverend Russell was her lover."

"Not possible."

"I'm positive, Nikki. I heard enough about it. And I think he killed her."

"No." I shook my head adamantly. *This couldn't be happening.*

"That's why I wouldn't take their money at first. I sure as hell didn't want his help defending me in a murder that *he committed*. I mean, I knew right away it was him. They had been fighting a lot, because she couldn't decide if she was going to keep the baby. He wanted her to, but she wasn't sure. He wanted her to leave her husband, and he was mad that it was taking her so long to decide. That's why I went after him."

"What do you mean?"

"I went to see him the morning after they found her body. I told him I thought he had killed her. And things got a little out of hand." I raised my eyebrow. "I hit him," he explained. "That's where this came from." He rubbed the cut on his forefinger.

"So what did he say when you confronted him?" I asked, sitting down heavily beside Marcellus. My head was spinning.

"He said he would never hurt her."

"What do you think?"

Marcellus clenched his fist reflectively. "I think he was lying."

Russell Jackson was standing alone at the lectern in the sanctuary of the Resurrection Church when I found him half an hour later. I walked slowly down the aisle of the church, stopping halfway.

"Nikki!" He looked up from the podium and smiled. "I thought you'd be at the game. You want to hear my sermon for tomorrow?"

I shook my head. "I'd rather hear about you and Amanda Fox."

His hand trembled slightly as he laid down the sheaf of papers he'd been holding. "Amanda Fox? What about her?"

"I'd like to hear about your affair with her. I'd like to hear about your unborn child." I waited until he'd stepped down from the podium before I continued.

"I'd like to hear about how you lured her over here and then stabbed her five times. Can we talk about that?"

"I don't know what you're talking about—" he began.

"I'm sure the cops will, once the DNA test comes back. You wanna wait? Or you wanna talk now?"

"I didn't kill her!" He spoke the words quietly, urgently.

"That's what you told Marcellus. He didn't believe it, either."

"I swear I didn't do it." His eyes were pleading with me.

"Not here, Russell." I looked around the sanctuary. "Don't lie here."

"I'm not lying." He took a deep breath. "Leroy said I'd be putting the noose around my own neck. He put his own reputation at risk to try to distract the media and the cops so that they wouldn't discover my relationship with Amanda. But we were wrong. This has been far worse than anything the cops could do to me."

"You've known Marcellus was innocent all along, haven't you?"

"Nikki, if I had come forward and told the cops about my relationship with her, it would have shamed this church. It would have shamed the community. So instead, we did everything we could to help Marcellus—a lawyer, bail, *everything*."

"Everything except telling the cops that *you* had a hell of a motive for killing her."

"You're wrong, I would never hurt her. I was trying to do right by her." The words echoed in the empty room. "I tried, but she was so—stubborn—" His voice cracked.

"Tell me," I said quietly. "Tell me what happened." *Make me believe you.*

"I met her when she stopped by the church one day," he began. "She was looking for a place to experiment with this idea she had for a legal clinic, and she said she'd heard about my after-school program from one of her students. She said the only hope for curing poverty was getting kids off on a better start, not giving them handouts." He smiled wryly. "I'll never forget the phrase she kept repeating: '*Give a man a fish and he eats for a day. Teach a man to fish and he eats for a lifetime.*' What she was proposing sounded great. So I accepted. Her only condition was that I not tell anyone about it. She said that she wanted this to be a real labor of love, out of the public eye. I don't think she even told her husband about it."

She must not have. Gary had certainly never mentioned it to me.

Sorrow crept into Russell's voice. "We started working on the clinic last spring, and I started getting to know her. Sometimes she would bring a senior professor, Talbot, along with her. But usually she would come alone. And gradually I realized that she was lonely. And angry. Her marriage was falling apart. Her husband was cheating on her, with a student, for pete's sake."

"And how did that make you feel?"

"Sorry for her."

"And?"

"And tempted."

"She was a rabid conservative who humiliated your boss on national television and was always running down black people, and you were *tempted?*"

"Say what you will about her, she was fiercely honest. She cared about the truth more than she cared about people's feelings. At first it drove me crazy. But later it seemed kind of sweet." He shrugged. "She was a beautiful, lonely woman. And I'm human."

"So what happened?" I prodded.

"It was just supposed to be for fun," he responded. "Neither one of us was really serious. We had some good times. And then she got pregnant. That was when the trouble started." He sighed heavily.

"What were you planning?"

"I wanted to do right by her. I don't believe in abortion, and I told her I wanted her to have the child. Even though I would have been kicked out of this church, I told her I'd marry her. It was my responsibility."

"To make an honest woman of her."

"Look, I'm not a saint. But there was no way I was going to desert a child of mine."

"How do you know it was yours?"

"It was. Her husband can't have kids."

"Did he know about this?" I demanded.

"Oh, yeah. She blurted it out in the middle of some fight they were having. Smart."

I stifled the surge of rage I felt at Gary. If Russell was telling the truth, then even last night, Gary had still been lying to me. "What did he say?"

"She said he tried to convince her to have an abortion so they could get on with their lives."

"He wanted to stay with her, even after that?" I asked skeptically.

"He's your friend. You know how badly he wants to be the Yale President. And he thinks he needs a solid marriage to make it happen."

"What about Amanda? What did she want?"

"She hadn't decided. But her husband was making some headway."

"Is that why you wrote those letters?"

He looked at me quizzically. "What letters?"

"The love letters. If you can call them that. I found about fifteen of them in her office."

He shook his head. "I don't know what you're talking about. But there was at least one other man who knew she was unhappy, and was trying to get her away from Gary."

"Poor Amanda," I drawled. "Surrounded by rejected swains whose only aim in life was to make her happy."

"You don't realize it, but it was lousy for her," he said sharply. "The attention she got was stifling. I think it was starting to make her a little crazy. And then I mean, Amanda said not to worry about it. But I saw bruises on her arm one day. And I realized that she was in trouble. This guy was crazy jealous. And he had no intention of letting her go. Especially not to a black man. And then she ended up dead. If that Lance O'Brien hadn't confessed, I would have thought it was him."

A chill went down my spine as I sorted through his words. Whatever Gary Fox might be, he was no bigot. And definitely no wife-beater. "You're not talking about her husband, are you?" I whispered.

"No," he said slowly. "I'm not."

As I ran through the names once more, I kept coming back to that afternoon in Amanda's office, and that cache of love letters. Who had written them? I'd seen that handwriting somewhere before. The theatrical flourishes, the elaborate strokes, all of it was maddeningly familiar. Then it hit me. I froze for a moment, paralyzed with shock. As the pieces fell into place, the shock turned to fury.

That was what got me moving.

"Where are you going?" Russell said sharply.

"Lance O'Brien didn't kill her."

"Wait, I'm coming with you."

"No, you're not," I said, picking up the pace, not even bothering to look back. "I'm doing this alone."

Russell shouted after me. "Don't be a fool, Nikki!"

As if I hadn't been one all along.

CHAPTER TWENTY-FOUR

Blue Blood

The courtyard of Branford College was deserted when I arrived there fifteen minutes after leaving Russell Jackson. The Game was still going on, and the silence of the quadrangle was broken only by the sound of the carillon. The melody sounded like "Ode to Joy."

Reid Talbot had always said that he preferred to play the classics.

If I was right, then he was up in Harkness Tower, the way he was every Saturday afternoon. If I was right, he was some two hundred feet over my head, looking mockingly down on the campus that he had roiled, certain that he was clever enough to get away with murder. I'd called Heaney and asked him to meet me at Branford. But now that I was here, I couldn't wait. Heaney would be along soon, but I had to know if Talbot had done it. I had to know now.

A minute of searching around the base of the bell tower led me to a thick black wooden door marked MEMORIAL ROOM. I ducked through it and found a narrow, winding stone staircase that appeared to lead up to the belfrey. Ditching my jacket and umbrella, I started climbing.

The redbrick walls surrounding the coiled staircase began to press in on me as I turned the pieces over in my mind. Reid Talbot had written those letters. I'd seen his handwriting on my visit to his office. He'd obviously been infatuated with Amanda. But she'd been with Russell. And maybe that had sent him over the edge. The sound of the bells grew louder with each step, and the air grew thicker and mustier. I could feel my heart starting to pound, and a feeling of unreality overtook me. All I could think about was getting to Talbot. Getting to him, and making sense out of this.

The stone staircase abruptly ended and I emerged suddenly into a small, carpeted room. I peered rapidly around the space, expecting the professor. But it was deserted. Apparently, it was a practice room, because there was a small console and stacks of sheet music. I took advantage of the unexpected respite to unload my backpack and catch my breath. Then I headed for an even narrower set of iron spiral stairs in the corner of the room. This had to be the way to the top.

The noise of the bells was nearly deafening now, and I had long since stopped trying to think. I climbed on, faster and faster, the tightening coils of the staircase dizzying me. Suddenly, a blast of cold air hit me full in the face and I realized that I had finally arrived. I was standing in a small stone room that felt almost like a prison cell, surrounded by a series of narrow doors and tall, ornate windows that revealed a panoramic view of the campus. Stretching endlessly above my head were rows of bells. Before me was a small green metal shelter encircled by a tangle of cords and ropes. Sitting at a console in the middle of this contraption, with his back to me, was Reid Talbot.

Resisting the urge to take a swing at his head, I politely tapped him on the shoulder.

The professor turned, startled, and the carillon came to a clangorous halt.

"I'm surprised you're not playing a dirge. After all, it hasn't even been a week since you killed her," I said sharply. I was bluffing. But I was betting it would work.

"Miss Chase, what are you doing here? How did you—"

"How does anyone?" I snapped. "I climbed, you SOB."

"I don't understand what you're—"

"Stop. We're not doing it that way."

"What way?" His kindly blue eyes narrowed quizzically.

"The 'I don't understand what you're talking about, there must be some misunderstanding' way."

Our eyes locked, and he swayed slightly, as if from a blow. "I deserve that," he said finally. "That and more."

I stifled the flood of emotions that his confession unleashed. *Keep him talking.*

"The cops are on their way here. But I want to hear it myself. Why? Why did you think you had to kill her?"

A frown passed like a shadow over his face, and then he sighed heavily. Swiveling on the ancient wooden bench, he looked pensively at the tangle of ropes and pulleys above him. Then he rubbed his chin, and almost seemed to smile. "I don't expect anyone to understand. I hardly understand it myself. But from the moment I met her, I had to have her."

There it was again. I'd seen the same look when Gary had spoken about Amanda: a mixture of longing and possessiveness and a tinge of anger at the impossibility of fully controlling her. Ever since I'd known her, I'd envied the effect she had on men. Perhaps I should have pitied her.

"It wasn't just her beauty," he continued, looking almost dazed. "Although of course, that was part of it. She looked so much like Margaret, my wife . . . but it wasn't just that. It was her fire. Her passion for exposing the truth, no matter what the consequences. She was like a glorious maelstrom, and I was desperate to be drawn in."

"*You* were the one who was calling her and harassing her right before she died. You wrote those letters, didn't you?"

He had the good grace to flush. "Yes. I thought you might have found them the day I discovered you in her office. I was always very gratified that she saved them."

"So was the feeling ever mutual?"

He snorted derisively. "No. No matter what I did, to Amanda I was just an elderly law professor. I believe that she pitied me." The pain in his eyes was so raw that I actually had to look away. I knew quite well what it felt like when one's desire was thwarted. I used to tell Dante that his unwillingness to commit was driving me mad.

I'd been exaggerating. But perhaps, for Talbot, it had been true.

A gust of freezing wind blew through the chamber and I rubbed my arms for warmth.

"Did Gary know how you felt about her?"

The professor's hands played idly across the carillon's massive keyboard. "No. Why should he? He had his own diversions. That silly girl, Giselle, actually played right into my hands."

"How did you get her to tell that 'black man in the bushes' story?"

Talbot smiled evilly. "I didn't. It was a stroke of pure luck. Apparently, the girl actually believed that Gary might have killed his wife. So she made up that story to send the police off in a different direction. The precise direction that I wanted."

"Toward Russell Jackson."

"Exactly. I mean, it would have been one thing if Amanda had been loyal to her husband. I would have respected that. But instead she chose to break her marriage vows. And with someone like him."

A chill went briefly through me at the expression on his face. If I'd had any doubts, they were gone now. This well-mannered Connecticut blue-blood was definitely capable of murder.

"Did you know that she was pregnant?"

He laughed harshly. "Of course. With his child. I saw the prenatal vitamins in her office one day, and I figured it out."

"And that's when you decided to kill her."

He looked directly at me, and for a moment I felt him soften. "I don't expect you to understand. But I believe I went slightly mad the afternoon I found out. I went over it and over it in my mind. It was clear that she was lost to me. Completely lost. And to a black man, of all people. I finally reached a decision early that evening. She'd hurt me for the last time."

"So you lured her over to Russell's church and did it there. Was that to frame him?"

"Why not?" he said. His tone was ice-cold again. "I felt that there was a certain poetic justice to it."

A certain wicked cruelty was more like it. He'd wanted Russell to find her body. Not to make him look guilty. To make him pay.

"I left her a note that night," he continued. "I made it look like it was from him. Asking her to meet there after class to discuss their plans. And she practically flew there. It was all terribly easy."

"And you wore blackface, just to make sure that the police would go after Russell."

A look of contempt flickered across Talbot's face. "The police. Even after I let that woman see part of my face, *see* that blackface, right outside his church, they still didn't get it. They arrested the wrong black man!"

"Why did you have to cut off her hand?"

"It was a diversionary tactic. I thought that if they didn't make the connection to the good reverend, then the police would assume there was some demented serial killer on the loose." He laughed bitterly, striking a few dramatic chords on the carillon for emphasis.

His theatrics were really starting to piss me off. "There's one thing I still don't understand. Why did you kill Lance O'Brien?"

"Because of that other reverend—Leroy, is that his name? He was actually starting to convince the police that the Tyler boy was innocent. And if they believed that, who knew if they'd be clever enough to go after Jackson? They might have looked in a different direction. So someone had to confess."

And what better way to humiliate Gary Fox? I thought. Make it look like he was having a torrid gay affair. It wasn't just Amanda who had to be punished. It was every man who'd ever had her.

"You were the one who chased me that night, weren't you?"

It took a moment for him to answer. Clearly, his mind was elsewhere. "Yes. I had to retrieve that knife. I had planned to plant it in Jackson's apartment. But you got there first."

"You're pretty fit for an old man," I taunted. That was something to keep in mind.

"I still can't believe any of this has happened," Talbot said, ignoring me. He was whispering, as if I wasn't even there. "And you know the worst part? I thought killing her would make the pain stop. But I've never felt worse in my life."

He walked slowly toward one of the tower's narrow doorways and pushed against it. The metal door swung obligingly open, and the wind swept even more strongly through the chamber. Talbot stepped out onto a small balcony and swung one foot over the railing.

"It's funny. I was sure that talking to someone about it would make it better. But it's hopeless. It'll never end." He leaned over and looked down.

"Professor Talbot!" I started toward him. He was a coward and a murderer. But I still couldn't let him kill himself.

I reached for his wrist as he leaned further over the balustrade.

That's when he grabbed me and twisted my arm roughly behind my back. And suddenly, he was safely on the balcony. And I was flat on my back and halfway over the railing.

"For a Harvard professor, you've been incredibly stupid," he said coldly, his face inches from mine. I could feel the rough stone of the railing scraping against my back.

Don't look down.

"Let go!" I shouted frantically. "You're not getting away with what you did to her. Don't make it worse."

"Of course I can get away with it, Professor Chase," he mocked. I could feel him edging me further off the railing. "You're the only one who heard my little confession. Without it, there's no evidence. And you're about to have a nasty fall. The police may end up convincing themselves that O'Brien killed Amanda. Or maybe they'll finally go after Jackson. Or they'll stick with that Tyler boy. But they've got nothing on me."

He paused for a self-satisfied grin and I took the opportunity to land a spit wad square in his eye. Not particularly elegant, but highly effective. His grip loosened for a crucial moment, and I got my right arm free. Then I raked my nails across the same eye until he screamed in pain. A knee to the groin and I was able to wrest my other arm out of his grasp and roll away from the ledge.

"You're right, Talbot. I have been an idiot," I snarled. "But I learn really fast, and you're going down."

Faster than light, he lunged at me and we crashed onto the floor of the balcony. Through a haze of pain and panic, one clear thought emerged. He might be almost sixty years old, but he was damn strong. I could easily lose this on physical strength. So I was going to have to mess with his mind.

"Come on, Talbot. Give me your best shot. You're a big man, aren't you?" I taunted breathlessly as I tried desperately to keep my arms free. "Stalking a defenseless woman and her unborn child and mutilating her just for the hell of it. Sneaking up on an innocent young man and hanging him from the rafters like a piece of meat. Tricking me into trying to save your cowardly ass so that you can toss me out a window. You've really got balls."

"Don't dare mock me, you little bitch," Talbot snarled. He straddled me and administered a blow to the side of my head that made the balcony spin a full revolution.

I swallowed hard and stared back defiantly. "It takes a real hero to slap a woman around, Professor. And let's not forget your truly gutless attempt to frame a black man for your crimes. You're not a man—you're a wimp. Amanda was right to reject you. No woman in her right mind would want you."

He let out a bellow of rage and frustration, and I saw my opening. With all my strength, I sent my fist into his jaw and landed a beautiful right uppercut. It probably hurt me as much as it did him, but he rolled to the side just far enough that I could wriggle out from under him and stumble toward the carillon keyboard. I needed a weapon, and the wooden bench he had been sitting on would have to do.

I grabbed it and turned back toward him.

He was actually grinning at me. A deranged, twisted grin, accented by the blood trickling from his mouth, but a grin nevertheless.

"That's it," he said. "It's over." He turned his back on me and started deliberately toward the railing.

"Oh no you don't," I hissed. With a single motion, I raised the bench over my head and brought it crashing down on his back. He collapsed to the floor, and I stood over him, nearly insane myself at that point. "If you think I'm letting you kill yourself, forget it," I screamed at his comatose form. "You're not getting off that easy."

I resisted the urge to administer a couple of

gratuitous kicks to his rib cage and started for the staircase to summon Heaney. I was confident that Talbot's fellow prison inmates could inflict more damage than I could dream of.

And that was the least that Amanda and Lance deserved.

EPILOGUE

The Road Ahead

"Make it fast, Juliet. Maggie's going to kill us if we're late."

Dante was behind the wheel of Maggie's car, and Lily was in the backseat. It was 10:00 A.M. Thanksgiving Day, and we were on our way to Cambridge to share dinner with Maggie, Rafe, Jess, and Ted. Despite the clamor from my department chairman, I had spent the past four days in New Haven, filling the police in on what I knew and attending Amanda's wake and funeral. We had stopped the car on High Street because I had one last task to complete before I left.

"It'll take one minute, *maximum*," I called over my shoulder as I jumped out of the front seat. The shadow of Harkness Tower loomed over me as I passed through the gates of Old Campus.

The quad was deserted, since most of the students had already departed for the holiday, and I reached my destination quickly. I stood before the celadon statue of President Woolsey, which was patiently keeping watch over his beloved campus. His face appeared worn, and lined, and for the first time, I saw that the years had chiseled rivulets of what looked like tears onto his cheeks. But still he persevered, steadfastly dispensing luck from the golden tip of his shoe.

Reid Talbot had been arrested for the murders of Amanda Fox and Lance O'Brien and was being held without bail on a suicide watch in a prison in New Haven. The charges against Marcellus had been dropped, and Gary had prodded the police into issuing a public apology. I'd seen him at the funeral, sans Giselle, and we'd agreed to try to repair our friendship. Given how lonely he'd seemed, it was the least I could do. Russell Jackson had announced that he was taking an indefinite leave of absence from the pulpit, to devote time to making Amanda's legal clinic a reality. He'd asked if I would come back and talk to the SOS girls again, and I'd promised that I would. He'd also asked me to have dinner with him when I returned. That I was still considering. *Vanity Fair* had announced that its January issue would carry Amanda's last article, co-authored by Jared

Fisch. An exposé of Max Fisch, Senior, it detailed the family's history and the fortune they had made trafficking in interstate pornography and prostitution. The word was that in light of this, the family was withdrawing its offer to fund an ethics curriculum at Yale. But the world would still know that Amanda had been here: her father had agreed to endow a chair in her name at the Law School.

A breeze from the north set the branches of the trees overhead asway, and I pulled my jacket a bit closer. It was time to go.

Solemnly, I reached out and rubbed the well-worn tip of President Woolsey's shoe.

I felt certain that he wouldn't begrudge me a tiny bit of Yale's magic for the road ahead.

ABOUT THE AUTHOR

Pamela Thomas-Graham is a Phi Beta Kappa graduate of Harvard-Radcliffe College, where she received a degree in Economics *magna cum laude* and was awarded the Captain Jonathan Fay Prize—the highest annual award bestowed by Radcliffe—as the young woman "showing the greatest promise" in her graduating class. A graduate of Harvard Business School and Harvard Law School, Pamela was an editor of the *Harvard Law Review.* At age thirty-two, she became one of the most influential women in American business when she was named the first black woman partner at McKinsey & Company, the world's largest management consulting firm. A leader of the firm's Media and Entertainment Practice, she advises Fortune 500 companies on a wide variety of strategic issues. Pamela serves on the boards of the New York City Opera, the American Red Cross of Greater New York, and the Harvard Alumni Association. A member of the Visiting Committee for Harvard College, she is also a board member of the

Center for Society and Health at the Harvard School of Public Health. She has been profiled in several leading publications, including *Time*, *Fortune*, *The New York Times* and *Black Enterprise*, and was named to the prestigious "40 Under 40" list of fast-track executives in *Crain's New York Business*. Her first novel, *A Darker Shade of Crimson*, was named a *People Magazine* "Page Turner of the Week." Originally from Detroit, she divides her time between Manhattan and Westchester County with her husband, writer and attorney Lawrence Otis Graham, and their son. *Blue Blood* is the second entry in her Ivy League mystery series.

A DARKER SHADE OF CRIMSON

Another riveting Ivy League mystery from

PAMELA THOMAS-GRAHAM

Pocket
Books

**Visit the
Simon & Schuster Web site:**

www.SimonSays.com

**and sign up for our
mystery e-mail updates!**

Keep up on the latest new releases,
author appearances, news, chats,
special offers, and more!
We'll deliver the information
right to your inbox—
if it's new, you'll know about it.

SIMON & SCHUSTER
A VIACOM COMPANY
www.SimonSays.com

2345